Confessions
of a
Prodigal Daughter

Confessions

of a

Prodigal Daughter

Mary Rose Callaghan

Marion Boyars . London . New York

First published in Great Britain and the United States in 1985
by Marion Boyars Publishers Ltd.
24 Lacy Road, London SW15 1NL
and by Marion Boyars Publishers Inc.
262 West 22nd Street, New York, NY 10011.

Distributed in the United States by
The Scribner Book Companies Inc.

Distributed in Canada by
Collier Macmillan Canada Inc.

Distributed in Australia by
Wild & Woolley Pty Ltd.

Distributed in Ireland by
Arlen House, Dublin

© Mary Rose Callaghan 1985

British Library Cataloguing in Publication Data

Callaghan, Mary Rose
   Confessions of a prodigal daughter.
   I. Title
   823'.914[F]   PR6053.A38/

Library of Congress Cataloging in Publication Data

Callaghan, Mary Rose
   Confessions of a prodigal daughter.
   I. Title
PR6053.A382C6   1985   823'.914   85-3809

ISBN 0-7145-2830-7 cloth

Typeset in 11 point Times
by Essex Photo Set, Rayleigh
Printed and bound in Great Britain by
Biddles Ltd, Guildford and King's Lynn

With Love to Sheila

He gave the little wealth he had
To build a house for fools and mad;
And showed, by one satiric touch,
No nation wanted it so much.

On the Death of Dr. Swift
Jonathan Swift

1

The bench by the duck pond was icy, but I preferred waiting there. Firstly it was quiet, and secondly ducks were impersonal, sort of, and I could feed them. In the streets outside the Green, cars braked and honked, and the pavements of Dublin were spilling over with people who knew I'd left school and was doing typing.

Three had already drifted up from Grafton Street: my ex-maths teacher, a girl from my old kindergarten, a chemist we owed money to. But I looked glassily past those sophisters, calculators and economists, and threw my last crust to the ducks.

'Shoo!' I shouted at a greedy seagull. 'Shoo!'

I hate seagulls.

So I looked at the trees, thinning against the pinkish sky.

As usual, my mother was late. And no telling how much longer the solicitor would take.

Soon the shops would shut and there'd be no time to buy my diary. From empties, I'd saved nearly £3 – £2/16/3 to be exact – enough for the five-year kind that locked. And with space at the back for my lists of quotations and titles of books read. My mother wanted me to spend the money on things for tomorrow's visit to Nicola, but I had picked out a diary in Combridge's. It was blue leatherette, with an epigraph by Longfellow: 'Look, then, into thine heart and write.' And a Foreword warning that perhaps only the most determined would achieve an entry for every day. But I would. It would be a sanctuary for my innermost thoughts and meditations, from that place inside me where no one else had trod. Not even my mother. Doone, my younger sister, was always asking me what I was writing. Or reading. Or

thinking. And she had a sneaky habit of reading my diary.

The trouble was, we shared a room. And since I had left school, the nuns wouldn't keep her. I can't go into it here, but they'd sent her home, keeping my trunk – initialled A.O'B, 16 – as hostage. So there was no hope for privacy now – in boarding school we'd had separate cubicles at least. Oh, there was some talk of our neighbours, the Freemans, taking her to a Kibbutz. And I fervently hoped they would.

So I'd have a room to myself.

Last year's diary was completely in Morse Code. I learned Morse Code when I was twelve because the Swallows and Amazons in Arthur Ransome knew it, and that seemed a good reason. It worked OK, except the dots and dashes were too difficult for poetry or cash accounts. That was another reason for the lock. If Doone knew I had money, she'd want it for comics with stories about midnight feasts in dormitories. Although she was nearly fourteen, I still couldn't get her onto books. Possibly her brain has been damaged from birth. Even reading aloud to her doesn't work. She has read one book on her own, and that's *The Ten Pound Pony* – she's obsessed with animals, too. Ironic, considering she had got her name from my reading *Lorna Doone* to her. I put Doone to her Lorna and Charlotte Emily in front of my Anne, and Doone had stuck but I was still just Anne. Ironic, not to say irritating.

I hated my name. The Hound, that's Mother Culhane, my ex-English teacher, says that's an X – according to her X equals your weak point. But whoever heard of an Anne O'Brien in a Georgette Heyer novel? Maybe George for Georgette . . . like Pen for Penelope in *The Corinthian*. And Yeats's wife had been George. Or maybe I should stick to my latest idea of Anne Brontë O'Brien. After all, my father's mother's name had been Brunty, the same as the Brontës' father's name before he changed it. The Brontës were Irish too and I secretly hoped we might be related way back. I have read that, although in humble circumstances, they were descended from an ancient lineage.

10

Which was definitely the case with us.

The darkness was gathering, the eventide falling fast. Near the gate a man was sweeping leaves. Soon they'd be burnt in piles, the smoke mingling with creeping mists. My hands were cold, so I blew on them. Not that I minded the cold. The melancholy chill meant winter was coming, and for me the pleasures of fire and candlelight far outweigh those of sun and sea. In summer everyone can see, so you've got to pretend to be happy; but in winter there's the blanket of the dark.

Besides, my mother says what the Irish call summer is a travesty. And life is more wintry really: people die and their earthly tenements return to the earth like the leaves. The Hound says their souls fly to heaven like gulls on the wing. My father had died in the summer, but I couldn't imagine him as one of those gulls squabbling on the pond.

I could barely imagine him dead.

The view from the humped bridge was better. So I moved to it, shuffling through the dead leaves which reminded me of Milton's angels and the brooks of Vallombrosa – although basically I'm a Dante person. My high heels were tricky to manage, but my mother insisted they matched my new scarf coat. It's an ugly green and too big by several sizes. I had wanted the French look: flat shoes and a belted camel coat – people in books always wear belted camel coats. But last week Aunt Allie had picked this from Clery's bargain rail, saying tweed would last. She is rich and always right, so I expected to be swimming round in it for the rest of my life. Not that I minded really; it covered things, especially my old school uniform. Anyway, I reminded myself firmly, the true life is the life of the spirit. So I concentrated on the leaves again and the brooks of Vallombrosa. Then I thought about my best friend Nicola and tomorrow's visit. She had written, saying it would be bliss to see me. Then I had rung her. And we'd arranged to meet in town after my typing class. I was to stay the night, as we hadn't seen each other since the end of the summer term, when she went to her sister in Paris. Paris is OK, I suppose . . . it must be lovely in the Autumn, but Rome is more my bag. Now I'd really be envious if Nicola had gone there – let me admit envy of Nicola as another of my Xs. Oh, she had left school too, although for different reasons than I had, so there was no need to envy her new copybooks and that. Like the time she spoke to Peter Finch in the Hibernian. I had seen him walking down Grafton Street, but that's not like having a conversation. If I met him, we'd probably talk about Dante . . . and Italy. Maybe he'd been there. 'Roma,' I whispered to myself. 'Firenze . . . Vallombrosa.' Which reminded me of the leaves again,

> *Yellow, and black, and pale, and hectic red,*
> *Pestilence stricken multitudes.*

After Dante, Shelley's my favourite poet. I mean, who else could've written so beautifully about the thorns of life? Then I got an idea for my own poem about the trees blackening the sky. Murkily blackening, I mean. And I heard a familiar shriek behind me.

'Annie! Annie, darling!'

Then a hand shot up, and my mother's green Jacqmar headscarf and balding leopard skin coat bobbed from the wrong gate. The leopard skin coat is the same as Jackie Kennedy's and always worn for our town shopping – my mother's an American too. I waved back and teetered towards her.

'Darling, I'm sorry! The bore kept me waiting! Not cold, are you?' Feeling my hands, she pulled me towards the Grafton Street gate.

'What did he say?' I tried to guess through her sunglasses, but her blue eyes were completely hidden. My mother's the spitting image of Lady Lavery, the beauty on the Irish pound note. And is renowned for her legs.

'Oh! . . . He said there's no case against Cousin William! Be nice to him!'

'But what'll we do for money?'

'Have you ever known your mother to be outwitted?'

Reluctantly I shook my head. My mother's as good as Mr Micawber for things turning up.

'I'll get us plenty of money! Although why I didn't strangle your wretched Cousin William in childhood, I'll never know!'

My wretched Cousin William is my brother, well half-brother really. But that's another story. And very sordid.

'I had the opportunity!' My mother went on in a dangerous whisper. Suddenly she brightened. 'Never mind! We'll have time for a quick cup of tea before your bra.'

I stopped dead. 'Then there won't be time for my diary.'

'We'll have tea in Brown Thomas', and then get the bra there.' And she linked her arm in mine, pulling me forwards.

'But it's my money! And there won't –.'

'Now look, Annie! I'll pay for the tea, and we can use Aunt Allie's account for the bra.'

'But I don't want a bra! And what will Aunt Allie think?'

'What will Nicola think, if she sees you don't wear a bra?'

'But you'll want my money for the tip. I know –.'

Angrily she pulled away. 'What do you want to waste it on a diary for? You could spend it on something normal!'

'Like what?'

'Get something done with your hair!'

'What's wrong with my hair?'

'It's not as fair as when you were a child.'

'But I'm not a child anymore.'

'Sometimes I doubt that! I really do.' Her mouth twitched dangerously. I knew the signs. Although we were more like sisters, she could often be *difficile*.

'Damn it, Annie! I go to all this trouble. Risking my neck. Getting you things. And what do you do? You put on a face!'

'I don't want you to risk your neck. I only want a diary.' Stubbornly I dug into my pocket to clutch my money. Usually she was understanding about my literary needs. Giving me her last penny for books.

'Anne,' she said in a dangerously low voice. 'I am *going* down the street to get you a bra. Now if you want to be normal, come! Otherwise go home.'

'OK, I'll go home.'

'Say another word, and I'll . . .' She lifted her hand, and then thought better of it, and stamped off towards the gate.

Oh, blister it!

I bit back tears. Sometimes there was no reasoning with her. Beside me, a duck waddled up to the pond and plopped in. I wanted to jump in too, envying its watery loveless life . . . beneath the murky trees.

At the gate my mother turned her head and, seeing me still standing there, rushed on. We had no permission to use Aunt Allie's account. There'd be ructions when she found out. And she'd blame me. She always blamed me for my mother. Oh . . . we had enough money for a Clery's bra, but not my mother. 'I never cross the Liffey, if I can avoid it!' she always said. If I left her alone on the rampage now, something awful would happen – our lack of money sometimes drove her mad. So, wishing myself a pillar of salt, I walked wobbily after her.

In the middle of Grafton Street, I caught up. At first she pretended not to notice, but after a few steps she stopped. 'Look at you!' she said, yanking off her sunglasses and pulling at my coat.

Miserably I looked down at it. 'It's not that bad.'

'Bad?' she shouted, stepping backwards. 'It's not bad; it's hideous!' And she charged on down the street.

Aunt Allie was only related by marriage, but she was always trying to help. She had sort of adopted me. I mean, she had paid my school fees to fifth year, sent me to Irish College one summer, arranged for the commercial course I started, and even promised to get me into a bank. Or Guinness's. 'But I'm not Aunt Allie's child,' I said, catching up.

My mother shoved open the shop door, shouting at the top of her voice, 'Her child? Indeed, you're not! Do you think she'd

14

have you typing if you were?'

I hopped to avoid the swinging door. If typing hadn't been Aunt Allie's idea, my mother would probably be agreeable. Between them, I felt like the baby in the King Solomon story. 'There's never been a typist in our family. And you're not going to be the first! No man has the right to say, "Thus far shalt thou go and no further!"' And she waved her arm dramatically.

The quotation was from Parnell's statue, and like 'footprints on the sands of time' and 'sticks and stones . . .' etc. was one of my mother's favourites. Catching the smirk of the girl behind the perfume counter, I tripped on the doormat but luckily recovered. My mother was standing at the foot of the stairs, in front of the mirrored wall. 'Look at you!' she wailed. 'I mean – look—.'

'I might grow into it,' I whispered at my reflection. The coat had a scarf collar which engulfed my chin, and the hem came to the top of my ankles. 'You don't stop growing till you're twenty-four. I read that in –.'

'Well, we can't wait that long!' And she dashed up the marble staircase, calling over her shoulder, 'At your age I was alone in Paris!' Then in a lowered voice, 'But not for long! Not for long!' And she disappeared into the raincoats.

Usually in the perfumy warmth of shops, I would imagine Italy and my future of travel with matching luggage. Or my long-dead grandparents. Although my mother's mother was Irish, her father was an ex-US ambassador, of all things. I had figured that between my mother and Doone and me there was a 100% Americanness – 50% for my mother, 25% for each of us. So America was definitely on my list for a visit. I loved imagining New York skyscrapers and white Southern beaches where I was meant to have relatives, but her commotion was making us too noticeable. I felt in my bones we'd never get out of the shop. It'd be like the time we stayed in a London Hotel and left wearing two sets of clothes. Only this time we'd both end up in prison with nothing to eat but bread and water . . . Crusts and water.

The underwear boudoir was through the twinsets and up some

15

steps to the back of the first floor. When I passed the rail of nighties guarding the entrance, my mother was dipping indiscriminately into a tub of panties.

'You'll need plenty of these. From now on, people will judge you by your underwear.'

I smiled weakly at the listening assistant behind the counter.

'Can I help you?' she enquired perkily.

My mother fished out an armful of panties and dumped them on the counter. 'Indeed, yes! We'll have these. And you can measure my daughter for a brassiere. Something a little *décolleté, n'est-ce-pas?*'

French was always a dangerous sign. A sign she was jeering me.

'You must grow up sometime, *chérie!*' She smiled brightly, her teeth white against her suntan makeup.

Then and there, I resolved to drop French and take up German. German, after all, is a much more spiritual language, the language of many great thinkers such as – how did you pronounce it? Surely not Goatey? Goeth? Geeth? Well, maybe I'd learn Italian. Then I could get started on my Dante translation. Which was to be my life's goal.

'You'd better take off your coat,' said the assistant, flicking a tape at me.

'My coat?' I stammered stupidly. But I obeyed, and instantly my shabby school skirt jumped out from a thousand mirrors.

'Hmm – 31½, almost 32,' the girl said, connecting the tape in front.

By now, my mother was perched on a tall stool, with her coat tucked in to hide the worn lining. 'What about a padded cup?' she suggested, peeling off her long leather gloves.

The girl nodded understandingly and, gliding behind the counter, deftly undid several packages. Then she showed me to a curtained box where she laid the things on a chair.

'When you're ready –,' she said, backing out.

I drew the curtains closely and picked out the cheapest, a

16

creation of snowy lace, priced three guineas. Then, pulling off my jumper and letting my ragged yellow vest flop over my skirt, I tried it on. I was still fumbling with the catch when the girl's head popped between the curtains.

'How are we doing? Here, let me.' She expertly did me up, then to my mortification hopped round me and pokily pinched the cups. 'Hmm,' she murmured and adjusted the straps.

Then my mother appeared through the curtains. 'No, she doesn't quite fill it.'

And they both stared sadly.

Nervously I fidgeted with my vest. It was mad, spending all this money on something that didn't fit.

'Never mind!' my mother said, waving grandly at the girl. 'We'll take three! An economical number. She'll grow into them.'

The assistant blinked doubtfully.

'People don't stop growing,' snapped my mother, 'until they're twenty-four.'

I glared at her.

'Don't be difficult, Anne! You're delaying this young woman!' She turned confidentially to the assistant. 'Children are so difficult.'

'Well,' said the assistant, blinking again, 'will she wear it? Shall I wrap her old one?'

'Yes,' I mumbled, pulling on my jumper and hiding under it until they'd gone. It was my first bra. Getting three instead of one was my mother's weird way of saving. Like the time she said her hysterectomy was to save on sanitary towels. 'The economy, darling! Think of the economy!'

Well, she could get me a million bras. I still wouldn't wear one. As soon as we got home, I'd give it to Doone.

'These are on account,' my mother was saying as I came out. 'Mrs Grubb-Healy's account.'

'Yes, Mrs Grubb-Healy,' said the assistant, looping a bag.

'No, I'm Mrs O'Brien. My daughter there is Mrs Grubb-

Healy's godchild, and this seemed the easiest way of coping with her birthday.'

'Of course, Mrs O'Brien.'

'She's the brains of the family,' my mother went on. 'She'll be off to the University one of these days.'

Groaning inwardly, I concentrated on buttoning my coat.

'Oh?' said the assistant. 'How nice. Now I'll just dash and check the account.' And she half hopped, half glided off in the direction of the stairs.

This was unexpected. For me, the minutes stretched out in agony, but my mother sauntered coolly about. She stopped by the dressing-gowned dummy and frowned over the tag. 'Tut! Tut!'

Now was the time to run for it. I paced as far as the balcony and stared down at the shopfloor. The chandelier hung from the ceiling and I had visions of us swinging on it out of the shop.

I walked quickly back to her. 'Mummy, I don't want them.'

'What, darling?'

'I said I don't want them.'

But she only gave me her brightest smile. Defeated, I fingered the sets of frothy underwear hanging embarrassingly from rails. I couldn't imagine the sort of people who'd judge me by something like that. Maybe sophisters, calculators and economists.

My heart began to gallop out of the top of my head, as the assistant came back up the stairs. At the top she stopped to talk to a striped-suited gentleman. They started over, and I frantically looked at my mother. She was poking noisily in her handbag. Oh, if the world were flooding, other people might panic, but my mother would casually put on her lipstick.

She was doing this when they came over.

'Eh – Mrs O'Brien – this is our manager.' The assistant stepped back from the tall, elegant looking gentleman.

He gave my mother a tight little smile. 'This is a little unusual, Madam –.'

'Unusual?' my mother said frostily, and then paused to

18

smudge her lips together. 'Is there something unusual about my daughter?'

He glanced lazily at me, then coughed politely. 'Ah, perhaps we could ring Mrs Grubb-Healy? Just to verify it.'

'Verify it? Certainly ring her! She's in the directory.' Defiantly my mother pulled on her gloves. 'Mrs Alice Grubb-Healy of Merrion Road.'

'It's just a formality,' he said silkily, padding off towards the stairs.

The girl busied herself behind the counter, and I looked quickly at my mother. She was pale, and I saw the corners of her mouth beginning to twitch. Oh, Angel of God, why had she done this? Just to get me something nobody could see anyway?

It was awful.

We waited.

Awful.

When he came back, his countenance was expressionless. 'I'm afraid there was no answer. How would it do if we delivered them tomorrow?'

'Delivered them? Tomorrow?' My mother pursed her lips. 'Well, now!'

'Yes, Madam. Our van delivers daily. If you give the assistant your address, we'd have them out in the morning.'

Instantly the girl pulled out a docket book.

'Well, perhaps that will do,' my mother said, leaning over the counter. 'Shelley.'

'The Chalet,' the girl scribbled down.

'No, Shelley,' my mother said. 'As in poet. S-H-E-L-L-E-Y.'

'The Shelley,' the girl wrote flustered.

My mother unbent slightly. 'Anne there named it,' she explained.

Usually I got mad when she told people things like that, but now I just laughed. Nothing terrible was going to happen. And I still had my diary money.

'Well,' she said, relaxing a little as we went down the stairs, 'I

19

suppose there's still time to get it.'

'Eh . . . What?'

'Your diary.'

I said nothing, feeling guilty about the tea.

'Combridge's will still be open, Annie.'

'No.' I squeezed her hand. 'I'll – I'll buy you a cup of tea.' It was terrible of me to still begrudge it, but I did.

'Well, not at Bewley's,' she said firmly. 'At the Shelbourne.' According to my mother, that was the place to see and be seen.

2

And that was where I met Chris.

He sat perusing a folded newspaper at the edge of the crowded Shelbourne lounge. Maybe I'm exaggerating, but he was the Peter Finch type: small, dark and wiry with curly greying hair, sort of balding at the back. And he had a biggish nose and sallow sort of pitted skin from acne or something. I suppose it wasn't quite love at first sight. But I had noticed his white button-on collar – my father occasionally wore one – and his shiny grey-striped suit before my mother stopped.

'Why! Good heavens!' she shrieked. 'It's Christopher Murphy!'

He looked oldish. So I thought he was someone from Paris. Or maybe some relation – I have oodles of cousins I've never met. But his grey-blue eyes registered nothing as they darted curiously from my mother to me. Renoir always judged people by their hands, but I judge them by their eyes, and Chris' were curious.

'It is Mr. Murphy?' my mother persisted, towering over him.

'Ah – ah – yes, yes!' He frowned, trying to remember her. Then suddenly he sprang up and shook hands. 'Ah – ah – who . . .?'

But my mother just talked on: 'It must be five years . . . Yes, we finally sold the land . . . The will was botched! . . . Botched! . . . Some solicitors . . . not all, now. I didn't say all . . .'

He listened, banging his paper behind and occasionally raking his hair. Once he peered past her to me, smiling slightly crookedly. I felt myself redden and decided to move on.

The Shelbourne has a big lounge, full of tables. I found a free one at the back, under the huge mirrors. As usual, people were mostly drinking, but one or two sipped tea and nibbled on sandwiches. I calculated we'd better stick to plain biscuits with

21

ours. In a hotel like that, they up the price of everything. But one thing: they give you hot water to stretch the tea.

There was no sign of a waiter, so I rang the bell on the wall. Then I just sat there, watching the smoke curl towards the high ornate ceiling and enjoying the warmth and babble and clink of glass. An occasional loud hoot of laughter rose above the rest. Suddenly there was a lull, and my mother's voice floated over: 'Bill would never have wanted his property left like that . . .'

Then her voice sank back, D.G.

Bill was my father. The cigary smell was reminding me this would be the first Christmas without him.

Soon his tenor voice was singing in my head:

> *Far, far away is my lovely Isabella;*
> *Far, far away is my pretty island home.*

Then my mother's voice rose to the top again. 'That's Anne . . . No . . . she's the second . . . William's the eldest.'

I concentrated on my song. 'Far, far away is my pretty Isabella.'

'Anne! Anne! Come and meet Mr. Murphy!'

'Far, far away is my lovely –.'

'Oh, she's very moody!' my mother shouted. 'It's her intelligence.'

People were definitely looking – my mother says my thinking this is just my adolescence, but they were. So I got up and wobbled over what seemed like miles of soft carpet, concentrating on another of her mottoes, 'People say. Let them say. What do they say?'

'This is my daughter Anne,' my mother said for the millionth time, when I arrived. 'Anne, shake hands with Mr. Murphy!'

'Ma'am.' He sort of clicked his heels and bowed. As we shook hands, he glanced all the way down my coat to my feet.

I went beetroot. Just beetroot.

The high heels made me taller and seemed even sillier.

He looked from me to my mother. 'Eh . . . would you both

22

join me for a drink?'

'Well . . .' my mother hesitated.

I tugged her arm. I was president of our school Pioneer Total Abstinence Society and knew drink to be a curse.

'Oh, Anne doesn't approve!' she laughed, rattling on, 'She's the brains of the family.' I want her to have a profession. Medicine or Law. What do you think of Law for a girl, Mr. Murphy? You're just the one to advise her!'

He arched an eyebrow dubiously.

I went even redder.

'Has she left school yet?' His voice had a nasal twang.

I couldn't bear him looking. Just couldn't bear it.

'Indeed, yes,' my mother crowed. 'She matriculated this year. With some extraordinary results. And do you know what she's doing now? Typing!' She suddenly shook my arm and then let it disgustedly go, turning to Chris. 'Typing!'

I wanted the ground to devour me.

He blinked, digging one hand deep into his pocket. 'Oh! Eh! Well –.'

'It's all her godmother's idea!' my mother wailed. I thought she was going to cry. It was a terrible blow to her that Aunt Allie hadn't left me in school for my last year.

'Her godmother's idea? Hmm . . . Well –.'

'Yes! Her godmother is Mrs. Alice Grubb-Healy.'

'Not Stephen Healy's widow?' His eyebrows shot up.

'Yes! All the Healys ever think about is money! Alice doesn't realize Annie has the bump of knowledge. She gets it from my father; he was a lawyer too!'

'Really!' he shook his head gravely, as if assimilating the information.

I studied the flecks of grey in his hair.

'The bump of knowledge!' my mother wailed.

With a smile lurking in his blue eyes, Chris scrutinized me for a bump. 'Are you any relation to the Howth O'Briens?'

'They're the other side of the family!' my mother snapped. 'We don't see much of them!'

More truthfully, *they* didn't see much of *us*. Not since we got poor. But my mother has the knack of twisting things. My brains are a typical example. Firstly, in our family there isn't much competition for the brainiest. Doone is still on comics. And Cousin William, well, I'll be coming to him. Secondly, I hadn't done well in the National University Matric – that's their entrance exam. Actually, I'd failed it. I'd done it a year before everyone else, OK, but I'd gone down in Irish and failed Maths completely. My mother wanted me to get a Maths grind and re-sit the Trinity Matric. But I'd never manage Maths. Indices always whizzed round with fractions, which were already jumbled up with surds and L.C.M.'s, and the result . . . I was just going to say this when a waiter carried a tray to Chris' table.

While he whispered something to the waiter, I nudged my mother.

She looked puzzled, so I mouthed, 'Come on!'

'What is it?' she whispered, deliberately stupidly.

I pointed to our table at the far end of the room.

She grabbed my arm. 'Don't point, Annie!' Then to Chris, 'We're off then, Mr. Murphy.'

Jangling the change in his pocket, he turned from the waiter. 'But I insist you join me for a cup of tea. I've ordered two more cups. And cakes. I'll bet my bottom dollar you like cakes?'

This was to me.

'We have a table, actually.' And I pointed to it again.

But my mother was already throwing off her coat and plonking down exhausted. 'We'd love to have tea with you. Phew! That's better!' Then, glaring at me, she said, 'Annie loves cakes! *Don't you,* darling?'

'But there's no chair. And –.'

'That can easily be remedied,' Chris said, laughing. He went to the next table, lifted a heavy armchair as if it were a feather, and put it down beside me. 'Now we can all sit comfortably.'

As I sat down, my mother started up again. 'Now, Mr.

Murphy, advise Annie!'

He coughed, frowned, then sitting back crossed his legs importantly. 'Well, frankly speaking, I mean, to be honest, it's a bit difficult for me to . . . ah . . . I'm afraid I don't know her background. Or ability.'

'Her background?' My mother's voice broke. 'Is American! American! And her ability –.' She flushed apoplectically. 'Her ability –.'

Just then the waiter came with another tray.

'Is not in dispute! I'll pour!' My mother shakily gripped the teapot. Then, as the tea wobbled orangely into each cup, 'Annie, do the milk. Sugar, Mr. Murphy?'

He said he'd have two, so she spooned them in and rattlingly held out his cup. Then, taking a sip, he pushed the plate of cakes towards me. 'Eat up, Annie.'

He had said my name.

Quickly I bit on an eclair.

'Well. Let's see now . . . Let's get to the point.' He put down his teacup. 'Let's see, you're doing typing now?'

'Yes. At Miss Halfpenny's. My aunt wants me to work in a bank. Or Guinness's. She has pull there.'

'Well, let's get to the point.' He shifted in his chair. 'Would you like that?'

'Maybe Guinness's wouldn't be so bad,' I said through a mouthful of cake.

'Well, frankly speaking.' He paused, a frown wrinkling his brow. 'I mean, to be honest – and there's no point in beating about the bush – I'd say candidly it'd be about the worst you could get.'

I was touched by his eloquence.

'There you are!' my mother butted in. 'Did you hear him, Annie?'

He picked up his teacup, a little finger elegantly extended. 'Now, I don't want to say anything about the *type* of person you'd meet there, but –.' And he shook his head disapprovingly.

25

'However, let's get to the point. No beating about the bush now. What are you interested in?'

'She's a bookworm!' my mother snapped. 'But for children's books! At seventeen!'

This finished me. Of course, I'd read other books. Dante's *Inferno*. And books on existentialism by Jean Paul Sartre and Camus. And Georgette Heyer hardly had children in mind.

Chris recrossed his legs. 'Well, that's legitimate enough. Frankly speaking, some of the best books were written for children. To be honest, reading – well – ah – improves the vocabulary and develops the imagination.'

He was definitely a person of sensibility.

My mother put down her cup. 'She's too much imagination already. Reading is all very well. But she needs to study something practical. Something at the university.'

According to her a degree is the one thing you can't lose.

'I studied art in Paris.' She thumped her bosom dramatically, looking from me to Chris. 'And where did it get me? Where?'

Her Parisian studies had lasted exactly two weeks. Then there had been rumblings of war and Aunt Allie had written, persuading her to come back to Dublin to do nursing. Friends had tried to dissuade her, saying she'd have to lay out dead bodies, but my mother wanted to justify her existence – she's that type. Now her dearest possession was her Mater Hospital badge dated 1939. Because of it, she could work to support us since Daddy got sick – except people never paid. It was ironic.

Chris was eyeing my mother cautiously over his teacup. Then, turning to me, 'Ah, let's get back to the point. What's your favourite book?'

'*The Children of the New Forest,*' I said quickly. It was one of those books I had read over and over.

'Oh, Robert Louis Stevenson. You like him?'

'Nearly as much as Captain Marryat,' I said, immediately regretting it.

He looked at me suspiciously. 'Good! Grand! Well, to get to

26

the point. If I were to say, no beating about the bush now, if I were to say: you can do anything you like. Anything. What would you, candidly speaking, do? Let's put our cards on the table.'

While they both awaited my answer, I studied the Georgian ceiling. I wanted to be Cuchulainn and fight the waves of the sea. To sing of arms and the man. But I couldn't say that.

'Maybe I'd translate Dante,' I said at last. 'There's no really good translation. Eh – they all make him sound like bad Milton.' That was what the Hound had told me.

'List –!' my mother exploded into her teacup. She slammed it down, wiping her mouth with a paper napkin. 'Listen to her! Now you can see –!' And she broke into coughing.

'Or else be a champion jockey.' This was for my father.

Chris just nodded, saying nothing.

My mother threw down her napkin. 'Where would we get a racehorse? And Dante! Dante!'

'Let's get to the bush now!' Chris said.

'Point!' my mother interrupted.

'Quite!' He turned to me. 'Can you speak Italian?'

'No, but I can read Latin. They're very alike.'

My mother groaned.

He gave her a quelling look. I think that's why I fell in love – he got so cross taking my side.

'You can't adopt that attitude, if I may be blunt,' he said. 'Candidly, frankly speaking, if a person has a bent for something, it's criminal to push them into something they mightn't be happy at. And to be honest, Law is very dull. And Medicine is – well –hardly the thing for a girl. Why can't she study Italian at the University?'

I didn't have the busfare to go home, never mind the University. But at that moment I crossed the Rubicon which divides the world of the child from that of the adult. A line was drawn across my life; I was in love.

He finished his cake.

My mother pondered on his suggestion.

'Ah, sure, she'll be getting married one of these days!' he joked, sneaking a look at his watch.

Abruptly I looked away, feeling him reading my thoughts.

'Well – could she earn her living at Italian?' My mother sighed heavily. 'The very thing I don't want her to do is marry! She'll be just another lamb to the slaughter then.' And she stared gloomily into space.

'A lamb to what?' Chris' eyes narrowed.

'A lamb to the slaughter. That's all marriage is for a girl.'

He suppressed a laugh, looking around for a waiter.

I was mortified, just mortified. Every time we passed a wedding, some demon would possess my mother and she'd hiss this under her breath. But I hated her saying it now. It was worse than her 'My daughtering' me. Anyway, he was looking at his watch again and getting bored with us.

'I have to go . . .' I got up abruptly, pointing towards the Ladies.

'Well, hurry!' my mother said. 'Mr. Murphy hasn't got all day.'

On the way, I passed two drunken men. They both leered at me. Then one nudged the other saying, 'No, too angular.'

'Bony,' his friend corrected.

I escaped into the Ladies, and sat at the low dressing-table wondering if this were true. 'Fine drawn,' I would have said. Or 'pale and interesting' was how my mother always described me. Once she'd written to me in school, saying I had a lovely smile and her American legs. Of course, the Hound had read the letter and gave out stink. Vanity, she said. I smiled vainly at my reflection. Was my mother right about my hair? It was mousy and cut boringly in a fringe. And should I wear make-up? Trying to see my profile, I noticed the attendant smirking in the corner. So I put sixpence on the plate and hurried back to the WC.

In the black glossy box it was quiet enough to think. As well as me failing the Matric, my lack of sophistication was the despair of my mother. Oh, she'd been brought up in Florida where they had dates from infancy. At my age, Raymond Stark, the high school heart-throb, had even proposed to her over a root beer. They'd skip school and go to the beach every day. I had never even had a date, so could only imagine all that hot white sand. I mean the only boys we ever saw in school were pimply altar boys. And at seven o'clock in the morning. So, without any practice, how could I be sophisticated? Oh, my mother had got the brilliant idea of sending me to an American university. And had written to an old boyfriend, who was something high-up now and whom I imagined to look like President Kennedy, asking him what he thought of Smith College for me? He sent back the prospectus OK, but hadn't offered to pay. His *whole* reply was about his boat, with not a hint of Kennedy's idealism. It was ironic . . . and probably just as well. My mother depended on me for advice. And I couldn't do without her. Oh, I had read books on psychology and that. It was something buried deep in my childhood. I had kicked her once, for which my father had hit me. But then at my First Communion, I had wanted a gaudy nylon dress and she insisted on a white smocked vyella. After a struggle, my mother had given in, saying tearfully, 'I hope getting your way makes you happy, Annie!' Of course, it hadn't. I couldn't bear to see her crying and would have done anything to bring the dress back.

My mother had a hold on me.

She had a hold on everyone because of her beauty. Even Father Mullane, Cousin William's ex-headmaster, was in love with her. Every Wednesday evening for years she'd visited the college. Doone or I would run her bath beforehand. 'Darlings,' she'd sigh from the soapy depths, 'I have to use my wits.'

How she was using them, I don't know. Or why she couldn't have loved my father. I mean he had such *élan,* and Father Mullane looked . . . well . . . countryish. Still, he was decorated by Franco for heroism in his youth. And he arranged for Cousin William's education. And wrote to me in school, sending me books on religion. Or growing up. But it was the way he looked at my mother which fascinated me. His eyes would light up and he'd sort of chuckle chestily. Of course, I understood him loving my mother for her courage and gaiety. It was ... oh, the mechanisms of love I couldn't imagine. I knew the facts of life OK – from Botany class. I just dreaded the whole idea. According to the Hound, men were after one thing, and I felt sure I couldn't supply it. When I asked my mother how she managed, her answer was, 'Spanish Fly, darling! Spanish Fly!'

This was some aphrodisiac from her youth. But whether you swallowed it, or rubbed it on, or both, I could never discover. Once his ardour cooled and we fled to London to bring him to his senses. Oh, there were bills too, but, like the poor, there were always bills. Basically my mother wanted Father Mullane to declare his love. It worked OK – I mean he was glad enough to see her back, but we had the most awful time. Awful. Back in school the next term, I found a quotation in my Latin book: 'Amatium irae, amoris integratio est.' (The quarrels of lovers are a renewal of love.) Which definitely wasn't the case with my mother and father.

For years I'd been in the Future Infinitive case: Amaratus Esse. (To be about to be loved.) Maybe now I could be in the Present Indicative Active: Amo. (I love) Chris was just my type: dark and broody, with muscles knotted like a root of heather – exactly what I'd read about in Emily and Georgette Heyer. *'Whoever loved that loved not at first sight?'* the poet has written. But for me it was love before sight. Chris was the composite of all the men I'd ever been attracted to: Dirk Bogarde, Alan Breck, Peter Finch, The Man in the Dark Brown Suit, and all the stern guardians in Georgette Heyer – Sir Richard, Sir Gavin, Mr. Marmaduke Shapely, Carlington, Sir Thomas Fort, Mr Lionel Winter, The Marquis of Vidal. Except we were doomed never to meet again. And even if we did, what would I say? I hadn't my mother's knack. I was alone and always would be, in my own suburban heath.

'Annie!' My mother rapped menacingly on the door. 'Is anything wrong?'

'I've a pain.'

'Is it a visit from Judy?'

'No!' This was our school's euphemism for the curse.

'Well, hurry! Come and say goodbye to Mr Murphy! He's in a rush!'

'OK.'

'Annie?' My mother sighed heavily. 'What's wrong?'

'Nothing!'

'But you've never behaved like this before.'

'I'm trying to go to the toilet!'

That made her go away. When I was washing my hands, she came back.

'He had to rush off and play football.'

'Football?' I grimaced into the mirror. 'But he's going grey!'

My mother snapped her handbag shut. 'At your age, I was white. But so long as I can lift my hand to my head!' And she proudly combed her hair. 'I'll be a brunette!'

'Who was he anyway?' I asked, yawning.

'A young friend of your father's.'

I made another face. 'Young?'

'He's a solicitor with Fossil Forsyth. He acted for us once. Lost the case.' She paused, concentrating on putting on lipstick. 'Your father could really pick them.'

'Still, it was nice of him to ask us.'

'The first of many, darling.' She smudged her lips together, and retied her scarf. 'Now, give me half-a-crown for a tip.'

'Eh – we'd better hurry home. There's your coat to be ironed.'

My mother was on a night case, and hadn't yet been abed.

'Give me half-a-crown, darling!'

'A half-a-crown?'

'The tip, darling!'

I know money doesn't matter, but her philanthropy was the bane of my life. 'But if he paid, he'll –.'

'We can't walk out without leaving a tip!'

The attendant was listening, so I gave in.

31

3

Our house was in utter darkness.

I banged the knocker harder, but still no one came. The echo just clattered hollowly over the rooftops, reminding me of the poem:

> *'Is anybody there,' said the traveller,*
> *Knocking on the moonlit door,*
> *And his horse in the silence . . .*

'Oh, open up!' My mother stamped down the garden path and pounded angrily on the side door. 'Doone! William!'

This brought howling barks from Pete, our half-Dalmatian. Then a light appeared in one of the new houses opposite.

If Pete were there, Doone must be. I stepped over the flower beds onto the squelchy grass and checked the upstairs windows. The venetian blinds were down. Lifeless. The white slats contrasting nicely with the dark cedar house. We were the only house in the row of four to have venetians – they were on H.P. like most of our furniture. The houses were a bit rickety, but because of the cedar, unique in Ireland. They were on a crossroads, facing the Dublin mountains and surrounded by suburban sprawl. The owner was a Plymouth Brethren minister who preached the love of God from Dun Laoghaire pier every Saturday night. My father often brought us to hear him, making Doone and me stand apart as if not with him. Because despite loving God, our landlord hated children. It was ironic. So, when he called for the rent, we had to pretend there was only one child: Cousin William – Doone and I hid with Pete. The Freemans had lived next door, but since getting rich on antiques, had moved up in the world to Foxrock. I don't know why – they were cosy little houses. Perhaps they'd been upset by the bulldozers slicing the front gardens to widen the road. Anyway they drove off one day, packing their antiques, endless washing machines, radios, and bikes into a huge van, and taking Doone, who was best friends with their daughter Susie, for the spin. Without them, it wasn't half the fun. They often had Doone to tea and when Daddy died they had offered my mother a job in their shop. Of course, she didn't need it with having her profession.

My mother was getting angrier and angrier, but I just stared at our house. It had been called 'Villa Rosa' when we came, but I thought 'Shelley' was better. Even minus the garden, it was a relief to live here. After we sold our farm, we'd wandered nomadically from flat to flat in Dublin, and to every seaside resort from Bettystown to Bray. Our family wasn't restless – we just had to move when the time came to pay.

The same with schools: I'd been to twelve – nine before I was eight.

'Doone! William!' My mother peered through the kitchen window.

In a minute she wouldn't just see red, but a kind of howling purple.

Pete was really yelping now. 'Y-i-i-ow-ow! Y-i-i-ow-ow!'

'Perhaps they've gone out,' I suggested. 'Or think we're creditors.'

'Hmpf!' My mother banged the knocker again.

Then, through the letterbox, I saw someone move in the hall. 'Doone! It's only us!'

Her blue eyes appeared in the slit. '*You?* Oh!' Then, holding Pete's collar, she warily opened the door.

My mother stormed into the house. 'Now! Why wouldn't you open that door?' Roughly she brushed off Pete's excited licks so, as was his wont, he goosed her. 'Oh, my God!' And she kicked him, turning on Doone.

Knowing what was coming, I turned my head.

It was a hard slap.

'It wasn't my fault!' Doone screamed.

As my mother lifted her hand again, she hopped nimbly out of the way. She looks like a foundling or a workhouse child. Her shabby outgrown skirt showed bony knees, and wisps of hay-coloured hair escaped from her untidy ponytail. Oh, I admit she's stubborn, but my mother's often too hard on her.

'Go to your room!' she raged, struggling out of her leopard-skin. 'And take that mutt with you!'

'But Cousin William wouldn't let me!' Doone sobbed, dragging Pete upstairs. 'He thought you were Nicola!'

'D-did she call?' I nearly died at Nicola seeing my house.

'Yes! Here, Pete! But you were out! Here, boy!' And she disappeared into our room.

I dreaded what Cousin William had said to Nicola.

Just then his dressing-gowned figure popped round the dining room door. As he never spoke to us now, there was no point in asking him. He's a tall boy with wild dark curly hair and handsome ruddy looks. Seeing us, he immediately slammed the door shut. 'I'm going to kill that dog! Kill him!'

He was always saying this – it was about all he ever said.

My mother was furiously examining the afternoon's post. 'Bills! Bills! Bills! Nobody ever writes to me!' And she flung them unopened into the waste basket.

I followed Doone upstairs. Our room was strictly divided: the tidy half with the bookshelf mine; the untidy half with the pictures of giraffes hers.

She was lying face-down on her bed, with Pete whimpering beneath it. I rubbed her back. 'Never mind, Mummy's just tired.'

'She's always tired to me!'

'You know she'll be sorry in a minute.' This was always her way.

'Where were you anyway?'

'Shopping. Eh – was Cousin William rude to Nicola?'

Doone just turned to the wall.

34

'Please, Doone! What did Nicola say?'

'You're to get the train out tomorrow. You go everywhere!'

'I don't! What did Cousin William say?'

'Oh . . . I didn't ask her in. He was mad 'cos she came.'

I sighed with relief.

Then Pete began licking me enthusiastically. He's an unfortunate looking animal, sort of biggish and spotted and hairy. His mother had been a pure-bred Dalmatian, but he resembled his mongrel father. Technically Cousin William owns him, but, as Doone took care of him, he was considered hers.

'Down boy.' I petted him, thinking on what she had said. True, I was my mother's favourite. She always told me things, about my father and her youth and Father Mullane. I thought I was just older and so a *confidante,* but Doone was fourteen now. Still, my mother never told her anything. Which left her a bit in the cold since my father's death. Then I remembered her weeping at his funeral, when I had just sort of watched myself. It was weird.

'*I* won't be going to a Kibbutz with the Freemans,' I said gently.

She still faced the wall. So I put my arms round her.

'Whatja get?' She sat up on her hunkers, her feet on the bed.

'Oh, just underwear. It's being delivered.'

'You get everything!'

As was her wont, she began sucking her thumb. It's a terrible habit, the cause of her prominent teeth, but I only said, 'I don't! And you wouldn't be objecting if we were buying Christmas presents.'

'You got that coat!'

'You'll be getting things when you leave school.'

'I have left!'

This was true. The reason, the Mount Prospect nuns had sent her home was that nobody had paid her fees. And her reports were so bad, my mother couldn't find another school willing to take her. It was tragic she had to leave school, far, far worse than my leaving. Now her lamp would never be lit by the torch of knowledge. Also the Sacred Heart nuns had convents all over the world, and a sort of empire of past pupils to help if need arose. Nicola and I were members. What would Doone do now that she was excluded?

'You'll be getting things when the Freemans take you to Israel,' I placated. 'Do you think I should shorten this coat?' I pirouetted round the room.

'They'll never take me to a Kabbage!'

'Kibbutz! And they will. Then you'll see real giraffes.' I tried to see my coat hem in the dressing table mirror. At least I had my mother's legs.

'There aren't any giraffes there. Only in Africa.'

'Maybe they'll have dead ones in the museums.'

'You think so?' Anything about giraffes always cheered her up.

'Yes. Now concentrate on my coat. We'll talk about the Kibbutz then.'

'OK, Sis.'

'Sis' was an irritating expression from *School Friend*. Or some other comic. 'Hols' was another. But for now I said nothing, just pinned up my hem. Of course, I had no idea what she'd be doing on the Kibbutz. I just made up stories about picking grapefruit and riding camels and petting giraffes and that.

'How's this length?' I had a pin in my mouth.

She was sucking her thumb and staring dreamily into space.

'Sis, I'd miss Pete too much if I was there.'

'If I *were* there. The conditional takes the subjunctive. Now –.'

Suddenly something crashed downstairs. So we both dashed down, followed by a yelping Pete.

Everything seemed OK. The sitting room door was shut and there was nobody in the dining room. Yesterday's dishes were still on the table, chop bones congealing on the plates and our remaining odd china cups half-filled with tea.

'Doone!' I scolded. 'It's your day!'

But she was already transfixed in front of the T.V.

Suddenly something cracked on my head. I saw stars like in the comics. Then I saw a cup lying broken on the floor.

'Leave her alone, you bully!' Doone shrieked.

Cousin William was doing a sort of jig at the door, his face lobster red.

'What's wrong?' I asked, shaken.

'You touched my *Financial Times!*' Then, looking as if he'd swallowed something the wrong way, he furiously waved a letter.

'I d-didn't!'

Doone was crying, while Pete growled and bared his teeth.

Cousin William crumpled the letter and flung it at me. 'I'm not paying that!'

It was my dentist's bill.

'He said there's no hurry!' I mumbled, uncrumpling the bill for four guineas.

Cousin William was biting his hand and getting madder. Pete growled louder, getting ready to pounce.

'Down, boy!' I patted his head. His was the opposite of all canine behaviour; he licked people when they came and growled at them when they left. And he'd never grasped that Cousin William was a member of the family. Odd, considering Cousin William had studied to be a vet.

'Why'd he send it to me?' Cousin William raged.

Pete flew at his pyjama leg.

'Cos you have the money!' I pulled the dog back.

Just then my mother came in saying, 'He shouldn't have sent it. And Annie won't go to the dentist again.' Then, seeing me, she fell in a swoon.

Doone and I rushed to catch her, but luckily she landed on a chair. Although a nurse, she cannot stand the sight of blood.

'Hunh!' Kicking Pete, Cousin William disappeared into the hall.

'Doone! A glass of water!' Frantically I loosened my mother's buttons.

'Blood! Blood!' she shrieked, opening her eyes.

37

'But you aren't bleeding,' I said.

'You are, you silly girl! Oh!'

I hadn't realized my face was bleeding.

Doone shakily handed me a glass of water.

My mother sipped a little, asking, 'Are you all right, Annie?'

I nodded, swallowing back tears. 'Come up to bed.'

'I'm sorry I fainted. And Doone darling, I'm sorry for getting mad.'

''s OK!' Doone shrugged magnanimously.

Then we hauled my mother up, staggering up the stairs. Cousin William had disappeared into his room. D.G.

'Don't judge him,' she groaned, half-way up. 'His genes are clashing.' Then in a whisper 'and we're completely in his power.'

'What're genes?' Doone swayed dangerously backwards.

'Careful! She means it's heredity.' I puffed under the weight.

It's a complicated story and the stuff of fiction. Cousin William's mother was someone who died before my father and mother met. I imagined her as a Russian spy or something, but she was someone ordinary. Cousin William had been ordinary too, only getting funny at our father's death. I mean, I had loved having a half-brother, like a heroine in Georgette Heyer. It was silly, but I'd even christened him Branny. The Brontës' brother had been odd too, and so had Prince Hal. I believed Cousin William was like him, 'Amongst a grove the very straightest plant,' and only chaffing under the yoke of inheritance. It's all to do with a Will. Basically, Cousin William's the heir to my father's property – like Mr Collins in *Pride and Prejudice* (a book I've always found dullish. I mean, Darcy Dullard?) Still, to get back: my father waited all his life for Cousin William to be twenty-one, to break the entail, sell the land, and go into some business that wouldn't fail. Then, just as Cousin William came into his majority, and we came into our kingdom, my father died and the lot went to Cousin William. With nothing for my mother or Doone or me. Nothing. It was a fluke, according to my mother. And the law, according to Aunt Allie, which is always right.

38

I didn't mind about the money so much as Cousin William not talking to us. My mother consulted Fr. Mullane about this, saying 'manners maketh man.' But he corrected her, saying it was 'morals'. And Cousin William's were OK as he didn't drink, smoke, or fornicate.

I wouldn't have minded him having some vices.

My mother lay on her bed, ashen-faced. She'd only an hour before work. So, thinking her not well enough to go, I decided to ring the people from our local pub – as usual our phone was cut off. But she opened her eyes and, rolling them, signalled.

Luckily Doone was straightening her quilt and didn't see.

My mother rolled her eyes again.

'Doone,' I said with heavy emphasis. 'Marcella's coming.'

She plonked on the bed, deliberately ignoring the hint.

'If the dishes are done, she'll have time to make scones.' I knew this would cheer her up.

'OK, I'm *going*,' she moaned, shuffling out.

My mother grabbed my hand. 'He didn't write!'

'Father Mullane?'

'Yes. It's all over!'

'You'll hear from him.' For the first time, I understood the pain in her eyes. 'You always do.'

'But he's being moved. And all because of me. She slumped back on her pillow.

'Where to?'

'Cork, he thinks. Might as well be the moon!'

This was true. We'd never, ever be able to afford the fare there. Not once a week. What could be wrong with Father Mullane loving my mother? Or vice versa? To love was the message of the gospels. Thinking of Chris, I felt a spasm myself. He was surely bespoken, either married or with a girlfriend. I'd certainly never meet him again. It'd be a case of unrequited love . . . *de rigeur* in books, but . . . I fiddled with the make-up and perfume bottles on her dressing table. Since childhood, I had resisted their charms, believing they held nothing for me. But now they seemed

39

to hold all the secrets of being grown up, which would never be revealed to me.

Then something made me confide in my mother. 'It's happened to me too.'

She sat bolt upright. 'What's happened? Tell me! You can tell your mother anything!'

I felt myself redden. 'It was that man –.'

'*What* man?' Her eyes rounded in horror.

'It – just happened.'

She pounced out of bed. 'When?'

'At the Shelbourne.'

'My God! That's why you wouldn't come out!' She pulled on her dressing gown. 'What'd he look like? I'll go to the police! Any distinguishing features? Thank God, your father didn't see this day!'

'Mummy –.'

'Where'd he attack you?'

'In the dining room.' I regretted telling her anything, so was deliberately obtuse. It was typical of her to nag me about being childish, and then worry if I was out of her sight for a minute.

'The dining room? *What* dining room?'

I felt my face. 'And I don't need a doctor. It's stopped bleeding.'

'Bleeding?' She gaped in horror.

'Nothing's happened! I'm in *love,* that's all.' I gave her a hug.

'Oh! . . . With *whom* are you in love?'

'With the man in the Shelbourne. The man who asked us to tea.'

'Christopher Murphy? Him?' She stared in disbelief, then went on slowly, 'Well . . . no finer man to be in love with. But darling, he's a man of the world. He wouldn't be interested in someone like you.'

'What's wrong with me?'

'You're only a baby. You wouldn't know what love meant.'

'I would.'

40

'Well,' she went on thoughtfully, 'if you felt that way, you should've given him the come-hither.'

'How?'

'Caught his eye, looked away, and then looked back.' And she demonstrated this. 'Let me see you do it!'

I did it.

'Good! Now practise that in the mirror. Of course,' she went on, 'you could get him interested. You may not *keep* him interested but –.'

'How?'

'Leave it with me.' She tapped her chin. 'He agreed to look in to the Will for me. Maybe –.'

'I'd better iron your coat.' I hopped nervously up, hearing Doone let Marcella in. 'There's not much time.' Oh, I wanted to meet Chris again, but the idea made me queasy.

Marcella's our maid from long ago. She's absolutely ancient, and before us had actually worked for my grandparents, nursing my mother as a baby. We couldn't afford her anymore, so nowadays she worked for a doctor in Merrion Square and came to us some free evenings. She was convinced we needed minding and couldn't manage alone.

It was ironic, *her* minding *us*. I mean, she's tiny and comes only to my elbow. Her wispy white hair is always carefully rolled to hide her bald head. And she's nearly blind. But we loved her coming: she always told us stories and brought leftovers from her other job.

She was unpacking these in the kitchen.

'I've a jiant, Miss Annie.' She rummaged in her big black bag. 'There's a good bit o' cuttin' on it.'

We all had titles: Miss Doone, Master William, and my mother was always Ma'am. They were relics from another age, like the cherries in her hat, her starched floral overall, and nunnish shoes and stockings.

'Is Ma'am sleeping?' She laid the things on the table: cold meat, a half a loaf of bread, an opened packet of butter, tea in an envelope, and a tin of Ajax.

41

I nodded, putting the iron on the gas – we heated it this way since it broke. If I said my mother had gone to town instead of to bed, Marcella would only scold – most days my mother took diet pills to stay awake.

Just then she appeared in the kitchen, giving the game away.

'There's no sleep with children.' She plonked down on a chair. 'Annie's staying overnight with the Jennings and needed things in town.'

'Hmm!' Marcella's mouth tightened, as she pulled on her dowdy apron.

'Now, we can't have her disgracing us,' my mother placated. 'Can we?'

'No Jennings could hold a candle to Miss Annie.' Marcella pinned a wisp of hair. 'What's bred in the bone . . .'

My mother winked at me, as Marcella's the most awful snob. 'Oh, Marcella! You're being old-fashioned. Nowadays –.'

'What's bred in the bone, Ma'am.'

'But Annie's reached the age when she needs to meet people. Why, already she's in love.'

'Mummy!'

'What, dear?' She smiled brightly. 'Sorry! As I was saying, Annie needs friends –.'

'It's time you had your tea, Ma'am.'

'Yes, I'd better get on my horse.' And my mother went upstairs singing a pop song.

As well as being a Jackie watcher, my mother's a pop song fan. I generally prefer the older songs: John McCormack singing 'Wearin' of the Green', or 'Just a Song at Twilight' – two of my father's favourites.

I ironed happily, while Marcella tore into the dining room. 'Look smart, Miss Doone! Clear that table, now!'

Pete growled, but Doone stayed glued to the snowy T.V.

So Marcella switched it off. 'Clear that table!'

'Oh, OK!' Doone petted Pete into quietude. 'If you tell us a story.'

42

'I'm hoarse tellin' yez things! Clear that table!' Marcella was clattering in the kitchen, making my mother's tea and toast – that was all she ever ate.

I finished her coat, then brought up the tray. Then, as usual, walked her to the bus stop. I always hated her going, but it had to be. And she'd be home in the morning.

Of course, Marcella gave in and told us a story before going home that evening. About her brush with death on Baggot Street Bridge. Her brother was in the British Army, so she'd been *for* the British in 1916. And had never since changed her mind. In the middle of the Rising, before my mother was born, she'd been walking with my grandmother and little uncle who died to their house on Pembroke Road – they lived there after Haiti where my grandfather was the American Ambassador, but that's another story . . . at the time my grandfather was *in* Kilmainham for Republican sympathies. But to get back: Marcella and my grandmother were crossing the bridge and got caught in crossfire. 'Come on, Marcella!' my grandmother had shouted, running for cover with her little boy. But Marcella had stood her ground, calling her brother's name. 'Come on, Marcella!' My grandmother had been nearly frantic. 'They wouldn't shoot a sympathiser!' Marcella had screamed, calling her brother again. And the soldiers had held their fire. Oh, I suppose it's an ordinary enough story. It's just the way she told it gave you goose pimples.

And she'd tell us about her childhood in County Clare where they made the linen for the sheets. She'd been very young when she went to work for my grandparents, travelling with them to New York, then Haiti where my grandfather had actually quelled a revolution. The story goes that an assassin had been hired to kill him but had killed himself instead. Marcella told us this. And about negroes, casting spells. And about my mother as an orphan baby.

In school Doone and I had been called 'the Americans', because of me always boasting about America – probably that's

43

another X. But I couldn't help mentioning it now and then. Like when my grandfather fell in love with my grandmother. He came to Ireland to speak at Wolfe Tone's grave and happened to see my grandmother riding to the Kilkenny hounds. 'That's the woman I'll marry,' he said to himself. And he did.

In bed that night I thought and thought about marriage. It sounds cracked, but the idea gave me a queer feeling. That I wouldn't know what to do. Like the time when I was little and the cat ate my rabbit. I had brought him to the cabbage patch for his lunch. But as I lay in the sun, our huge Tom dragged him off. And I'd been too frightened to do anything. Even to tell my mother and father. I think I just said it ran away. And I dreaded marriage for the same reason: not knowing what to do. I asked Aunt Allie if this was normal, and she said marriage came naturally. But when I told my mother, she said it was natural OK, naturally boring. And not to marry an Irishman. Or if I had to, to pick someone kind like Father Mullane – which was a bit unfair to my father.

Chris was Irish, but definitely looked kind. I was in a turmoil of unhappiness and couldn't sleep at all, thinking a Man of the World was most probably married. Still . . . they never were in Georgette Heyer. Then I imagined him as Sir Christopher with close-cropped hair, sporting neck-cloth and gleaming Hessian boots – the signs of the Corinthian. And myself as a Bath Miss fleeing in my chaise from his curricle. We were on the road to London . . . As the gap between us narrowed, my post boys lashed my horses. This foolish gesture of defiance enraged his Lordship and he passed me at the first opportunity, blocking the narrow road ahead with his curricle. As my chaise pulled up, I awaited inside in trepidation. Sir Christopher stalked over, wrenching open the door with a crack of sardonic laughter. 'Well, Miss!' And a muscle quivered at the corner of his mouth. And I had no time to escape, but was locked in a crushing embrace and kissed so hard and so often that I had no breath left to expostulate. Sir Christopher at last stopped his kissing, but showed not the least inclination to let me go. He just looked into my eyes saying in an awe-inspiring voice, 'Well? Are you going to marry me?'

But it wouldn't happen like that. I had an anguish, which could only be soothed by writing Hamlet's Soliloquy: 'To be or not to be . . .' Or a poem, or something. So I decided to grasp the nettle and write Chris a letter. After all, Virgil has written, *Audentis Fortuna iuvat.* (Fortune favours the brave.)

So I put on my light, tiptoeing to my bookshelf for paper.

'Dear Mr Murphy,' I began. 'It was awfully nice of you to ask us to tea today. I am still in a quandary careerwise, and wonder if –.'

'Whaja doing?' Doone sat up, blinking.

'Writing an important letter! Go back to sleep!'

She groaned, pulling the blankets over her head. 'You never sleep!'

'I don't need to!' My mother had told me you needed less as you got older. And a nurse should know.

My train of thought was interrupted, so I chewed the end of my biro.

'Don't forget a punctuation mark every four words.' Doone's voice was muffled.

'It's not always necessary.' I'd only told her this as a general rule.

'But, you said –.'

'Oh, go to sleep!'

At times like this, I really wanted the room to myself.

'Turn out the light!' she grumped.

So quickly I finished my letter: 'I'm still in a quandary careerwise, and wonder if you'd think of advising me again sometime. Listen, I must close now, as my sister wants the light out.

　　Sincerely,
　　　　Your friend,
　　　　　　Anne O'Brien.'

45

Sleep had deserted me, and I lay awake until that hour when,

the morn in russet mantle clad
Walks o'er the dew of yon high eastern hill.

4

Fossil Forsyth Solicitors were in the telephone directory. So, after typing the next day, I delivered my *billet* to the top of Dawson Street.

Then I caught the train to Nicola's.

She lives in Dalkey, a seaside village on the south side. Her Georgian house is tucked beneath a big hill about fifteen minutes dark walk from the station. So I ran nervously ahead of the other passengers and was soon through the barricades, past the village, and alone in the scary dusk of Sorrento Road. According to my father, the railway here is haunted. He was always telling stories about headless men, and the Widow Gamble in Monkstown, and beds moving in hotels, and black dogs appearing. But I banished them. The mind, after all, is its own place.

My suitcase contained only my blanket-bit, toothbrush, asthma inhaler, nightie and *Wuthering Heights*. So I didn't mind the hill. 'Sorrento' reminded me of Dante, and I prayed the first lines of his *Inferno:*

> *Nel mezzo del camin di nostra vita*
> *mi ritrovai per una selva oscura.*
> (In the middle of my life's journey
> I found myself in a dark wood.)

I'd lived for years, OK, but wasn't quite in my journey's middle. Although there were trees about, so *per una selva oscura* could apply. Now that I was in love, the next line definitely did – it's about losing the straight way:

'Che . . . Che . . .'

I couldn't remember it. But the communion with my hero

47

made the smitten sky and spidery trees actually comforting. Not far off the sea lapped. And when I turned inland over the railway bridge, its still sad music followed me, inexorably, eerily, to Nicola's gate.

Then I got the fright of my life.

A big black dog was behind it.

'Yi--ow--ow!' he howled, his eyes glinting red, his long thin tail lashing the night.

Dante had passed Cerebus by throwing dirt in his eyes. Orpheus soothed wild beasts with his music. Even Cuchulainn throttled a dog. But I just shivered.

'Down, boy!' I whispered.

But he howled again, snarling.

He's only a dog like Pete, I told myself and slipped through the gate. But as I edged up the avenue, he sniffed me hungrily.

Then he jumped on me. His huge paws thumping my shoulders. His breath hot on my face.

I dropped my suitcase and ran back.

It's the devil in disguise, I thought, as my footsteps echoed clatteringly in the distance. The trees were claws now, grabbing me. The sea hissed sinisterly. The sky closed in. I was alone on the road, running.

Why hadn't Nicola met me in town?

Blindly I ran on, my legs weak, sweating.

On the bridge a sportscar screeched to a halt.

'Anne?' a voice called from the driver's seat. 'Where are you going?'

It was Nicola.

'I was – a bit early.' I crossed over.

She looked at me in puzzlement. Although she's on a permanent diet, her face was still fattish and her brownish shoulder-length hair was backcombed. She hitched her pink silk headscarf forward, knotting it under her chin. 'But mother's home! You should've gone in!' Then throwing her parcels into the back, she opened the passenger door.

I clambered into perfumy safety. 'Actually – there was a dog.'

'Oh, Caesar wouldn't hurt you.' She released the handbrake and we jolted forward. 'His teeth've been pulled,' she shouted over the engine.

'What? He has no teeth!'

'But how can he eat?'

Incredulously she shook her head. 'One minute you're running for your life, and the next you're feeling sorry for the brute. It boggles the mind.'

I definitely wouldn't tell Doone.

On the hill she shifted gears. 'What do you think of the car?'

'It's fast.'

'Should be! It's an MG. A present for college. And my eighteenth.'

Although in the same class, Nicola's a year older than I – her eighteenth was last January, mine is next. We're both Aquarians, the sign of many distinguished people. And we both left school early. Two of the reasons she liked me.

At the gate she honked. 'Now hurry up!'

A light went on outside the gate lodge.

Nervously I peered through the window. 'Eh – will I open –?'

'No!' She honked again. 'That's why we pay Mrs Conroy. You could've rung her bell. It's on the side wall. Remember?'

'It was always daylight before. I – eh – dropped . . . My case – it's out there somewhere.' But it was gone.

She was honking. 'God, I'm whacked!' She rubbed the back of her neck.

'Is the University tiring?'

'No! That's super! Occasional students have great fun. It's Poise and Personality that gets me. I spent the whole afternoon learning to walk in and out of a room.'

'How do you do it?'

This difficulty had never occurred to me.

Finally a thin woman in an apron opened the gates.

'About time too!' Nicola waved as we zipped through.

49

'But my case! Nicola, I dropped my case!'

'Well! The mind boggles!' She braked screechily, backing to Mrs Conroy who had found it.

I struggled with the door.

'Here!' Nicola stretched to open it. 'Thanks, Mrs Conroy! – Gosh, what've you got in that?'

The huge case rattled emptily as I took it on my knees. 'My night things.'

'You'd think you were staying for a year!' Laughing, she banged the door and sped up the avenue.

As it was my only suitcase, I thought this a bit catty. But I stared silently ahead. It was eerie outside with no sign of the dog. D.G. The towering trees became spectres again in our headlights and I was glad to be in the car, and gladder when we scrunched to a halt on the wide front gravel.

Getting out, I heard a whinny in the darkness. Then galloping. Then a horse appeared at the paddock railings. A real horse. Its coat was inky black and a white star marked its forehead. 'Look, Nicola!'

'I'm sick of looking at the brute!' Grumpily she gathered her parcels.

I patted the horse's nose through the railings. 'There, boy!'

'It's a mare! Daddy wants me to hunt!'

'Oh! . . . You lucky thing! Here, girl!' The horse butted me affectionately. 'Could I've a ride sometime?'

'We'll have to ask Daddy. The stupid thing's valuable.'

'But I can ride.'

She was swaggering over the gravel to the house. I followed with my case, thinking how much Doone would love a ride too, and picturing myself galloping across the paddock like Rembrandt's Polish Rider – it was in a school library book of Dutch paintings.

We walked through the plant-filled porch to the hall. Nicola dropped her parcels by the table and thumbed through the bundle of letters on a silver platter.

She grimaced drolly. 'Nothing from Anton! Hmm! . . . We'll see about that.'

For the millionth time, I envied her her house. It was so rich. Much richer than our country house, where we lived before all our moving. A dark red carpet stretched the length of the hall and up a wide stairway. And there were drawings of Dublin on the walls – Trinity College and the Bank of Ireland and that.

'You haven't met Anton, have you?'

'Eh – no!'

'Never mind, you will! Come on upstairs. You can leave your things.'

On the landing she paused. 'Oh, did I tell you? I'm coming out in two weeks.'

'Coming out of what?'

'Nothing, stupid! I'm having a *début!* We're having caterers. And a band. You're invited of course.'

'Oh!'

'But it's formal. You'll need a long dress.'

'I have one,' I lied.

'And an escort! Mother insists on being stuffy.'

As we went into her bedroom, I concentrated on the *décor*. The walls were newly decorated in powder blue, and dark blue chintz bed quilts matched the curtains and kidney dressing-table.

'Never mind. I'll dig you up someone.'

'Eh – what?'

'I'll find you a partner. Take the far bed. Unless you want the guest room?'

'No!' I blurted, remembering the dog. 'Eh – there is someone I could ask.'

She took off her scarf and brown suede coat. 'I didn't know you went in for men.'

'I – eh – your room's lovely, Nicola.'

'It's dire. That blue boggles the mind.' She hung her coat in the wardrobe. 'Mother's idea of a surprise!' She went into the connecting bathroom and turned on the taps. 'I'd prefer

51

something a little less frumpy. Tell me about your mystery man!'
'I've only just met him,' I called. 'It hasn't – really – progressed.'
'Invite him to my *début!* That'll be progress!'
'Well . . . maybe, I shouldn't.' I shouted over the taps.
'Why on earth not?'
'We only met once.'
She came out, rubbing on face cream. 'Where'd he take you?'
'The Shelbourne.'
'He took you *there*?' Quickly she blotched on more cream.
'How far did he go afterwards?'
'All the way – to the bus stop.' I was going to say home, but
bus stop was less of a lie.
'*All* the way to the bus stop?' She scrutinized me, then went on
quickly, 'What happened then? Did you feel anything?'
'Well . . . I felt great!'
Her eyes widened. 'You *did?* Well! . . . Anton and I – we've
gone "all the way to the bus stop" a few times too. Of course we're
getting engaged! Tell me,' she asked darkly, 'how long did it last?'
'The bus came in a few minutes.'
'Annie!' She flung herself on the bed, giggling. 'I never knew
you would! What's his name?'
'Christopher. Christopher Murphy.'
'Hmm . . . sounds familiar. What school did he go to?'
I shrugged.
'I only go out with Glenstal boys! Anton went to Glenstal. Is he
at university?'
I was praying she'd stop. 'No. He's a solicitor.'
'A solicitor? Well!' She sat bolt upright. 'No wonder he took
you to the Shelbourne!'
Feeling her prying into my very soul, I fiddled with the jar of
cream on her telephone table. 'Is this good?' The label said, 'Skin
Food.'
'Should be. It's Elizabeth Arden. Try some!'
I dabbed my chin.
'You'd better cleanse first.'

52

I went into the bathroom.

'What brand do you use?' She called after me.

'Ponds!' This was my mother's brand.

'Junk!' Nicola appeared in the doorway, reaching for an expensive bottle. 'Try this cleanser. But take off your coat!'

I was wearing my school skirt, but D.G. she hung up my coat without comment.

Then she put cream on a tissue and, while I cleansed, watched me, saying, 'Rub in circular movements . . . you should look after your skin, Anne. You've got open pores . . . Now, Tonic!' And she dabbed tingly stuff on my face. 'A little does. Can you feel it working?'

I nodded.

'Now for the "Visible Difference".' She dabbed it sparingly on my face and neck. 'Rub upwards, Anne! Always upwards! It prevents sagging.'

'Is it expensive cream?'

'Don't be put off by the price!' She looked approvingly at my reflection. 'You can buy it in Brown Thomas's. Or any good chemist. You know, you could be good-looking Anne. If you took more trouble. And held yourself properly.'

I straightened my shoulders. 'Mummy wants me to dye my hair.'

'Maybe a few streaks. Like mine.'

'I don't see any.'

'You're not meant to, silly!'

'Oh.'

'There's still a lot to be done!' She rooted in the cupboard for a tube of make-up and rubbed it on my face. Then she put on lipstick and eyeshadow. Then spread glue on a false eyelash. 'Close your eyes!'

I did.

She pressed on the lash. 'Hold that a sec! I'll glue the other one.'

She pressed on the second lash.

I peeped out of the first eye.

'Keep your eyes closed!' Noisily she rooted in the cupboard.

'Can I look now?' I said at last.

'Oh, all right.'

I blinked droopingly into the mirror. 'Do I not look funny?'

'There's still a lot to be done!' She began backcombing my hair, and, when it was all on end like a golly, smoothed it into a pudding shape. Then she painted a thin line over each eyelash, rouged my cheeks and put on lipstick.

Dumbly I stared at the new me.

'You look terrific, Anne!' She nodded admiringly in the mirror. Then reached to the back of the cupboard for a gold lighter and a packet of cigarettes. 'Have a ciggy.'

I took one.

She lit me. 'Anton gave me this.'

I puffed and broke into a cough.

She inhaled expertly. 'You need to work on your image, Anne. Keep up with the latest fashions. In clothes, hair styles, even books. I'll bet you haven't read Colin Wilson?'

'Well –.' I shook my head. I'd never even heard of him.

'He's the thing now! I'll show you his book.' Taking an ashtray from the cupboard, she made for the bedroom. 'I'll just open a window. Mother's stupid rules.'

I sat on my bed, smoking.

'Here!' She gave me two books. 'That's his masterpiece, *The Outsider*. And Sylvia Plath's the latest poet.'

I flicked through *The Colossus*.

Nicola blew out a cloud of smoke. 'She's thirty. I'll be finished by thirty.'

'Dante wasn't finished by thirty. Or Doctor Johnson. Remember . . .'

She was looking at me vacantly.

'Remember, the Hound used to tell us about him leaving Oxford because of his shoes.'

'What about his shoes?'

54

'He hadn't any.'

Nicola rolled her eyes. 'That woman bored me! Utterly!'

The Hound's real name is Mother Culhane. Which we changed to Cuchulainn – the Hound of Ireland, and then just the Hound. She told me about Dante and Shelley and Keats whose name was writ in water, but I still said, 'I suppose she was boring.'

Nicola grimaced. 'She was dire! Thank God, I don't have to listen to any more of her drivel!'

I took a puff of my cigarette.

Then Mrs Jennings appeared in the doorway. 'I thought I heard you come in.'

I stood up, smiling. She's the model type: tall, and thin and always perfectly made up. She wore a red wool shirt dress and her hair was in a French roll.

But she was glaring at Nicola. 'What do you think you're doing?'

Slowly, sullenly Nicola stubbed out her cigarette. 'Anne gave it to me.'

I felt myself redden.

Mrs Jennings turned icily to me. 'I don't allow smoking in the house, dear.'

I stubbed out mine.

'Bring Anne down to the study!'

Nicola didn't answer.

Mrs Jennings forced a smile at me. 'You've grown up a lot! But – haven't you got thin?'

'I – eh –.'

'Remember, no smoking in the house, dear!' And she went out.

Immediately Nicola flung the ashtray at the closed door. 'Bitch! Bloody bitch!'

'But, Nicola!'

The hairbrush went flying.

'Nicola!'

Then a box of trinkets from the dressing table.

55

'She – just thinks you'll get cancer,' I whispered.

She just stood there, shaking.

I was shaking too. It reminded me of my row with Cousin William. Except it was worse with a mother. I never had such a row with mine. Oh, we disagreed sometimes. I mean, she went mad in shops and talked too loudly in hotels, but she'd never, ever, embarrass me in front of a friend. Ironically, she'd probably be relieved to see me smoking. Think I was growing up at last.

'Bitch! Bloody bitch!' Nicola choked.

'But she's just worried about you.'

She ignored me, putting her head in her hands.

I began picking up the stuff from the floor. I wanted to stand by Nicola. To impart friendship to her, as she did to me. Because of her aura, everyone in school wanted to be her best friend, but she chose me. She said I had a quality which made people want to confide in me. And I pictured our friendship as remaining the one untrammelled snow-patch in the sludgy street of life.

I got everything off the floor. 'Cheer up Nicola.'

She still wouldn't move or speak.

I tried reading *The Outsider,* but it wasn't a story. Then I tried the poetry which was OK. If they were great books, Nicola might be like the sailors in Ulysses, taking bags of wind for sacks of treasure.

'Oh, I'd better take you down!' Nicola said at last. And without even looking at me, she tidied her hair and led the way down the stairs.

The real dining and drawing rooms were huge deserted galleries at the front of the house, used only for special occasions – for instance Nicola's birthday parties. The Jennings used the study for everything else: sitting, eating, TV, etc. Although in the basement near the kitchen, it was furnished with a Persian carpet, lamps on side tables, a round dining table in one corner, and a chaise longue on one side of the roaring fire.

Mr Jennings sat on this, perusing the *Evening Herald.* He's a portly, redfaced man, but only his bald head with its funny strand of black hair was visible. And his shortish trousered legs.

Nicola kissed him behind the paper. 'How's darling Daddy?'

'How's the chicken?' he muttered, going on reading.

Nicola pointed me to an armchair on the opposite side of the fire. Then she swaggered to the drinks cabinet, calling, 'Can we've a sherry, Daddy?'

Irritably Mr Jennings rustled his evening paper. 'Ask your mother!'

'Oh, Daddy! Please! Anne's here!'

His red face popped momentarily over the paper. 'Hmm . . . All right!'

Dreamily I stared into the fire. Blue and copper flames licked each other hungrily, sort of pre-historically, primordially . . .

'Here!' Nicola passed my sherry. Then, sipping hers, she rooted among the coffee table magazines and sat down.

Then and there, I decided to break my Confirmation pledge. After all I had left school now.

My first mouthful trickled warmly to my tummy.

I took another.

Then another.

Everything was so nice. The firelight reflected in gorgeous orange in the brass bucket and fender. Over the mantelpiece hung a painting of Mrs Jennings holding a red rose. I have read that a picture requires of the spectator a surrender. I looked more closely, remembering the lines:

> *Nature, I loved, and next to nature Art;*
> *I warmed both hands before the fire of life;*
> *It sinks, and I am ready to depart.*

'I'd jail 'em! Jail the lot of 'em!' Mr Jennings suddenly shouted.

Nicola arched her eyebrows. 'Jail who, Daddy?'

'The tinkers! That bloody Boylan let a woman off with a warning!'

Nicola giggled, going back to her magazine.

I sipped my remaining sherry, meditating on the tinkers and

finally asking, 'What about their children?'

Nicola looked at me curiously. Mr Jennings peered momentarily over his paper.

'What happens to tinker children,' I asked again, 'while their parents are in jail?'

Mr Jennings rustled his paper. 'I'd jail 'em too! Yes, by God! Yes!' He broke into alarming coughing, then gasped, 'Nicola, talk to your little friend!'

Nicola giggled. 'It's Anne from school, Daddy.'

'Hello, Anne from school!' he snarled behind the paper.

'Hello, Mr Jennings.' I went over to shake hands, feeling relieved to be remembered.

Reluctantly he lowered his paper and shook hands. 'Hmm . . . How are you?'

'Very well,' I chatted. 'And so's Cousin William. He's given up Vet. There's no money in it!'

'Isn't there?' Mr Jennings was gaping at me.

'Mummy and Doone are – well, since Daddy's –.'

'Nicola, talk to your little friend!'

She frowned warningly. I finished my sherry, feeling sad. Why hadn't Mr Jennings mentioned Daddy dying? After all, they'd been best friends in school like Nicola and I. And millions of times my father had told me the story of how Mr Jennings had made a fortune from inventing concrete or something.

Then Mrs Jennings appeared with a trolley, wheeling it to the table. A white coated maid followed her with another dish.

'Nicola, the napkins!' Mrs Jennings snapped.

Nicola got them from the sideboard drawer. Then we all sat down and Mrs Jennings ladled the soup. When we were served, Nicola passed me a basket of fried bread bits. I popped one in my mouth, but she whispered, 'They're meant to float in the broth!'

I floated another, but it went soggy and sank.

'And what did the chicken learn today?' Mr Jennings asked, tucking in his napkin.

'Well . . . there was French at the University –.'

'Hope you're not meeting riffraff at U.C.D.' He slurped a spoonful of soup.

'Oh, Daddy!'

Gravely he shook his head, 'Trinity are letting in a lot of wogs. I see them from my office window. Brown, black, yellow . . .' He slurped again. 'Don't know why they come here!'

'An education,' I suggested tactfully.

He looked up sharply. 'Hmm! . . . I'd educate them all right! Back to the paddy fields!'

'But what about the Greeks? . . .' I felt everyone's eyes on me. There was a pregnant silence.

'What about them?' Mr Jennings broke it.

'They believed the pursuit of knowledge to be man's noblest activity!'

'Did they now?' Mr Jennings began coughing.

Nicola nudged me into silence, asking brightly, 'Did you get the tickets, Daddy?'

Recovering his breath, he tapped his breast pocket. 'Ahem, yes. . . . A skiing holiday was promised, and a skiing holiday will be delivered.'

'Tell your father when you had your last cigarette!' Mrs Jennings snapped.

'They were Anne's!' Nicola kicked me under the table. 'She tempted me!'

Mr Jennings' eyes bulged, his face lobster red. 'You shouldn't corrupt others! No sir!' Irritably he finished his soup.

'But –.' Another sharp kick made me finish in silence.

Then, while Nicola cleared the plates, Mrs Jennings served prawns and rice. 'Start on that, dear! We'll have to fatten you up,' she said, passing mine first. 'I hear you're taking a secretarial course?'

'Yes. At Miss Halfpenny's.' I studied the lines of cutlery flanking my plate.

'Typing's so useful, dear!' Mrs Jennings chatted. 'And I'll bet it's fun.'

59

I nodded, noticing the fish knife on the outside.

'And I hear Doone's left school?'

'She's going to a Kibbutz. She's not the school type.'

'What a good idea!' Mrs Jennings finished serving and sat down.

'Who's she going with?' Nicola quizzed.

'The Freemans.'

Nicola giggled. 'Not those funny furniture people?'

I nodded. 'Our neighbours.'

'The Jewish furniture dealers?' Mr Jennings jumped in. 'A story in tonight's *Herald* about them! Passing off reproductions as antiques!'

'They're –.' I wanted to say the only neighbours who've ever talked to us.

'What fun for Doone!' Mrs Jennings mused. 'Nicola loves to go abroad. Have you ever been, dear?'

'She hasn't.' Nicola cut in.

'I have! I was born abroad!'

As Nicola gaped in disbelief, Mrs Jennings smiled encouragingly. 'Where were you born, dear?'

'The West Indies! The same island as Mrs Rochester!'

'How unusual. Is she one of your teachers, dear?'

'She's the mad wife in *Jane Eyre.*'

Mr and Mrs Jennings eyed each other warily, but I went on, 'My grandfather was American ambassador in the West Indies . . . And my parents just happened to be visiting . . . when I was born . . . accidentally.'

'You were born accidentally?' Mrs Jennings frowned.

'I was premature,' I blurted. Actually both sets of my grandparents were dead before my parents even met but I don't know what got into me. 'My mother almost died.'

'Hmm . . . Didn't know your Dad got to the West Indies,' Mr Jennings mused.

My heart hammered happily. 'You remember him then?'

'Remember him? In the third line in Clongowes together! How is he?'

'He . . . he died.'

'Did he? By George! . . . So he did! . . . Nicola, pass the salt.'

I poked at my prawns and rice wondering how I'd finish them.

Mrs Jennings reached for my plate. 'More, dear?'

As I shook my head, Nicola burst out laughing. 'Annie! Ha! Ha! Ha!'

'Wh-what is it?'

She laughed louder. 'I don't believe it! I don't!'

Her parents laughed too.

My face felt on fire. 'But – wh-what?'

'Your eyelash! It's –.' But she collapsed into more giggling.

'Your false eyelash is hanging off, dear.' Mrs Jennings smiled. 'Go and fix it. There's a cloakroom next door.'

Just then, the maid opened the door. 'Mrs O'Brien's on the telephone for Anne.'

'You know your way, dear?' Mrs Jennings said.

I fled the room, going upstairs to the hall.

My mother always rang from work.

'Hello, darling!' she said through the receiver. 'I had to ring with the news. Mr Murphy's taking a case against Cousin William. Thinks we've got a good chance! . . . Darling, are you there?'

'Yes.'

'Well, what do you think?'

'About what?' Maybe Cousin William was in shock. Or hadn't been loved enough.

'About Mr Murphy taking the case!'

'Shouldn't we try talking again?' I always thought my father had preferred Doone and me.

'Talking? The boy's untalkable to! There's something very odd about him. He didn't say anything till he was five! Tonight he even kicked Pete. The poor fellow yapped so hysterically, I mixed sleepers in his doggy food. He lapped them up. I left him snoring on Doone's bed. She's off with the Freeman's for the evening –.'

61

'Mummy! Mr Jennings says there's something about them in tonight's *Herald.*' I paused, whispering, 'Something to do with the police.'

'The police? Don't worry darling. Mr Freeman's a genius!'

'In what sense?'

'In the same way as you have the gift of language, he has the gift of money.'

'I don't have the gift of language.'

'You do, darling! I wish Doone was half as clever. The Kibbutz idea is all very well, but can she read?'

'She can,' I explained patiently. 'I taught her.'

'I see her flicking through comics. But can she read the words?'

'Yes.' I sighed heavily.

'Well, Killiney convent are seeing me tomorrow. If they take her, it'll be another blasted uniform! Never mind –!'

'Mummy! Listen – there's another problem. They're having a *début* for Nicola. And –.'

'You need a dress?'

'Yes! But that's not it! I – I said I knew someone to ask!'

'Mr Murphy?'

'Yes. What'll I do?'

'Do? I'll wangle it! Just tell me one thing. Does Mrs Jennings look younger than me? The truth now!'

'No.' I didn't correct her grammar. 'Years older.'

'But she was the beauty of her day.'

'Not any more.'

'You're sure?'

'She couldn't hold a candle to you.'

'Oh! . . . thanks, darling! Now don't worry about the dance. I'll fix it. You couldn't be going with a nicer young man. I hear the Major calling now. He says he's only hanging on by his eyelashes!' She giggled. 'Bye, now, darling!'

And click went the receiver.

Standing over the cloakroom sink, I pulled off both lashes and pocketed them. It was such a relief to talk to my mother. She gave me such a safe feeling. And if anyone could persuade Chris, she could. My tummy was still queasy at the thought of the prawns, but I hoped they'd be cleared away by now.

'Bill O'Brien – decent poor drunk,' Mr Jennings was saying when I came back in. 'Married a mad Amer –.'

'Anne,' Mrs Jennings shouted. 'Eh – how pretty you've grown, dear!' And she frantically spooned dessert.

Mr Jennings coughed loudly, while Mrs Jennings and Nicola talked excitedly about the *début*. My plate was still there, horrible pink wriggly things, staring up at me. I poked at the rice, wondering if Mr Jennings ever took Nicola to the races. And then on to the Dolphin or the Red Bank if he had a win. It was rude of me, but the prawns were really sickening.

'Anne! . . . Anne! Nicola says you're coming with Christopher Murphy!' Mrs Jennings broke into my thoughts. 'How nice! Can't you finish, dear? Never mind!' And she spooned me out some trifle. 'Your mother doesn't worry about your thinness, dear?'

'Eh . . . No!' And I ate my dessert with intense relief.

Then I helped clear the table. And we sipped coffee, watching T.V. In the middle of *The Fugitive* Mr Jennings started snoring stertorously, but we sat on till half ten when Nicola made moves towards bed.

'Let's phone your man!' she said, opening her bedroom door.

'Who?' I was suspicious.

'Christopher!' she giggled.

'I – eh – it's too late!'

She flicked through her directory. 'He should be here . . . Mother says he lives with his mother in Blackrock . . . Yes! C. Murphy, 15, Waltham Terrace. Is that him?'

'It is – he. But it's too late!'

'Mother says he's a chancer. Owes everyone in Dublin money!' Then, picking up the receiver, she dialled and gigglingly thrust it at me.

I backed away. 'Please, Nicola! It's ringing! Hang up!'

Then a woman's icy voice said, 'Hello?'

'Hello,' Nicola said mincingly. 'Could I speak to Christopher?'

'I'm afraid he's at the theatre,' the woman said. 'Who's speaking?'

'Anne!' Nicola gasped. 'Anne O'Brien.' Then, still giggling, she banged the receiver down.

I was speechless.

She ran into the bathroom, shouting, 'Your Romeo's a bit of a mother's boy!'

If anything, Chris is an Antony. Romeo, I've always considered a complete fool. But I was too shaken to speak. I just unpacked my nightie, hiding my blanket-bit and inhaler between the sheets.

'Wonder who he took to the theatre?' Nicola came out, wearing a nightie.

'Oh – His sister! He goes regularly with a married sister!'

She scrutinized me narrowly. 'Have a bath if you want.'

So I did, *aussitôt que possible.*

Usually on visits, Nicola and I had a heart to heart till the small hours. But she was asleep when I came out. So I switched off my light and lay awake for hours thinking of Chris. He'd hear about the phone call. And he'd have my letter by now. I imagined a look of *faint hauteur* as he opened it, then him muttering *en effet* the girl loves me *en désespéré* . . . But whom had he gone to the theatre with? His *fiancée?* And if he hadn't one, why not? And why wasn't he married? Everyone was married by his age. Maybe he'd had a tragic clandestine *affaire* with a girl of low estate in his youth. His mother had objected to the *mésalliance* as she'd soon object to me. 'He loved a girl called Anne,' people would whisper one day. 'A pilgrim soul who beggared all description . . . she's old now, living with her sister Doone. A brother disappeared to America . . . Christopher remained a bachelor all his days . . . or did he die soon after they met? . . . No, they met after a life-long quarrel . . . she's completely grey? . . . Oh, age cannot wither her . . . she has that within which surpasseth show.' Then I was

Cleopatra burning the water, and Chris was Antony calling, 'I am dying Egypt, dying.'

'Husband, I come!' I sobbed, reaching into the dark.

My bedside lamp crashed to the floor.

'Anne.' Nicola sat up. 'You've been talking to yourself!'

'Sorry!' I jumped out of bed for the lamp.

'Talking to yourself is the first sign of madness! I'm putting you in the guest room!' She flicked on her light and got up, storming across the room.

'Please, let me stay! I – I –.'

But she was already going out the door. Clutching my blanket-bit and inhaler, I followed. All the doors in the murky corridor were closed, and it seemed miles and miles to the one Nicola had opened.

'Blast it! The bulb's gone!' She madly flicked the switch. 'Never mind! You'll be better in there!' And she pushed me in.

And slammed the door, leaving me to darkness and to woe.

5

The rest of my night was plagued by a visitation from the demon asthma. As well as being banished from sleep, I was cold and filled with a perturbation of having lost Nicola's friendship.

Now there might be no *début* invitation.

And no excuse for asking Chris.

Then the sun rose, D.G. Majestically, powerfully, gloriously . . . words fail me altogether. But as the cold clear dawn lit the sleeping world, I pictured Nicola begging my forgiveness. And me granting it as Joseph did to his brethren.

I would be magnanimous: 'To err is human; to forgive divine.'

But at breakfast she ignored my reddish eyes, chatting gaily as if nothing whatsoever had happened.

Then, on her way to university, she left me off at typing.

As I got out of the car, she presented me with an invitation (gold-lettered and gilt-edged) in which Mr and Mrs Richard Jennings requested the pleasure of my ˙and my partner's company on the occasion of their daughter Nicola's *début*.

I stared at it, remembering the words, 'Weeping may endure for a night; but joy cometh in the morning.'

Now I had to forgive her.

Just had to.

'Nicola, I –.'

But she waved me into silence. 'I *know* you're sorry!'

'Well – I –.'

'But in future you'll be in the guest room!' She grimaced drolly. 'Now hurry up! I'm causing a traffic jam.'

A car honked behind us, so I got out.

'We'll see you on the 31st then?' she shouted across the

passenger seat. 'Hopefully in a better mood!'

Hopefully isn't good English, but I was too transported to speak. I just nodded, slamming the door shut and waving her off into the morning traffic.

Then I went into Miss Halfpenny's.

It occupies the third floor of a tall Georgian house in Clare Street, nearly opposite Greene's famous bookshop. The words on the brass door plate are now almost indecipherable: 'Miss Halfpenny's Commercial Academy' in big letters, and 'Gentlewomen trained in secretarial skills; prepared for Bank and Civil Service Examinations' in smaller letters. But it hardly qualifies as an Academy, which in my book is something bigger. Firstly, there were only six pupils, including me. And secondly, it was only one partitioned room. The rest of the house is let: there's a dentist on the ground floor – the reason for the queer antiseptic smell in the hall; a solicitor on the second; an accountant with us on the third; and some sort of recluse in the dismal top of the house.

The Academy's run by two old maids, the Misses Halfpenny and their young maid and niece, Miss Fortune. The two sisters are like Jack Spratt and wife, one thin, the other fat. Hope, the elder, dourer, bigger is always called Miss Halfpenny, while Faith, the younger, thinner, chirpier is called Miss Faith. The niece Toni's just called Toni and reminded me of a wrinkled unpicked apple – a cooker. All three are Protestant looking – grey, grey-haired and tweedy.

Normally I wouldn't mention a thing like religion, but Miss Halfpenny's a bit of a maniac for it. Although technically the 'Directress' to whom everyone had to defer while Miss Faith and Toni did all the teaching, she just sat in the partitioned corner office, reading the Bible aloud.

'Why are you downcast, oh my soul?' her mannish voice droned, as I tiptoed to my place that day. 'Why is my pain unceasing, my wound incurable, refusing to be healed?'

I wondered why she always read out such sad things. What

tragedy had blighted her youth? A fiancé killed in the war? Or was she a Miss Havisham, jilted and overcome by the Bible and cobwebby crumbs? As her voice droned on, the other girls clattered away at their big black typewriters. Their desks were spaced far apart in an effort to fill the emptiness. It's difficult to describe the bleakness of that room. Except for Miss Faith's throne, a blackboard, and a postage stamp of a carpet in front of the empty grate, the desks were the only furniture. The floor was covered with cold lino. And even the coat rail in the corner was empty that morning as most of the girls wore their coats – the fire isn't lit till December (Thrift is the Academy's motto). Oh, there's a picture of the Mountains of Mourne over the mantlepiece, but it's drabbish too.

The only cheering thing was Toni's parrot, Birdie.

My desk was near its cage at the top of the room.

As usual Miss Faith and Toni were quarrelling about Birdie and didn't notice I had come in late. I flicked idly through my manual, listening to Miss Halfpenny's droning voice.

'Why did I not die at birth? Come forth from the womb and expire?'

She was more lugubrious than usual this morning.

Oh, I had known religious maniacs before, but only Catholics: nuns, etc. And Aunt Allie. She's a Republican and actually believes Protestants go to Hell. And you'd go with them, if you ever set foot in their churches. She's decent enough about going to a Protestant neighbour's funeral (in fact, she likes funerals), but she always makes sure to stand in the porch. It's as well to be safe. She couldn't risk her soul. She probably didn't even realize she was risking mine by association. Oh, I don't suppose it mattered – once you were baptised there was no escape; you were a Catholic whether you liked it or not. The original plan was to send me to the Loreto Commercial College in North Great George's Street. But without my having a Matric, Miss Halfpenny's was probably the only place I could get in.

'So we do not lose heart,' Miss Halfpenny warned. 'Though

our outer nature is fading away, our inner nature is being renewed.'

The inner and outer would be good for my diary.

'Don't use last night's *Herald!'* Miss Faith's voice broke into my musings. 'I haven't read it yet!'

Irritably she rubbed her glasses with a spotless hanky. She's a small neat person who always wears grey: blouse, suit and stockings. Even her bun is grey, and she has buck teeth like Joyce Grenfell.

'I said I hadn't read it yet!' she hissed, replacing her glasses.

Toni went on spreading the newspaper on the cage floor.

'I don't get time for the papers till the weekend!' Miss Faith stamped her foot. 'I'm still on last week's! There's a year's bundle in the cupboard!'

They threw out nothing.

Toni still ignored her.

'What are you doing?' Miss Faith turned on me.

'Eh – I'm –.'

'Listening!'

'I just heard.'

'Listening!' Miss Faith wagged a finger. 'Those who listen never hear good of themselves!'

At that moment Miss Faith's awful cat Trigger jumped from the top of the blackboard to the top of the cage, causing a terrible to-do. As the cat clawed the cage, the parrot squawkingly flapped its green wings.

'Get down! Get down!' Toni shrieked, batting the cat with a ruler.

There were green feathers everywhere.

'Yii--oww! Yii-ow!' The cat darted behind Miss Halfpenny's partition.

Her voice stopped droning.

And everyone had stopped typing to stare.

While Miss Faith scuttled after her cat, Toni comforted her squawking bird. 'Poor Birdie! Poor Birdie!' She smiled and tapped the cage until the bird folded its wings. 'There's my Birdie.'

Toni only smiled for her Birdie. I wondered about her too. Why hadn't she escaped from her aunts and got married? She's pretty still. And not old, but old-looking because of her sallow, wrinkly skin. And her clothes were always miles too big, emphasizing her smallness. While her tightly permed grey-blond hair seemed to shrink her head.

Miss Faith reappeared from behind the partition, holding her cat. 'Carry on, girls!' She faced the class. 'Anne, it's a quarter to eleven and you haven't started yet!'

I inserted a page.

'Will you mind Birdie, Anne?' Toni pleaded. 'Chase Trigger away?'

I nodded, hissing into the cage, 'Hello bird brain!'

'Hello bird!' it squawked stupidly back, momentarily spreading its wings.

Miss Faith stormed over. 'Why are you always late?'

'Late? I –.'

'Hello brain!' The parrot beadily eyed Miss Faith.

'The other girls are working since nine o'clock!' She handed me yesterday's page covered with red underlinings. 'This won't do, Anne! What kept you this morning?'

'I was staying in Dalkey overnight. I had to wait for a lift.'

'And Monday afternoon?'

'I had to go shopping with my mother.'

'Well,' she sighed heavily, 'I'm afraid Mrs Grubb-Healy phoned me this morning.'

'Oh – I –.'

'I had to tell her you're not trying!'

'But I am!'

'You miss part of every day!'

This was because of doing things with my mother.

'Every second counts, Anne.' She cocked her head sideways, peering at me over her glasses. 'If you go on like this, you'll never

70

be fit for a pensionable job! Take a lesson from Fidelma!'

Fidelma was clattering at breakneck speed. She was a dumpy round-faced girl with shoulder length hair cut in a fringe and a frightening efficiency. Although we had started together she was already on words.

'But it never sort of clicks – in my mind.'

'And why, Anne?' Miss Faith breathed unpleasantly in my face. 'Why? Because you don't concentrate! What's this suitcase doing here? And this book?'

'It's *Wuthering Heights.*' I swallowed nervously. 'I read at lunch.'

'Isn't it heavy?' she picked it up. 'You're not tempted to read it during class?'

I shook my head. Only a person of the meanest intelligence would call Emily Brontë heavy.

'I'm confiscating it! You'll have no lunch if you don't work.'

I wanted to grab it back. No wonder she'd been left on the shelf.

'Now do yesterday's exercises again! I'm putting this case in the corner.' And she went off, calling over her shoulder, 'I almost forgot, Mrs Grubb-Healy invited you to dinner tomorrow!'

My heart went thump in my chest.

Aunt Allie knew about our shopping in Brown Thomas's.

I was fed up. My mother had an awful habit of doing things in a temper against Aunt Allie and leaving me to face her.

I hated charity's crumb, just hated it.

And it was so unfair of Miss Faith, confiscating my book. I'd never ever read during class. To pass the time, I sometimes made up stories about Qwerty Uiop, a character I'd invented from the top line typewriter letters. Qwerty was a good German, parachuting into Ireland. My father had often told me about meeting good Germans. He'd met them at the Munich Olympic Games in 1936 where he'd caught a glimpse of Hitler, too. The thought made me shiver, but I put everything out of my head and concentrated on my typing. After a few letters the ribbon got stuck. I fiddled with it, but to no avail. I couldn't fix it.

'Fidelma!' I hissed across the room.

But she continued clattering.

'Hello, brain!' the parrot fluttered to life.

Then I pulled at the ribbon, trying to rewind it. But it just spilled all over the place like entrails.

'Fidelma!' I pleaded.

'Hello, bird brain!' came from the cage.

'Anne!' Miss Faith snapped from the throne. 'I might have guessed! Not content to waste your own time, you distract others!' And she stormed down, moving my desk right under the throne.

'What have you done to your ribbon!' she scolded, rewinding it miraculously. 'Bring up that page when you correct it!'

With Miss Halfpenny still droning in the background, I finished the page and showed it to Miss Faith.

She marked it, looking at me oddly as she handed it back.

jfg, jfh, *why,* esd, esf, esd, *are,* esdfg, esdfg, edsfg,
you, jhl, jhl, jhl, *down,* ikj, ikj, ikj, *cast,* fgf, fgf,
oh, jhj, jhj, jhj, *my,* asd, ads, asd, *soul,* jgf, jgf, fjg . . .

'Do the whole page again, Anne!' she ordered, disappearing behind the partition to hush up Miss Halfpenny.

'Bird brain! Bird brain!' came triumphantly from the cage.

At break, Toni appeared with the tray of tea and buns. 'Did you bring your bun money, Anne?'

I felt myself reddening. 'Eh – no!'

'In that case, you won't have a bun!' Miss Faith chimed in, wagging her finger. 'It's for your own good! You've had over a month to remember it! Actually, you don't deserve a break!'

D.G. I faced away from the other girls. It wasn't that I'd forgotten – you were meant to pay £5 together for the whole term if you wanted refreshments. And, well . . . my mother just didn't have it to spare. I hoped they'd put it on my bill which Aunt Allie had paid. Anyway, I wasn't hungry. I never was. Ignoring the chatting and stretching and yawning and clinking cups behind me, I typed the page again. This time, I had only a few mistakes and was allowed to proceed, satisfying Miss Faith sufficiently to be allowed out for lunch.

As usual, I ate an apple on the bench by the Stephen's Green duckpond. Those yellowing bowers were by far the best place for meditating on Chris. My love for him, Dear Reader, resembled Cathy's for Heathcliff. 'If all else perished and he remained, I should still continue to be; and, if all else remained and he were annihilated, the universe would turn to a mighty stranger.' I could never express myself like Emily Brontë, but like Cathy *was* Heathcliff, I *was* Chris. He was always, always in my mind.

With no sleep the night before, a whole afternoon at Miss Halfpenny's was *de trop*. But if I didn't go back, Aunt Allie would be the first to hear. So I decided on a strategy.

As fortune would have it, Wednesday was Miss Faith's afternoon for shopping for cat food, etc. After lunch Toni would be alone in the cold and unpitying room, taking the shorthand class. Now what could she say if I were genuinely sick and had to go home.

Oh, I know a lie's always sinful, even a white one blackens the heart. In school girls had often been doubled up with period pains, but I'd never had one in my life. Never. Still, half-an-hour into the afternoon shorthand class, I fell on the desk groaning.

At first everyone kept working at Pitman's awful squiggles.

So I groaned louder.

Still nobody noticed.

Only Birdie threateningly ruffled his feathers.

I groaned again and was almost dead when Fidelma leaned across the aisle, whispering, 'are you all right, Anne?'

'Agh!' I clutched myself. 'Agh!'

'Hello bird!' came from the cage.

'Toni!' Fidelma called. 'Anne's sick.'

Everyone stopped working to stare.

Toni blinked nervously from the throne.

73

'Agh!' I gasped, writhing.

The cat jumped from his blackboard perch, scuttling behind the partition. Even Birdie eyed me beadily.

'Agh! Agh!'

'Goodness!' Toni hurried to my place. 'What's wrong, Anne?'

'Just – agh! – my tummy!'

'Oh, dear,' she wrung her hands. 'Is it appendicitis?'

I managed a brave smile. 'It's just – the usual.'

'The usual? . . . Oh!' She cleared her throat politely. 'You're unwell? Miss Halfpenny has aspirin for such an emergency. At a penny each.'

I rocked back and forth in agony.

'Eh – I'll – Oh dear, I'll get you an aspirin, you can pay later.'

'I-I think, I'd better go home.'

Nervously she glanced at the clock. 'It's only twenty-five to three.'

'Agh!' I clutched myself. 'Agh!'

She went sallower. 'Goodness! . . . Maybe you'd better go . . . Yes – definitely! Miss Faith would agree.' She glanced nervously around the room, whispering, 'someone will accompany you.'

I shook my head vehemently. Then heaved myself up, clutched my tummy and hobbled to the coat-rail for my suit case.

'Fidelma's willing to see you home,' Toni tiptoed up behind me.

'I'm all right!' I managed a brave smile, struggling into my coat.

Just then Miss Halfpenny limped out of her office and, leaning on her stick, ogled me with bulging bloodshot eyes. There is an impression of yellowness in the hue of her skin and in the tips of her short white hair, and the front of her old-fashioned black dress is always carelessly stained.

'Anne is unwell,' Toni explained. 'Eh – can she go home?'

The bloodshot eyes moved slowly down my body to my case and then up again to my face. At last she wheezed, 'In sorrow shalt thou bring forth children.'

'No, Auntie! It's –.'

'Be sure our sins will find us out,' the old woman chanted, a lump moving under the skin of her neck as she swallowed.

I went beetroot. Miss Halfpenny had seen through me. Next thing she'd forbid me to leave.

But she just hobbled wearily back to her office, mumbling, 'Man that is born of woman is of few days and full of trouble.'

At this Toni sharply nodded goodbye and ushered me out. I hobbled stoopingly down the rickety stairs to the street. But once outside and out of sight, I ran singing all the way to the bus stop in Dawson Street.

As usual, the buses were on a go-slow. To pass the time, I mentally typed the surrounding shop names: Elvery's, Hodges Figgis, Browne and Nolan, and behind me my mother's hairdressers, Jacqmal. But my little finger was too weak for Q's. And I'd never learn to type. Never. Never. Never.

I looked nervously up the street to Chris' office; what would he be doing now? Seeing a customer? Typing? No, I was sure he'd have a secretary for that. What if I applied for a job with him one day? Then, Dear Reader, whom should I see hurrying down the street towards me? It was Chris. Yes, Chris. I couldn't get over the coincidence. Unbelievingly I blinked my eyes shut, opening them immediately. But it was he. Wearing a grubby raincoat. The same curly greyish hair. The same blue eyes. His sallow countenance in a brown study as he hurried along, a battered briefcase banging his side.

Then and there I decided not to marry a doctor. Or even someone rich. But someone small and dark. A Man of the World like Chris.

I wondered if he'd mention my letter.

But, as I said hello from the queue, he looked right through me, sailing on round the corner to Nassau Street.

6

My typing wasn't the basic cause of the war between my mother and Aunt Allie.

It was ongoing, like Caesar's Gallic wars. God, oh God, in Ireland you can never get away from the past. It went back to Parnell: he was my mother's hero while Aunt Allie insists he was an English traitor. They even quarrelled about the Civil War and 1916 and that. Aunt Allie was a Republican and for de Valera, while my mother's father told her Collins was the better man and the Irish always destroyed their great. Also Aunt Allie's a maniac for the Irish language, and my mother cannot speak a word. And, too, my mother's an orphan and married my father against Aunt Allie's expressed wish. It was ironic: although she herself had married, Aunt Allie abhorred marriage. She was a suffragette and in Cumann na mBan in 1916. It was the first women's army in the world – although armies were another thing she abhorred as they contained men (cannon fodder) and were violent; and violence was the one thing she'd changed her mind about as she'd witnessed two wars, and two were enough.

I suppose a Gaelgóir like Aunt Allie was bound to clash with someone brought up non-denominationally in America. But religion was another thing they quarrelled over – my mother's always threatening to become a Protestant. And America was another topic – Aunt Allie says they're the scum of Europe, while my mother insists they're the cream. Also Aunt Allie doesn't like Marcella, and is always calling her a thief. Then there was the family brawn secret – brawn's a slippery sickening cold meat. Ugh. . . the very thought makes my skin crawl. Well, Aunt Allie has the secret recipe. When my mother was getting married she asked for it. (I don't know why, she only cooks fudge and iced tea and French toast.) But Aunt Allie refused, saying my mother had married into trade, and it might get out. But my father was a gentleman farmer who only had hobbies: greyhounds and horses, etc. His only connection to trade was a sister who eloped with a shopkeeper and nobody spoke to her. Anyway Aunt Allie had no right to refuse. She'd only married into the Healys, (keeping her own name Grubb) whereas my mother's a niece. Her mother, my grandmother, was a real Healy who went to school in England and rode to hounds and that.

Except she also married unfortunately (my American grandfather Marcus O'Neill) and then more unfortunately died. So nothing came to us. Still, Aunt Allie says it's something to be related to the Healys and I have 'the look'.

As I'd hardly ever met them, I didn't know what this was. My mother says they all look 'down at heel', but I don't believe that. They helped us OK but, except for Aunt Allie, very reluctantly: the cousin who took on Cousin William was always disappearing, and Doone's had just died intestate. So in emergencies my mother had to resort to blackmail. The treacherous Tim Healy was no relation, but my mother was convinced the Healys were descended from Pigott, the man who betrayed Parnell. And they'd pay her anything, just anything, to keep it quiet.

Usually a letter threatening exposure did the trick. But if not, she'd remind them again of her gun with the three bullets: one for Cousin –, one for Cousin –, and the last for Cousin –. (I'm funny about mentioning names.) Of course the gun was a lie. And the Pigott story only a guess. But one or the other always produced a cheque by return post.

Even Aunt Allie wasn't exempt from getting letters.

'Another begging letter!' She'd wave it at me in the school parlour. 'What do you want with electricity! Why not use candles?'

Basically Aunt Allie believes God rewards the rich for frugality. So she cannot bear waste. And naturally my mother's

77

extravagance is a red rag to her. Also she has to blame someone, and I'm always nearest – like now. By her next school visit she'd always be calmed down and have sent my mother a cheque. Marcella says Aunt Allie helped us because she was haunted by my mother's little dead brother, but she wasn't the type. I think she's just good. 'It is in men as in soils, where sometimes there is a vein of gold which the owner knows not of.' Swift.

I don't know if her vein of gold would be too happy about our shopping. The bras and pants had been delivered OK, but I hadn't worn them. I felt too queasy. My mother had bumped cheques at Christmas, but had never done anything quite like this. Still, I decided to face Aunt Allie the next evening.

Her house is in Blackrock, on the corner of Merrion Avenue and Merrion Road. From the top of the bus you can see over the high garden wall: there's a croquet pitch, a front lawn with beautiful weeping willows, a fishpond, a vegetable garden, and a green-house with plants from every corner of the world and Latin names which nobody but me can pronounce: Lactuca sativa, Allium Porrum, and Apium graveolens, to name but a few. Great Uncle Stephen, R.I.P., Aunt Allie's husband, roamed the world for them. He unfortunately died after slipping on some seaweed in Monte Carlo – that's what we were told . . but I think he was a gambler. Aunt Allie flew for the first time to collect the body. Other times she'd always stayed home. She just couldn't leave her garden. Her fingers are as green as her politics and can make anything grow. Just anything.

Even our cherry tree. A cow had lumbered through the fence of our country house and gobbled its top. To me it was a symbol of our family's luck: if it recovered, so would we. Aunt Allie had got it to leaf, saying it might flower. Like the Bolingbrokes, the O'Briens might one day bloom again from a broken bough.

Aunt Allie was gardening as I opened the side gate that evening. As usual she wore mourning, her black garden coat and black wool headscarf giving her a stooped, bird-like look. The scarf must've affected her hearing, because she didn't look up as the gate clanged shut.

Not even when I stopped beside her. She just kept snipping shrubs, her thin lips pursed absorbedly, her wrinkled weather-beaten face expressionless.

'Eh – hello, Aunt Allie.'

She kept on snipping. She'd been to the hairdressers. Under her scarf, her bluish hair was set in rigid curls and a net cut across her widow's peak arrowing to a beaky nose. After a few more snips, she glanced up, sighing. 'Cad ta uaith?'

'Eh – what?' Although I was doing typing, I had let her down about learning Irish.

'Cad ta uaith?' she repeated crossly.

I groped for words.

'Oh! What is it?' She nipped the top of a shrub.

'I – eh – Miss Halfpenny said –.'

'Said what? Don't mumble!'

'To come for dinner, Aunt Allie,' I blurted. 'She said you said.'

'Oh!' she just threw the scissors into her gardening basket and staked a broken shrub.

Thinking she'd most probably forgotten, I held the shrub. 'What happened to it?'

Her knobbly fingers worked deftly. 'Last night's wind. Here! Hold this!' And she thrust the twine ball so hard at me that it dropped.

I retrieved it, chatting on, 'I didn't hear anything.'

'Typical!' She grabbed the twine, throwing it into her basket.

'Poor ruined choir,' I sighed, to myself really.

'Poor what?' She spat the words at me. 'What?'

'It's a poem by Shakespeare. "Poor ruined choirs where late the –".'

'Why do you always have to speak in quotation? When did poetry ever pay a bill?' She snipped madly at a flower. 'When?' She beheaded another flower, throwing it on the grass. 'When?' Then another flower went.

The mad blue of her eyes terrified me.

'Don't just stand there! Pick up those flowers!' Then she scattered the weeds in her garden basket in every direction. 'Pick up all of that! You don't know the meaning of work! Your mother has you ruined!' And she tore off towards the croquet pitch.

God, Oh God, I thought, she knows about our shopping.

I went for a rake.

'Now, where are you going?' she screamed after me.

'For a rake, Aunt Allie.'

'Pick them up by hand!'

'OK, Aunt Allie!'

'And don't say OK! It's American slang! Put those weeds in the wheelbarrow! Then get these!' And she flung another handful of weeds. 'A rake indeed! Your mother has you ruined!' And she flung more weeds afar.

She definitely knew.

I put the debris in the wheelbarrow, wheeling it towards the croquet pitch.

Aunt Allie was weeding the cracks in the little stone steps leading to the manicured grass. As I approached, she flung more bits of moss. 'Get every bit of that!'

I decided to confess everything. 'But Aunt Allie, Mummy didn't mean it. I can –.'

'Don't call me Aunt! I'm only your aunt by marriage! Your mother means it, all right! She means to ruin you!' She yanked up another weed, flinging it. 'Ruin you!'

'But Aunt –.'

'Don't call me Aunt!'

I swallowed back tears. 'Sorry! I mean –.'

'Don't stand there mumbling! Pick up!'

I picked up a weed. Then another. Then I saw some in the middle of the croquet lawn.

'Why didn't you live with me last summer?' Aunt Allie shrilled as I passed back. 'You could've taken that job!' She barred my way, her hands on her broad hips, her head sticking out like a turtle. 'What's wrong with being normal?' She lowered her voice. 'Answer me, Annie! What's wrong with being normal?'

'Eh – nothing!'

'What did you do all summer?'

'I read.'

'All summer? What did you read?'

'Well . . . Dante and –.'

'Stop boasting! You can't read Dante!'

I was afraid to argue with her.

'And where were you yesterday afternoon? Miss Halfpenny phoned me about you!'

'I wasn't well, Aunt – eh –.'

'And Monday afternoon?'

'At the solicitors!' I blurted. 'Cousin William won't give us any money!'

'Clever boy. Always thought he had something to him! Unlike most men!' Her stealy blue eyes narrowed alarmingly. 'What did you promise me in September?'

'To do my best, Aunt Allie.'

'Don't call me Aunt! Just tell me! Is missing two afternoons a week your best?'

I was crying.

'Answer me, Annie! Answer me!'

I was crying and couldn't.

'Answer me!'

I still couldn't.

'It's what comes of educating you,' she sighed, returning to her weeds. 'I see now what a mistake that was.'

'Oh no, Aunt – eh – sorry.'

'Oh, call me Aunt! I felt for you, Annie, because we both like plants.' She began weeding again. 'I felt for you, and was even going to leave you Uncle Stephen's leather suitcase. And the French Encyclopedia! But not now! Not now!' Her voice rose higher and higher as she scattered handfuls of weeds. 'It's about time you realized your father was a nogood who lived on capital, and your mother is a beggar! Stop that crying! I said stop it this minute!'

I managed to. According to Aunt Allie, living on capital's the eighth deadly sin. And she'd rather be dead than do it.

'And don't just stand there! Pick up! Pick up!' Like the sower in the gospel, she flung a weed. 'Sow a thought and reap an act!' She hurled another. 'Sow a habit and reap a character!' Then with a mighty fling. 'Sow a character and reap a destiny!'

I ran after them, her words sounding in my ears, 'A destiny, Anne, a destiny!'

I imagined mine as a typist in Guinness' garret. Withering and shrinking like Toni.

It was dark now and hard to see, but I finally gathered all the weeds into the wheel barrow.

'What's that Doone doing?' Aunt Allie's voice came from somewhere.

'At home,' I sobbed into the dark.

'She can stay there! I'll not make the same mistake twice! I'll fold my tent and disappear! There's a poem! Ha!'

We almost collided on the little stone steps.

'Oh, get out of my sight!' she snapped, rushing towards the house.

Blindly I headed for the side gate.

'Now where are you going?'

'Home, Aunt –.' It was unfair.

'Well, the ingratitude! When poor Frog has cooked your dinner!'

'But – you –.' So unfair.

'Stop mumbling and pick some mint! Then make the sauce! And hurry! I'll not eat lamb without mint!' And she disappeared into the house.

I tipped the barrow onto the dump, then went to the vegetable garden in search of mint. Oh, I will not dip my pen in gall and write against Aunt Allie. Upset as I was that day, I told myself she couldn't know about our shopping or she'd have mentioned it. She was annoyed about Miss Halfpenny's. I had let her down about that. And about Irish. And she didn't mean that about my father. She once told me he was a gentle man, which was better than being a gentleman. Although he was that too. And I wasn't to worry about marrying an Irishman. That although my mother was right about kindness being important, her views of Irishmen were biased. And if I *had* to get married to marry someone like Frog. Frog was kind.

I searched rows of vegetables for mint. As usual, the thought of my father started him singing in my head.

> *Oh, I met with Napper Tandy,*
> *And he took me by the hand,*
> *And he said, how's poor Old Ireland?*
> *And how does she stand?*
> *Oh, she's the most distressful country*
> *That ever yet was seen.*
> *For they're hanging men and women,*
> *For the wearin' of the green . . .*

I stopped by the glasshouse, trying to stop crying. My father would say, have understanding for Aunt Allie, that she was a nervous girl. To look for the truth hidden beneath the surface, like Mr Pickwick, his favourite character. That I had never ladled soup with the Countess, or ended up in Kilmainham in 1916 like Aunt Allie. That I didn't understand what fire had wrought her.

Oh, I loved Ireland and Emmet was my hero, but D.G. I wasn't alive in 1916. Tired, I searched the glass house, but nothing looked like mint. Nothing. Then, just as I was giving up, I saw some growing in a nearby bed and picked it.

Frog would help me cook it. She's Aunt Allie's cook-companion – and a poor relation like us. Since girlhood she'd gone from one branch of the Healys to the other, housekeeping, etc. She'd even cooked my grandmother's last meal of two boiled eggs. But she's been with Aunt Allie for years now, or I should

83

say the target of her spleen. For what is a poor relation, but the most irrelevant thing in nature? Calling her 'Poor Frog' now meant Aunt Allie was really mad with me. I was always 'Poor Annie', if my mother did something. In rare moments we were the 'Poor O'Briens,' singularly and collectively: Doone was poor for being born at all; Cousin William for being the heir; my father for dying, or for marrying my mother; and occasionally my mother was 'poor Oonagh', I suppose for marrying him.

Aunt Allie has a thing about her parquet hall floor getting wet, so I went in the back door.

Frog was stirring gravy at the huge Aga stove. She's small with the heavy rotund look of a good cook. As usual she wore a navy nylon housecoat over her tweedy skirt and jumper. Frog's a funny name. I mean, she was christened Elizabeth de Lacey, but ironically the nickname Frog had stuck. I don't know how she got it. Probably because of her jumpy limp and the way her shoulders came up to her ears.

'Frog!' I nudged her.

Abruptly she turned, pressing a finger conspiratorially to her lips. Then she pulled me into the big walk-in pantry.

'What is it?' I asked as she shut the door and opened the flour bin.

We were surrounded by shelves and shelves of homemade jam and bottled plums and things – Aunt Allie buys nothing tinned. Frog pulled a bottle of whiskey from the flour bin. Dusting it off, she uncorked it and took a swig before passing it to me. 'Battle fuel, pet!'

I reluctantly took some, coughing as it went down. It wasn't nearly as nice as sherry.

'Battle fuel!' Frog grabbed it back, swigging again.

My tummy went queasy. Aunt Allie hadn't mentioned Brown Thomas's ringing, but they must've. Otherwise why would Frog be giving me sustenance? Why would I need it?

'Frog, did a shop ring Aunt Allie?'

But she had the bottle in her mouth.

84

I grabbed it back. 'Frog, please think! Did a shop ring up?'

'More pet! Take more!'

I did, breaking into coughing. 'Think! . . Did Brown Thomas's ring about Mummy?'

Thoughtfully, she blinked hooded lids, but then jerked the bottle back. And was guzzling before I could stop her.

'Frog! Aunt Allie'll be mad!' I grabbed the bottle and corked it. Then, with Frog watching sadly, buried it in the flour bin. Blister it, I shouldn't have come in with her. If we were caught I'd be blamed. Frog's an alcoholic and only allowed a pint of medicinal Guinness after supper.

'Frog, how do you cook mint?' I waved the leaves.

She belched, peering at it in puzzlement.

'Frog, please tell me!'

She just belched again.

I felt like crying.

Her knobbly hand grabbed my arm. 'Chop, chop!'

'Chop it?' I heard footsteps in the kitchen. 'Frog, we're walking out as if you're sober!'

'Shhh!' She placed a finger to her lips. Then shouted at the top of her voice. 'Ash if I'm shober! Shtone Shober!'

Cautiously I opened the door and we went out.

Brigid Birch, the new maid, was in the kitchen. Aunt Allie usually had the most awful luck with maids – either they'd leave after one day, or refuse to wear a uniform. But six months ago she'd found Brigid Birch in an orphanage and offered her a job. I suppose working for Aunt Allie was better than an orphanage. Oh, I shouldn't say this, but Brigid terrifies me. I mean, she's huge. And wears a ribbon in her hair. Like some giant's child. And her great stumpy legs almost creak as she walks. Also she's missing a forefinger. And she never speaks. Just giggles nerve-rackingly.

'Frog's showing me.' I waved my mint in her face.

Her pale pig-like eyes moved from Frog to me. Then her fat white cheeks exploded in giggles, as she loaded the

dining room tray.

'Chop, chop.' Frog wobbled towards the Aga.

I grabbed her, hauling her staggeringly towards the door. I'd hide her in bed. But she wriggled free, stumbling towards the Aga.

I closed my eyes, waiting for a crash.

But there was none.

When I looked again, Frog was swaying with the gravy pan to the scullery. And Brigid Birch was stalking out with the tray.

Then Aunt Allie appeared in the doorway, her face like the wrath of God.

'Sauce made, Anne?' She glanced suspiciously around the kitchen.

'Nearly!' I backed towards the scullery, the mint behind my back.

'Watch out!' Aunt Allie warned, as I almost collided with Frog, who carried the gravy jug back. Then, looking keenly at Frog, she went ahead of her to the dining room.

Frantically I chopped the mint in the scullery. I'd no idea what to do next. So I boiled it in water on the gas cooker – it's used when the other maids let the Aga out. The concoction was soon bubbling away. It looked like greenish bile, nothing you could eat. Madly, I sprinkled in salt and pepper. Then added herbs from the spice rack. Then crumbled in a bay leaf. Then boiled it all again.

I blew on a teaspoonful, tasting it. It was acidy, but I supposed it was OK and carried it upstairs.

When I came into the dining room, Aunt Allie was carving at the sideboard. Brigid Birch stood sentry beside her. And Frog, having shed her nylon coat, was sitting on a tall hard chair with a napkin expectantly around her neck. She looked perfectly sober now and winked.

Three places had been set at one end of the long polished table, and I took mine on the right hand of Aunt Allie.

'Pass Miss de Lacey's plate!' Aunt Allie ordered.

86

Brigid passed Frog's meat. Then I was served. Then Brigid's and Tommy the gardener-chauffeur's plates were piled high. Then Aunt Allie sat down with her plate.

Frog poured herself some of my mint. Then, winking, passed the jug to me.

I took some, a little. Then passed it to Aunt Allie.

'Mint, Brigid?' Aunt Allie peered suspiciously at it, as she poured Brigid's. 'Did you put vinegar in this, Anne?'

'Eh – vinegar?'

'Yes! Vinegar and sugar?'

'I boiled it.'

Cautiously she tasted it, immediately spitting into her napkin. 'What *is* this?'

'Mint, Aunt Allie! I found it by the glasshouse.'

'And delicious too, my pet!' Frog butted in, spreading it over her meat.

Dumbly Aunt Allie gaped at the sauce. 'That's not mint!' she roared at last. 'You've boiled nettles! Nettles! You stupid girl!'

'And delicious too!' Frog smacked her lips together.

'Dún do bheal!' Aunt Allie lowered her voice threateningly. 'Or you know what'll happen.'

Aunt Allie was always threatening to sack Frog for drinking.

Brigid was sniggering as usual, but, seeing Aunt Allie's mood, quickly composed her face.

'Here! Give me that!' Aunt Allie grabbed Brigid's plate and scraped off the sauce. 'I'll not waste good food! Frog, pass your plate!'

But Frog hugged hers. 'They ate nettles in the Famine! Delicious! Delicious!'

'With your background you'd know that!' Aunt Allie snapped. 'Well, mind you don't get sick. I'm not paying for the doctor!'

As Brigid departed to the kitchen, we ate in deadly silence. Deadly silence.

Then I noticed hives all over my hands. And stinging brought tears to my eyes. It must've happened when I picked the nettles, but I was afraid to say anything.

Munching was the only noise throughout.

I tried to stop myself crying, but tears ran down my face onto my plate.

Aunt Allie pretended not to notice, while Frog kept inclining her head and mumbling, 'Up, down and flying around.'

Finally Aunt Allie shrieked. 'Stop it! Both of you! Stop it at once!'

'But – my hands are stung, Aunt Allie!'

'Well, get some calamine lotion in the bathroom!' Angrily she rang the little silver bell for dessert.

Just then the phone went in the hall.

'I'll get it!' I staggered up, but Brigid was there first.

'It's the young wan's mammy, Ma'am,' she shouted.

Aunt Allie straightened her back. 'Mrs O'Brien to you, Brigid! Say I'm not at home to her!'

'It's for the young wan,' Brigid called.

'Ask your mother not to ring this house, Anne!' Aunt Allie snapped.

I fled to the phone, fuming. Even when they were on the ins, Aunt Allie treated my mother as if she had the plague. She wouldn't even come into our house on visits; she'd just hold court outside in her car. With Tommy listening to every word.

'Mummy,' I whispered into the receiver. 'I –.'

'Darling! Is that lizard in earshot? Just say yes or no!'

'No. They're in the dining room.'

'Good! Now listen, carefully. I've good news. Mr Murphy thinks you're a sweet girl. And guess what?'

I was trying to stop another wave of tears.

'Annie, what is it? Are you there?'

'Yes! I . . .'

'Are you all right?'

'Yes. I'm just glad . . .'

Brigid passed, sniggering.

'Silly girl! You knew I'd ring from work! Mr Murphy's

delighted to take you to the dance, darling!'

The thought of spending a whole evening with Chris suddenly made my blood run cold.

'He knows Nicola's father . . . Darling, are you still there?'

'Mummy – what'll we talk about?'

'Just be yourself, darling! You couldn't be going with a nicer young man! Annie, you sound down. Has that lizard been niggling you?'

'Eh – no!'

'Well *don't* stay the night! And pull a face at her –.'

'Mummy!'

'For me! Bye now, darling!'

And click went the receiver.

I went upstairs to the bathroom. It's a big room on the second floor with a big deep old-fashioned tub on a sort of platform. On previous visits, I'd always have the deepest bubble baths in it. Then go downstairs and play cards with Aunt Allie – Rummy or Whist before bed. But since I left school, my mother made a fuss if I stayed the night. I found the calamine lotion, although in my excitement about the dance I'd completely forgotten the pain. Then I stood smiling into the full length mirror, imagining myself dancing with Chris. I'd stood at the edge of a tennis hop once, but I'd never been to a real dance. Soon, I'd be at one, wearing a long dress . . . And Chris would be in tails . . . And the people . . . and the gaiety . . . the gaiety. It would only be the beginning. On other evenings Chris would call casually. Or he'd meet me in town after typing for a meal and the theatre. What if, after the show, Nicola happened to be in the audience and saw him helping me into my coat?

When I came downstairs they were in the drawing room. As usual Aunt Allie was entrenched with her knitting in an armchair on one side of the fire, while Frog was hunched in another sipping her medicinal Guinness.

A slice of apple tart and cream waited for me on a little table beside my usual chair. Also a glass of water and, as usual, an iron pill.

'We went on, dear,' Frog dabbed her frothy lips.

'Eat every bit of that!' Aunt Allie snapped, her needles clicking. 'And take that iron pill!' She stopped to count her stitches. 'Has your mother not noticed you're run down?'

I shook my head, my mouth full. Aunt Allie has a thing about iron pills, and women needing them and that – she also thinks coffee rots your stomach. I think the pills are sickening, but took it anyway.

'Aunt Allie was shaking her head, muttering, 'Typical! Typical! I suppose she won't let you stay the night?'

I shook my head again.

'Well . . . never mind! We'll say the rosary, then Tommy can drive you home.'

'Take care that Guinness lasts the evening!' Aunt Allie snapped, her needles going clickety-clack.

When I'd finished desert, Aunt Allie cleared her throat. 'Anne, I've something serious to say.' She paused portentously, her fingers dancing on. 'Now, Frog has pleaded for you. And for her sake, I'm prepared –,' she stopped at the end of a row. 'For her sake, I'm prepared, Anne, to give you one more chance. The question is,' she peered over her glasses, one needle in her mouth. 'The question is, are you prepared to take it?'

'Yes, Aunt Allie.'

'You're sure?' She didn't look up from her knitting.

I nodded. Frog held up her glass in a triumphant toast.

'Well, in that case,' Aunt Allie's voice lowered, 'in that case, I'll continue to pay for you at Miss Halfpenny's. And if you continue to work *all* year, I'll use my influence to get you into Guinness's in the summer.'

'Do I have to go *there*?' I blurted, out of the blue.

Frantically Frog wagged a finger.

Aunt Allie concentrated on picking up a fallen stitch. 'Pray, what's your objection?' she asked in a deadly quiet voice, 'to going *there*?'

90

'I was told it was the worst job you could get.'

Frog's shoulders were above her ears, and her eyes were closed.

'And pray, who told you that?' Aunt Allie probed.

'A friend.'

Aunt Allie sighed deeply, resignedly. 'That *nouveau* child, Nicola, I suppose. Ridiculous sending her to Trinity! Such notions! If she's not excommunicated!'

'She's at U.C.D.'

'Still ridiculous! But tell me, why does she object to Guinness's?'

'She doesn't! It's Christopher Murphy!' I was surprised at my own daring, but I knew Aunt Allie was sorry and so at a disadvantage.

'Christopher Murphy, the solicitor?' Aunt Allie was looking genuinely puzzled.

I nodded, looking uneasily at Frog who sat with closed eyes and her short fat legs elevated.

'And how, pray, is he a friend of yours?'

I shrugged. 'He just is. He's taking me to a dance. I have a letter from him at home.' Of course he'd never even answered me.

Her mouth clammed shut. Silently she knitted on, saying at last, 'Played bridge with his parents. Mother's a decent stick. Father was always chatting. No good. Did himself in finally.'

'Succumbed,' Frog bleated.

'How, Aunt Allie?'

'With a knife and fork!'

'Hari Kari?'

'He ate himself to death! Ah, poor woman's probably better off without him. Won't be so lucky about getting rid of that son of hers! It surprises me,' she went on grimly, 'how –.'

'But he's nice, Aunt Allie.'

'How people who chat at bridge are so amazed when they produce children like him. He's no business taking a child like you to a dance! No good can come of it! What dance is it?'

'Nicola's *début!* I got a *printed* invitation.'

'Have you answered it?'

'I told them I was coming.'

She shook her head. 'You must answer formally! Get some writing paper from my desk.'

I did.

And Aunt Allie dictated a reply, 'Miss Anne O'Brien has great pleasure in accepting the invitation of Mr and Mrs Jennings for the night of – when is it?'

'October 31st! Halloween!'

'For the night of October 31st.'

'How will I sign it. Sincerely, Anne?'

'No! Just post it! Now go and get your beads!'

'It sounds a bit Victorian to me.'

'Hmm! I'm not Victorian, I'm Edwardian! How many times have I told you that? Frog! Frog! Wake up!' And she threw down her knitting and shook Frog awake. 'Time for the Rosary!'

We said the Joyful Mysteries that night, and I danced all through them in a whirlwind of happiness.

Afterwards I got my coat.

'Bye, Frog,' I pecked her cheek.

''Bye, Aunt Allie,' I backed out.

'All this physicality is nauseating!' she shrieked. 'Nauseating! But if you're kissing one, you might as well kiss the other!'

And she proffered thin hard lips, shuddering as I did.

As Tommy had gone out, Brigid was rooted out of the kitchen and made to walk me to the taxi in Blackrock. Luckily we got one easily.

And so ended my visit with Aunt Allie.

7

Despite Aunt Allie's dire predictions, eight o'clock on the night of Nicola's *début* found me in evening dress, waiting on our staircase for Chris.

Pete was at my feet. His small spotted head rested on his big paws. His brown eyes soulful, knowing something was up. I must've transmitted my nerves to him, because he was acting oddly all evening. He'd go to the hall door, scratch and wag his tail as if he wanted to pee. But then, when I opened the door, he'd refuse to budge.

'Oh, what is it?' I shouted, as he did this for the millionth time. 'All right! Go out!'

I opened the door again.

But again he refused to budge.

'Out! Pete! Go on!'

But it was no use. He just grinned, whiningly thumping the stair with his tail. So I gave up, settling back on the stairs. I'd more to think about. Tonight I could barely control my own nerves.

For weeks I couldn't eat or sleep.

'My love,' I believed, 'was begotten by despair, upon impossibility.'

But such notions were utterly foreign to my mother. She busied herself with the problem of getting me dance clothes. She even tried to sell her fur coat. Although one fur dealer actually gave her a tenner, no one would buy it – to my intense relief. So my mother solved the problem in a roundabout way. By a quirk of fate, she was buying hankies in Walpole's – the world famous linen shop in Suffolk Street – when it came out that one of their ancient attendants remembered her mother, my grandmother, ordering curtains in 1918. And was so delighted with my mother's custom that she gave us three dresses on approval – of which this was by far the best.

I hitched up the bust.

It was a shiny greenish affair and too big there – a problem my mother solved by the judicious use of cotton wool. But my shawl, long gloves and spangled evening bag were the required white. And for shoes I whitened my high heels.

I hated waiting. I'd been waiting for ages, crossing off the calendar like in school. I passed the time imagining my future life with Chris. And sometimes after typing, I'd walk up Dawson Street, hoping for a glimpse of him. But I never saw him. One day I even walked past his house in Blackrock, but he didn't come out. I'd have said, 'What a coincidence!' or something, if he did. Only for that circled day on my calendar – October 31st, Nicola's *début* . . .– I would've been in despair. On that hallowed day I would enter into a kingdom. The Hound says the birth of Christ's the apex of history, everything before it led up to it and everything after it's the result of it. And even unbelievers have to acknowledge this by using the initials B.C. and A.D.

In a way Nicola's *début* was my apex.

I had wanted to meet Chris at the Pillar or the Metropole in town, but my mother said it was *de rigeur* to be collected. So the day was a swirl of activity getting me and the house ready. Then Doone went overnight to the Freeman's. Marcella to her doctor. And my mother, as usual, to work. Which, except for Cousin William and Pete, left me alone in the house.

'Pete!' I shouted as he slank suspiciously into the hall corner.

But it was too late. He lifted his leg and wet.

'Oh, Pete!'

Whiningly he hung his head, scratching the floor.

'Bad dog!' I hit him. 'Bad dog!'

Then, remembering Cousin William was upstairs, I went for a mop.

As I hastily wiped, a car honked outside.

But it roared away.

Back on the stairs, Pete licked me wetly. But I pushed him away. He'd finished himself with me. And tonight of all nights. I mean what if Chris forgot? He'd promised my mother to bring me, but since the Shelbourne he'd never spoken to me. And there was no guarantee that he'd ever reciprocate my feelings. According to my mother, that would come with propinquity.

The Hound says love is born of God and cannot rest but in God.

I sighed heavily and Pete nuzzled me consolingly.

So I hugged him, avoiding his licks. He was an ill favoured thing, but mine own.

Dogs are canny and know what's happening and who likes them. He was probably nervous about staying alone with Cousin William. As they didn't get on, he was to be locked in the garage till I got back. Then, as usual, he'd spend the rest of the night on Doone's bed. I smiled at the irony of me still sharing the room with him and all the giraffes. Oh, he's an awful eejety dog who barks at all the wrong people and pulls your arms out on a lead, but my love for him equalled Doone's. My big worry was him being killed on the road and then how would I console her?

'Make time count, don't count time,' is the Hound's maxim. So I should've done something constructive, like read a book. But I just sat there thinking of other Halloween nights when we'd sicken ourselves on nuts and my father would make us sweep up the shells so the Holy Souls wouldn't hurt their feet. Besides, my tummy was too wriggly to do anything. I was sick, literally sick with a mixture of happiness about the *début*. Trepidation about Chris being late. And my dress being OK.

I hitched it up again. How would anyone be attracted to such bony shoulders as mine?

Then another car honked.

But it too was a false alarm.

Pete's breathing and the clock's ticking eerily filled the silence.

As usual Cousin William was in his room, reading his newspapers. At least I presumed he was reading them. As he never let anyone in, not even Marcella to clean, it was impossible to be sure. What if I ran upstairs, knocked on his door and said, 'I'm off, wish me luck.' After all, he brought me to *The Horse Soldiers* in the Savoy last year. It was a super flick with William Holden as the doctor. And I had felt so grown up, hoping people would think we were on a date. Oh, it was silly, but I loved having a half-brother. No one else in school did. And I always imagined marrying someone handsome and bossy like Cousin William. But that was then. And the difference between then and now was a mystery to me. Why had things changed so utterly? I mean, my mother's wedding ring was out of the barm brack because ages ago she sold her real one for Cousin William's lunch money. And she gave my father's watch to Cousin William after he died – although Daddy lent it to me for the Matric and I wanted it for a keepsake. And now, although Cousin William got everything, he wouldn't speak to *us*. And I was going to a dance with a solicitor my mother had hired to sue him. And all because of money. *Radix malorem est,* etc.

Then another car screeched outside.

I ran to the landing window, but it wasn't Chris.

'Tickety-tock, nine o'clock,' mocked the clock.

Oh God, he was an hour late.

In the bathroom mirror I combed my permy orange hair. My mother had got her way, making an appointment in Lionel's of Wicklow Street for a coldwave and tint. It had cost £5.19.11, and taken an afternoon. My mother insisted it brightened me, but it definitely looked funny. And Doone had made a face. And Marcella too. But it was done now.

My pores looked smaller though.

For a week I'd been following Nicola's advice, and reading hints on skincare in October's *Seventeen,* an American –.

The bell went.

I froze.

96

And Pete yelped so hysterically at the hall door that Cousin William shouted, 'Shut that dog up! Or, I'll kill him! I'll kill him!'

I hurried down the stairs.

Chris' contour showed through the glass halldoor.

'Be there in a tick!' I whispered through the letter box. Opening the door might result in a chase down to the Stillorgan Road. So wrapping my shawl round me and clutching my bag, I dragged Pete through the kitchen and locked him in the garage. Then, ignoring his barks, I teetered through the side door and down the garden path to the grey-blue Volkswagen.

Chris stood in a halo of headlight.

He looked so *distingué* in a black evening suit that I lost my power of speech. Seeing him was always a shock. As if I'd never met him. Or had forgotten his muscular smallness. His curly greying hair, cut and slicked over his bald patch for the occasion. Or hadn't memorized the lineaments of his countenance. His greyish eyes. His beaky nose, beakier tonight. His sallow, pitted skin, sallower too against the white scarf.

'That's quite a din!' he joked, opening the passenger door. His voice was still nasal. And there was a slight smell of drink off his breath.

'He gets lonely,' I heard myself say, getting in.

'Sorry, I'm late!'. He tucked in the hem of my dress. 'Couldn't get this old banger started! Say, don't you need a coat?'

'Eh – no!' I pulled my shawl round me. Nothing could persuade me to wear my green tweed coat.

'Well – eh – you're looking, frankly – very nice.' He looked at me quizzically for a second, then, smiling crookedly, banged the door.

He glanced over. 'We won't be too late. To be honest, these affairs never start on time.'

At the apex of my life, I was struck dumb.

'Let me see –.' He stopped for the crossroad lights. 'It's Dalkey, isn't it? We'll go out to Blackrock and out that way. Now – eh – what's this girl's name?'

'Nicola.'

'Your Ma mentioned she's one of the Jennings? I was a pal of her sister Susie.'

'Sally. She's living in Paris now.'

'That's right! Married a diplomat. One of the Murrays from Ailesbury Road.'

'Were you in college with her?'

'Ah . . . Yes!' He suddenly thumped the steering wheel with the heel of his hand. 'Dammit! Should've bought you a box of chocolates!'

'I don't like them!'

'All girls like chocolates!' He smiled crookedly, rubbing his shorn neck. 'The law's a bitch –.'

'Do you have many customers?' It was a coincidence my grandfather being a lawyer too.

'Clients! Run off our feet!' He sighed heavily. Then looking right at me, 'Say – ah – did your Ma happen to give you a cheque?'

'A cheque?' I looked vague.

'Yes. For me. She promised to leave it with you.'

'Oh! . . . You know my grandfather was a lawyer too,' I blurted, changing the subject. 'He was on the Thaw case.' It was something I'd heard from the cradle's arms. About the American architect Stanford White shooting his wife's lover and getting off because it was a crime of passion. 'He was an ambassador as well! We have letters from Woodrow Wilson!'

'The Thaw Case?' He frowned in puzzlement. 'How do you spell it?'

It'd be funny if I married a lawyer too, I thought dreamily.

'How do you spell Thaw?' he persisted.

'Eh – I don't know!' If I ever had, I'd forgotten. My thoughts kept slipping away from me like bits of dreams. Or the fish wriggling off my father's rod.

'Your Ma didn't mention *anything* about a cheque?' His voice rose in irritation.

'Eh – she probably forgot! She had to rush off to a party!'

He perused my face. 'A party?'

'Yes! She goes to one every night. She's very popular!'

'Hmm . . . I'll bet she is!'

My mother never had any money, so how could she give him a cheque?

'Do you happen to like fishing?' I asked brightly, changing the subject again.

'Fishing?' He gave me a funny look.

'My Dad did! He caught a mackerel once. And do you know what?'

'What?'

'He threw it back.'

Chris raised his eyebrows. 'Didn't he like mackerel?'

'It wasn't that! He felt sorry for it!' I looked to Chris for some sort of response. But my story must've fallen flat, because he just stared ahead.

'We could give you his rods,' I said after a pause. 'No one uses them now.'

'Ah . . . what?' He frowned angrily. 'Listen, tell your Ma I need that cheque!' Then he accelerated sharply, speeding towards Dun Laoghaire.

I didn't know what to say about the cheque. My mother must've told him that in desperation. But just as I hated him seeing my house, I hated any mention of money. Or him knowing about Cousin William.

At the other side of Dun Laoghaire, he broke the silence. 'The Jennings' live off the Sorrento Road, if I remember rightly. A big house on the right.'

'It's Georgian,' I added.

'Should be with all the old man's lolly!' He let out an appreciative whistle. 'Frankly, one of the richest men in Ireland.'

He slowed for Dalkey village, grinding the gears as we pulled up the Sorrento Road. Then, just before Nicola's turn, he braked and jumped out of the car and plucked a flower from a garden.

99

'For my lady!' He handed it to me, getting back in.

It was a brownish chrysanthemum.

'Should've bought you one!' He started the engine. 'But a client held me up. Missed the shops, to be frank.'

I buried my face in bitter-smelling petals. I'd press them in one of my poetry books.

After the railway bridge, Chris changed gears for the hill. 'Here we are! I see the lights of the house!'

As we slowed for Nicola's gate, everything looked completely different from my last visit. For one thing, the gates were wide open. Secondly, no sign of the dog. Thirdly, the house blazed with happy light, completely dispersing the gloom of the trees.

A torch flashed us to parking in the stable yard.

'Watch your step!' Chris bossed, taking my elbow across the cobble-stones. I bore a charmed life, Dear Reader. And again I seemed to watch us walk together through the huge gates and over the front gravel to the hall door.

'The cloakrooms are upstairs,' a maid said, letting us into the crowded hall. 'And drinks are being served in the dining room.'

Mr Jennings stood guard at the foot of the stairs. His huge tummy was tucked into a red cummerbund, and his hands were clasped behind his back.

I waved hello, but he turned and paced to the back of the hall.

'Do you want to powder your nose?' Chris shouted over the music.

I shook my head deafly, hugging my shawl round me. So, saying he wouldn't be a tick, he ran up the red-carpeted stairs, leaving me to wonder how Nicola knew so many people. The house rang, just rang, with laughter and song. Heavily made-up girls in strapless dresses and their black suited escorts milled past me between the two huge front rooms. In the drawing room the carpet had been removed, and dancers jived to deafening music: 'Lipstick on your c-o-l-l-a-r . . . Told a tale on yo-ou-ou . . .' And in the dining room tailcoated waiters flitted behind the dark mahogany table, uncorking bottles and pouring endless drinks

100

for the thirsty revellers.

'It's Anne-Marie!' Mr Jennings paced past me. 'The cigarette girl! Ha! Having fun? Having fun?'

'I – eh –.' I just stood there. Explaining that I hated even the smell of cigarettes would implicate Nicola.

And he disappeared into the dining room crowd.

'Ah, there you are!' Chris took my elbow, steering me towards the drinks. 'First things first!'

We bumped into Mrs Jennings. A slinky black dress made her arms look scraggy and her face was a mask of make-up.

'Anne! Don't you look pretty!' She gave me a lipsticked smile, turning curious eyes to Chris.

'Christopher Murphy!' He held out his hand. Then, as she didn't shake it, plunged it quickly into his pocket. 'Ah – the wrong generation, I'm afraid. I was a chum of Sally's.'

Mrs Jennings just smiled glassily, gliding silently on.

Chris arched an eyebrow, seemed amused and again negotiated the crowd.

Then Nicola's shrieking laugh came from a nearby group.

'Anne!' She ran over, pursued by a tall boy in a skimpy dress suit, whom I guessed to be Anton. 'You're very late!' She kissed me exaggeratedly, whispering, 'Is that him?'

'It is – he.' Turning to make introductions, I stepped on Chris.

He winced, bowing admiringly to Nicola. 'Christopher Murphy, Ma'am.'

As they shook hands, Nicola giggled again. Truly I had never seen her look more lovely. Her full strapless white frock showed off her tanned shoulders. And her brown hair was set into a casual flick. She even looked thinner, glowing with the aura of money.

'How's Sally?' Chris was asking.

Between giggles, Nicola made an arc over her stomach to indicate pregnancy.

'Happens to the best of us!' Chris joked. 'Can't play with fire!'

This sent Nicola into more giggles. Even in school, I'd never seen her so giddy. Then Chris became infected with giggling too.

I smiled at Anton who definitely wasn't amused.

'C-Come and have a drink,' Nicola gasped, getting her breath. Then she pulled Chris towards the drinks table.

Anton looked after them, his face on fire. His arms were folded and he swayed back and forth slightly on his long legs.

'It's very crowded,' I said brightly.

He looked down, as if seeing me for the first time. 'Want a drink?'

I nodded.

So we weaved our way slowly after them to the table.

Chris was already handing Nicola hers. 'A gin and tonic!'

'I can't bear things floating in my drink!' She dipped her hand in, thrusting the wet lemon back at the startled waiter.

Chris suppressed a laugh. 'Eh – what'll you have, Anne?'

'She doesn't!' Nicola shrieked. 'There's punch for the children!'.

'I'd like a sherry.' I said quietly.

So Chris turned his back, hailing the waiter.

'But there's punch!' Nicola insisted. 'Anton's having that, aren't you?' She nudged him meaningfully. 'Why don't you two go and play!'

'Bitch!' he hissed, storming off.

'Go away, Anne!' Nicola mouthed at me.

'Eh – what?'

She pushed me in the direction of Anton's back. 'Go *away!*'

Then Chris turned with my drink. 'Oops! Sorry. It didn't get on your dress!'

'Eh – I'm fine!' I'd sponge it when I got home.

But he patted me dry with his hanky.

'Anne says you took her to the Shelbourne!' Nicola started up again.

As Chris smiled at her over his drink, I prayed for the ground to open and swallow me.

'Did you really take her there?' She laughed cattily.

My head was thudding so loudly, I didn't hear Chris' answer. I didn't want to hear it. I just sipped my sherry, thinking on the irony of nemesis, and grateful for the chatter surrounding me.

'Tony O'Reilly's in training again . . . Can I get you another drink? . . . Oh, it's likely he'll be picked for the team . . . What, a gin and tonic? . . . He might be just keeping his weight down . . . Oh, you're drinking vodka? . . . Not at all, he's a cert for the team . . . Two vodkas and a scotch here, please! . . . Listen, O'Reilly has no equal! . . .'

Nicola's hand was now cupped over Chris' ear. Nervously I gulped the last of my sherry.

'Look, if I was Kennedy, I'd blast Castro into the Carribbean! And his missiles with him! . . . Make things worse? Not at all! Strength is the only thing the Russians understand! . . . Do you want them to take over the world? . . . Ah, no. U Thant won't work anything out . . . He's calling a meeting of the security council? . . . War? The Russians have too many problems of their own! . . . Georgina! Where did you disappear to? . . . Let's have a dance . . .'

'Got myself a sleep-in', walk-in', cry-in', talk-in', liv -in' doll!' A singer drawled from the other room, reminding me of a doll I once had which did everything. Even wet its pants. And which was stolen from me later on a beach.

'Like this dance?' Anton was looking down at me.

'Eh – yes!' I saw Nicola still busy with Chris.

'Cliff Richard's old hat, isn't he?' Anton clicked his thumbs as we made for the music.

I nodded. I hadn't an iota of whom he was talking.

'The Crystals grab me!' And he wiggled his hips, singing, 'Why m-u-s-t I be-e-e a teen-ag-er in l-o-v-e!'

As we passed through the hall, I pulled my shawl round me.

'Give me that!' he tried to take it off. 'I'll give it to the maid!'

'I'll wear it!' I shouted over the music.

In the drawing room the band was ear-splitting, and people wiggled violently to faster music. I moved nervously to the centre where Anton immediately grabbed me and flung me to arm's length.

I stumbled, immediately recovering.

'Can't you dance?' he snapped.

'Yes!' But I stumbled again, my high heels no help.

He grabbed me again. I stumbled again. But somehow I blundered on, carefully copying the people round me, until finally the music stopped.

'Thank you!' Breathless, I made for the dining room.

'Wait!' He grabbed my elbow. 'Let's have another!'

'But they'll be wondering –.'

'They've more to think about!' And held me in a tight embrace, gyrating to the slower music.

Looking back, I should've broken loose then – Anton and Nicola were plighted after all. But the music lulled me into a timeless trance. Also I'd never danced with a man before. Only with Nicola in school.

We danced another.

'Bitch!' Someone hissed half-way through. 'Bloody bitch!'

'Wh-what?' I turned deafly.

It was Nicola. Her face red. Her hands angrily on her hips.

'Bitch!' She stamped her foot.

'Well, now!' Anton smirked, pulling me closer. 'Two can play!' And he buried his face in my hair.

'Oh, Anton,' she pleaded tearfully.

But he just danced on, smiling triumphantly.

'Please, Anton!'

'Oh . . . well, all right!' And pushing me away, he grabbed her wrist and ran off the floor.

'Bitch!' she shouted from the door. 'Bitch!'

Feeling my sins as scarlet, I stayed glued to the floor. Everyone was looking, I thought. But apart from a few curious stares, people danced normally. I noticed my flower trampled under-foot and bent to retrieve it. It was completely crushed, so I put it in my bag. Then, prodded by dancers, I went in search of Chris.

But he had vanished.

Two men occupied his place by the drinks table.

'A drink, Miss?' The waiter flitted back and forth behind the table.

Thinking Chris was in the loo, I had another sherry. Sipping slowly, I looked up the crammed room as far as the stately bay windows for even one familiar face. But there was none. A hum of chatter rose and fell, interrupted occasionally by a yelp of laughter. There was nobody from school. The older people must be Mr and Mrs Jennings' friends, I thought. The middle-aged, Sally's Paris friends. And the people my age Nicola's friends. But why hadn't I ever met them? I'd always thought Nicola and I were bosoms.

'What do you think of Ultima for tomorrow's St. Leger?' the baldish man beside me asked his tall friend.

'Princely Portion!' he answered, flicking cigarette ash on the floor.

'But Crystal Clear looks good!'

'Princely Portion!' The tall man inhaled deeply. 'And Silver Green for the 1.45.'

I noticed a cigarette burning the table beside me and picked it up. Who had left it there? I rubbed at the black mark. The table was ruined. I looked for the two men's ashtray, but they hadn't one. And there was nowhere to put the burning cigarette.

Then I saw Mr Jennings watching me across the room.

God, oh God, he'd seen me rubbing the table. And I was still holding the cigarette. I didn't know what to do, so quenched it in a glass.

Quickly downing my sherry, I plunged into the multitude. Chris might be looking for me in the other room. With Mr Jennings prowling around and Nicola in that mood, I'd feel safer with him.

But no sign of him anywhere.

He wasn't in the hall. Nor among the group sitting on the stairs. Nor the group watching the dancers. So I wandered down to the basement.

People had trickled down there. And white-coated waiters flitted around with plates of food. Long tables had been erected in the big old-fashioned kitchen. They were covered with whole cold salmons, plates of sliced ham decorated with pineapples, plates of sliced turkey, and dish after dish of delicious salads.

I'd never seen anything so sumptuous in my life.

'Anne, dear! You look lost!' Mrs Jennings appeared behind me, smelling perfumy.

'I'm looking for the loo,' I lied.

'Upstairs, dear!' She squeezed my arm gently. 'You know the guestroom! You've even slept in it!'

As I turned nervously, she said, 'You're enjoying yourself, dear?'

'Yes!' I couldn't tell her it was the apex of my life.

'Remember this party is for you too!'

I felt myself redden.

'After all, it's your first dance as well as Nicola's.' And, smiling, she turned to a waiter.

It was the nicest thing I'd ever heard. Except what would she think of me when Mr Jennings told her about the burnt table?

I searched the hall again. The dining room. Among the dancers. But Chris had vanished. I was too nervous to stand still, so stepped through the guests sitting on the stairs. I went on up, past the sprinkling on the landing and down a long lit corridor of closed doors to the room where I had spent the bleak night of my last visit.

The two beds were piled high with coats, and the adjoining bathroom was occupied. I smiled at a girl combing her hair at the dressing table mirror and waited for the bathroom. If I hid in there for awhile, Chris would have time to return.

When the bathroom was free, I went in.

Apart from the grave, Dear Reader, there's no safer place on this earth. I mean, there's no other place where you can be alone. I sat on the loo, staring into the vast unfilled spaces in my bosom. The dress was hickish compared to other peoples', I could see that. It looked as if it was my mother's, or grandmother's with those drab brocadish flowers. Still, I wouldn't even have it, but for my grandmother. What kind of a woman could still possibly be remembered in a Dublin shop, I wondered again. My mother had absolutely no memory of her. Marcella said she was a saint. Aunt Allie that she was soft. Frog that the whites of her eyes were very white and she never raised her voice. But I wanted to know her favourite book. Or if she had a Kilkenny accent. We had a faded brownish photo of her and her little son, staring from the front of an old-fashioned hoodless car, completely unaware of their doomed fate. Her hair was up and she wore a *pince-nez* and a Victorian dress. And, although fiveish, my dark pretty little uncle wore a dress too. Funny . . . Donal Dubh was his name (Dark Donal in Irish). I had always thought it the most beautiful name in the world. Like Owen Roe O'Neill, or Red Hugh O'Donnell, or O'Sullivan Beare. 'No one say pretty Donal,' was one of his childish sayings, from being the centre of attention on the ship home. It became a description in the Healy family for people looking for notice. And it was true, soon no one would. When he got black flu in 1918 (typhoid from bad drains, according to Aunt Allie), a ghoulish priest uncle had told him he was lucky to be going to Heaven. But the little boy didn't think so and sobbed for his Mama to come too. So she promised. Then he died. And three weeks later, she went to bed with a headache and never got up.

> *The fairest things have fleetest end*
> *Their scent survives their close.*
> *But the rose's scent is bitterness*
> *To him that loved the rose.*

Of course, my grandfather had nearly gone crazy. He'd been in America, and Aunt Allie's husband broke the news at the Cobh dock.

I asked the Hound, why was life so unfair? But she said it was my grandmother's fate to go to the nurseries of Heaven. Like

Francis Thompson. A huge chestnut tree still flowered in the garden of their Pembroke Road house. I had often stood outside imagining my grandmother and pondering on the line: 'Generations pass while some trees stand, and old families last not three oaks.' It may have been her fate, still it was unfair that she lay in an early grave, while I enjoyed myself at a *début*. I didn't want to go to Heaven either, not without my mother, or Doone, or even Cousin William – wanting a room's different.

Someone turned the doorknob, but I ignored it.

I combed my hair and put on more lipstick. My flower was badly trampled, but a few petals could still be pressed. I'd have them buried with my ashes, along with my Dante and other poetry books. I'd definitely made the decision to be cremated. And have my ashes buried in a cask, in a coffin. Beside Daddy. And across the graveyard from my grandmother.

'Who's in there?' someone shouted.

The doorknob turned angrily back and forth.

'It's been occupied for the last half-hour!'

There was knocking on the door.

So I came out, letting another girl in. I ignored the odd stares from the line of girls in the guest room and wandered out to the corridor.

A group had gathered at Nicola's bedroom door. So I went to see if Chris was among them.

'There's no room inside!' A girl at the edge peered on tiptoe over heads.

'What's going on?' I couldn't see anything.

'They're playing a record!' She laughed coyly.

'Oh!' I tried to see if Chris was in the crammed room.

Then people in front of me moved away, laughing. I saw the room was packed with giggling, laughing, squealing couples. Some necked on the bed, while others sprawled and squatted on the floor.

Nicola sat on Anton's knee. He nuzzled her hair, as a sort of talking song played on the stereo, 'I spanked my

108

daughter till she came . . .'

'What's the record?' I whispered to the girl.

She put a finger to her lips, giggling. 'Sshh!'

'I spanked my daughter till she came,' the husky man's voice sang.

Then Nicola looked up, so I fled.

I went back downstairs. Panic was overtaking me. And a terrible loneliness. If only I knew someone to talk to. Maybe Chris was under my nose and I couldn't see him? Maybe I was going mad?

I stood at the dining room door again.

'Has anyone seen the Abbey? . . . *A Jew Called Sammy?* . . . Don't want to see anything about Jews, thanks! . . . *Fursey's* on at the Olympia? . . . It's boring? . . . Oh, I heard it was from a good novel . . . Never read novels! Too many of them published! . . . I saw the *Birdman of Alcatraz!* . . . Did anyone hear John O'Donovan's play on the radio last night? . . . It was about Swift and Handel . . . Who were they? . . . He's a journalist . . . What, Swift is a journalist? . . . Now, *which* Swift is that? . . .'

Then I saw Chris.

He was at the far end of the drinks table.

When I came up to him, he wobblingly held up his drink. 'Ah, there you are!'

'I looked for you everywhere!' I suspected he was a little drunk but didn't care. I was nearly crying with relief.

'A drink?' He hailed a flitting waiter. 'Andy, a sherry here! A sherry!' His voice slurred suspiciously. 'He works in Davy Byrne's!'

'Here you are, Sir!'

Then, handing me my drink, Chris spilled his own.

He was definitely drunk.

'K-kn-ow any of these people?' He focused his eyes on a nearby group.

'There's no one from school.'

'School?' He looked at me blearily, then laughed. 'You're a s-s-sweet kid.'

I felt myself redden.

'But f-f-funny. Wh-why didn't you ask me yourself?'

'I – eh – my mother's –.'

'Your Ma's a terrible woman!' He turned again to the crowd. 'I s-see some of the law crowd. And a few d-diplomats!'

'Vodka and tonic! Irish and Water! . . . Scotch and ginger!' voices around us shouted.

Chris called for another too, insisting on yet another sherry for me.

'Why, Anne!' A voice said behind me.

Turning, I looked into the heavier features and thickened body of Nicola's older sister, Sally. 'Eh – hello!'

At last I knew someone.

'How lovely to see you! Are you enjoying yourself?' She looked curiously at Chris. 'And who's this?'

'You know me! Christopher Murphy!' he tried to bow, but stumbled.

'Hmm!' She turned to me. 'Is *he* with *you?*'

I nodded. There was an awkward pause.

'Well, it's lovely to see you again, Anne!' And she moved on.

Chris shrugged. 'Per-p-persona non grata.'

I was indignant at her treatment of him.

Then Nicola and Anton appeared, out of breath. I smiled, hoping she'd have forgotten or forgiven our misunderstanding. But she ignored me, smiling coyly at Chris. 'I just rescued Anton in time!'

Chris hicupped. 'Y-you rescued him? G-good! Ah . . . from what?'

'From her!' Nicola pointed tremblingly at me. 'They were necking!'

'Hmm! . . . Well now! Frankly . . . Hiccup.' Chris looked blearily at me.

'They were!' Nicola poked Anton angrily in the ribs.

110

He just folded his arms and stared bored over the crowd.

Nicola bit her lower lip. 'You were!'

Chris frowned, slowly comprehending the situation. 'W-well now. . . . Th-that's hardly fair! . . . Hiccup!' He covered his mouth with his hand. 'Ah, s-sorry!' Then, winking at Nicola, he slammed down his drink and grabbed my wrist. 'C-come and dance with your own partner!'

I followed his swaying figure, wanting to die of embarassment. I thought we'd never make it. But in the middle of the dance floor he took me in his arms and my troubles vanished. I forgot about Nicola. About everything. As his cheek touched mine and we moved gently to the music, it was . . . oh . . .

'I found my thrill-ll . . . On Blueberry Hill-ll.' The singer's voice rose above the band.

'Oops! Sorry!' Chris swayed, stepping on my foot.

'It's OK!' I wanted his face to touch mine again.

'On Blueberry Hi-ll-ll . . . When I found you-ou-ou . . .'

Chris stepped on me again. 'Let me s-s-see now, William's your father's awful child?'

'Oh, Cousin William's OK! I mean he can be awful!'

'The wind in the willow's play . . . a sweet melody-y-y- . . .'

'Lawful! L-l-lawful!' He steered me right into someone. 'Y-you mean he's your cousin?'

'And all of the vows we made-de-de . . .'

'We only call him that!'

'. . . were never to be-be-be . . .'

Chris was looking puzzled.

'We had different mothers!'

'But he is your father's legal son?'

I nodded, concentrating on the song. 'You were my thrill-ll . . .'

'I've checked the will,' Chris shouted. 'It's a straightforward case of male entail!'

'On Blueberry hill-ll-ll . . .'

'But we might get him on equity! There's just a question

of c-costs!'

'Costs?'

'Yes. Money. LSD!'

'Oh! . . .'

'What do you mean, *oh*?'

'Nothing! Just love of money's the root of all evil. *Radix malorem* and that.'

The music had stopped and Chris stood, blinking at me.

A gong went and a waiter announced supper was being served in the kitchen.

'Good! Let's get some grub!' And Chris walked off the floor, swaying wildly.

I followed, remembering a time my father had come home drunk. Doone and I had hidden in the bathroom. He banged on the door, shouting for us to come out. So we opened it, slipping past him and running out to the garden. 'Come back! Come back!' he shouted, stumbling after us. And all that night, after he had fallen safely asleep, I lay awake sobbing and reciting 'Lord Ullin's Daughter':

'Come back, come back!' he cried in grief.

'And I'll forgive your highland chief.

My daughter, Oh, my daughter.'

In the kitchen Chris handed me a plate and cutlery wrapped in a napkin. 'Help yourself!'

Then a peculiar thing happened: as Chris heaped his plate, I began crying.

'The s-s-salmon is scrumptious!' he said, not noticing me.

I tried to stop, but couldn't. Tears just poured down my face. Frantically wiping them, I concentrated on what to have. I walked up to the table, peering at the plates of food and finally opted for the salmon. Then other guests clamoured in, yelping and gobbling hungrily. One boy, his tie askew, grabbed a handful of turkey and stuffed it directly into his mouth. Then he dipped his hand into the potato salad and, messing his dinner jacket, crammed a handful of that.

112

'Red or white, Sir?' A waiter weaved through the crowd with a tray of wine.

Chris took red.

And I white.

He immediately quaffed his and took another. Then a girl beside me spilled hers, a wine-red stain spreading angrily over the cloth. As I tried to soak it up with my paper napkin, she laughed and stubbed out her cigarette in the potato salad.

She was dead drunk.

'Bitch!' someone hissed behind me.

Nicola.

I ate some salmon, biting back more tears.

She lurched dangerously towards the food. 'Bitch!'

Anton was behind her, steadying her. As he raised his eyebrows at me, Chris stared at Nicola as if comprehending her drunken state.

He coughed importantly, turning to me. 'That-t-t's no w-way to behave. Upsetting your hostess!' He shook his head disapprovingly.

I should've stuck up for myself, but I just stood there.

'F-frankly! Oops! Hicupp!' He dropped food down his front.

He was getting drunker. People in books would loosen his tie, or bring him out to the fresh air. But I couldn't do either.

He focused his eyes on me. 'And there's no need for all those lies!'

'Lies?'

'Yes! Your mother's parties! The Thaw case!'

'But that's true!'

Nicola shrieked with laughter. 'She was born in San Domingo! Before her parents ever met!'

Then everyone laughed.

'And her aunt is Emily Brontë!' Nicola went on. 'And her relations are shop-keepers from Kilkenny! With a crest!'

I hated her now. In a weak moment I'd told her about the Healy Crest: a pelican bleeding its breast for its young. With the motto: 'Omnia vincit amor.'

A loud crash came from the door, as someone fell off a chair.

'Boasting runs in the family!' Chris jeered. 'Her mother –.'

I put down my plate and made for the loo.

'Have her.' Nicola shrieked, pushing Anton after me. And I saw her nuzzling up to Chris, and him kissing her passionately.

In the hall someone was getting sick.

'Don't mind them!' A voice said behind me. Then a hand was on my shoulder. 'They're just tight!'

It was Anton.

'Don't be silly! They're just tight. Come on back!' he pleaded.

I hesitated, but allowed myself to be led back through the jostling crowds. On the way I saw a kitten picking its way gingerly through giant legs across the kitchen floor.

'Here, puss. Puss, puss!' I ran after it, picking it up.

'Now she's raping a kitten,' Nicola screamed.

'Where'd you get that?' Chris was heaping his plate again.

I hugged my bundle. It was the sweetest little marmalade kitten. Suddenly it clawed my face and wriggled playfully free, landing on Chris's plate.

'Christ!' He flung it squealing across the room.

'I hate animals!' Nicola yelled, as I went after it. 'Pregnant cats! Horses!'

Everyone stopped eating to laugh.

Then, at the instigation of Nicola, Chris swayed over to me. As I stood dumbfounded, he took the kitten from me and put it in the fridge.

The laughter rose to a crescendo.

'Everyone come out to the stables!' Nicola shrieked, standing on a kitchen chair and brandishing a scissors. 'I'm docking my horse's tail!'

A chain of guests formed behind her, shrieking and chanting around the kitchen and out the door to the stable yard.

Nobody saw me rescue the dazed kitten and pop it into my bosom with the cotton wool. Then I walked casually up the lit

114

house to the hall door and escaped into the night.

The pitch black of the avenue terrified me.

There was no moon. And icy fingers of twigs scratched my face. In the distance the sea roared hoarsely. And somewhere behind me the dog howled devilishly. But I stumbled on, ignoring the kitten's ticklish wriggling, my eyes fixed on Mrs Conroy's light.

Then a car started up in the stable yard.

I ran faster, stumbling and falling.

Light flooded the avenue as the engine got louder.

I thought of hiding in the bushes, but the avenue was fenced. Then honking and squeaking breaks made me turn into blinding headlights. The passenger door of a big car was pushed open and someone shouted, 'Get in!'

Anton again.

I ran on.

With the door swinging open, he drove after me. 'Get in! For heaven's sake!'

I ignored him.

'Let me drive you home!'

'But Nicola –.'

'She's just drunk! She's been at it all day! In the morning she'll have forgotten everything. Now *please* get in!'

So I did.

At the end of the avenue he braked. Then, leaning over the seat, kissed me wetly. 'This's better.'

'Wh-what?' I pulled back.

He kissed me again.

'St-stop it!'

But he wouldn't. The next thing he was on top of me, trying to pull off my shawl which hid the kitten. Then, with his elbow pressing agonisingly into my chest, he groped under my dress and up my legs into my underwear.

'Stop!' As I struggled, the kitten jumped free.

'Christ! What was that?'

115

'A kitten!' I could hear my heart thumping. 'Now you've frightened it! Here, puss!' I picked it up from the car floor. It was terrified too. 'Please let me out!'

I tried to open the door, but he held it shut.

'I suppose you're too pure!' he jeered. 'Then what are you doing with that fortune hunter? He was even too old for Nicola's older sister!'

Somehow I clambered out of the car.

'But, I'm leaving you home.' He looked aggrieved.

'You're not.'

In the confusion the kitten jumped free, disappearing into the dark. So I left it to its fate, fleeing down the avenue and through the gates to the road.

Anton drove after me.

'But everyone thinks you're with me!' he wailed, pulling up beside me. 'And how'll you get home?'

I ran on, not stopping till the Dalkey bus stop.

The last bus was pulling out, but, seeing me, the driver stopped.

'Out dancing, were you?' He gaped at my spattered dress and broken high heels. Then seeing my tears, 'Are you all right, love?'

'It's just my dress!'

'A brush will fix that! Mud brushes off!'

I couldn't explain the dress had to go back to Walpole's. As I'd no money he took my name and address, letting me off at Aunt Allie's house at the end of Merrion Avenue. I'd walk home from there. I wanted to call in to Aunt Allie, but she'd be abed by now. And anyway she'd only say Nicola was *nouveau* or something. That the Jennings were right to laugh at me. Or that she was right about Chris. She could've told me all men were drunkards like my father. So I passed her gates, looking at the old-world garden with its beautiful bending willows which made no melody now.

I felt an aching emptiness. What I had waited weeks for was

116

over. Does love alter when it alteration finds? Where Chris'
cheek had touched mine felt anointed. Dear Reader, in spite of
everything I had had my hour. When we danced there were
palms before my feet . . . My mother says I feel things too
much. Imagine insult where none is intended. Maybe that's
another X, I don't know. Looking back, I should've stood up to
Nicola. Replied to her jibes about my relations with one of my
mother's cracks about the Healy's being the hams that made
Kilkenny famous. That would've been good, but I didn't think
of it.

> *True wit is nature to advantage dressed*
> *What oft was thought, but ne'er so well expressed.*

But I was young then, and not wise in the ways of the world.
Other sorrows were awaiting me from which I would learn.
That night I could only trudge miserably up the long Merrion
Avenue, along the main road to Stillorgan, and up to
Kilmacud, consoling myself by reciting the only lines of Virgil I
knew:

> *Ibant obscuri sola sub nocte per umbram*
> *Perque domos Ditis vacuas et inania regna.*
> (On they went darkly beneath the lonely night in the
> gloom, through the empty halls of Dis and his ghostly
> kingdom.)

There was consolation in beautiful words.

My mother would be back in the morning, and Pete would
be waiting for me at home.

'Pete!' I shouted, opening our garage door.

There was no replying bark. Everything was eerily silent.

He's escaped, I thought, picturing Doone's face.

Then a warm furry bundle brushed my face.

I groped for the light.

Pete was hanging, strangled by his lead, strangled, hanging
from the eaves.

Strangled.
Dead.

His labours o'er
Stretched his stiff limbs, to rise no more.

'Pete!' I fell to my knees, sobbing. 'Pete! Pete! Pete! Pete! Pete!'

8

'Annie, come out!' my mother shouted, thumping the bathroom door the next morning. 'It was an accident!'

If I didn't answer, she'd go away.

I had locked myself in.

'It was an accident. Annie!'

I still didn't answer. The grisly spectre of poor Pete haunted me. And I found myself in a dark wood, as savage and harsh and dense as any Dante had known. I didn't cry for Pete, anymore than I cried for my father. I felt cold and dead inside. A drowsy numbness pained and I couldn't sleep at all. I imagined the Jennings were all laughing at me. That Chris had told them about the cheque. So towards morning I moved my bedclothes into the bathroom, deciding there was no place for me in the world of calculators, sophisters and economists. I'd give up Miss Halfpenny's and carry out my life's ambition of translating Dante.

The bathroom was as secluded as Robinson Crusoe's island. It had a bolt and a lock and all mod cons: running water – hot and cold, a toilet, a bathtub for a bed – my mattress sort of sagged into this, making it coffin-like to lie in, but it was quite comfy. I even cleared the medicine cupboard for my poetry books and dictionaries, putting the various bottles, soap and shaving equipment outside.

Already I had started my translation.

'I'll count to five! If you're not out, there'll be trouble! One!'

My mother giving me trouble was nothing new. Just the kind she was threatening now.

'Two!'

119

I concentrated on my Dante.

'Three!' This was followed by a sharp rap on the door and, 'I'm warning you, Anne!'

Her calling me Anne was a dangerous sign.

'Four! You have two more seconds!'

Hitting me was as laughable as stopping my non-existent pocket money. But maybe she'd some other grislier torture planned.

'Five!'

I waited for sentence to be passed.

But there was only a brooding silence.

'This is very adolescent, Annie!' she pleaded after a few minutes. 'Please answer me, darling! Cousin William says it was an accident!'

To prevent myself weakening, I intoned aloud from the first canto, rolling the r's extravagantly. 'Una lonza leggiera e presta molto.'

According to the notes, 'una lonza' – that's the leopard – stood for lust.

'What? Una? . . . Look, Annie, don't get fresh with me!'

'Che di pel maculata ere converta.'

'I'm! – My God! She's completely cracking up!' And she ran back down the stairs.

This was exactly what I wanted her to think. I was perfectly sane. But if I pretended to be mad like Hamlet, people would leave me alone. Already my mother suspected I wasn't normal for being unsophisticated. Aunt Allie was convinced of it. And even Nicola said talking to yourself was the first sign of madness. So it would take very little more to persuade them.

Cousin William tried to get in earlier, but I'd answered him with a bark.

Looking up every word was hard work, but I was determined not to cheat by reading the English on the opposite page.

> *A little learning is a dang'rous thing,*
> *Drink deep, or taste not the Pierian spring.* Pope.

The Hound said Dante was the central man of the world. He'd only seen Beatrice once. And had written the whole *Divine Comedy* to find out what love meant. In his day there was a row about whether you could love without knowledge. Or whether you had to know something to love it.

Basically this was my problem with Chris.

'Darling, I've made you a cup of tea.'

My mother's new tone was hard to resist. But she was the *very* one who always talked about 'footprints on the sands of time' and 'lives of great men.'

'Darling, please!'

'Temp'era dal principio del mattino,' I read haltingly back. Hmm . . . The time was the beginning of the morning . . .

'Annie, please stop this nonsense!'

I didn't answer.

'I've left my only pair of nylons drying in the hot-press.'

I checked. She had.

But I wasn't falling for that. Quickly I threw them out the window, watching as they floated wavily onto the grass below. Then I bundled the remaining clothes in the press (Cousin William's chillproof underpants and vests, and some things of Doone and my mother) into a towel, tied it carefully at the corners and lowered it from the window into the flower bed.

As I shut the window, my mother flew out the front door.

'Oh, Annie!' she shrieked.

I got back into the bath tub, hearing her gather the clothes and go back in.

I returned to the first canto. Why on earth didn't we learn Italian in school, instead of boring old Latin? Amo, amas, amat is all a cod; Latin's really all about wars. The hours, absolutely hours, I'd spent on Livy and Caesar were absolutely wasted. Who cares what Cnaeus Fulvius did to Publius Scipio? Or Vice versa? Oh, Dante was mad about Virgil, but I didn't care for

121

him. Maybe I was too young to appreciate him – but I doubt it. Or maybe nobody had ever said he was great, just so many lines for an exam. I mean Pius Aeneas, what a drip . . .

Then I must've fallen asleep, because I awoke to the sound of Marcella's voice. 'Miss Annie! I've buried him in the rose garden! You can come out!'

The memory of Pete made me queasy.

'He's in the rose garden, Miss,' she whispered through the keyhole.

Our back garden had only one scrawny rosebush. At least Doone could visit his grave there, but I didn't want to think of her.

'You can't take things so serious, Miss! You'll have some supper, now!' And she pattered down the stairs, returning with a rattling tray. 'Open the door, now, Miss Annie!'

This was only a ruse. I could hear my mother hovering in the background. 'Mi ripigneva là dove 'l sol tace!' I shouted, concentrating on translating the line. Driving me back to . . . step by step . . . to where the sun is silent.

There was whispering. Then silence. Then more whispering. 'She's always been highly strung . . . This is just boldness . . . I don't think it's a crack-up . . .'

'Annie, I've had enough of this!' my mother screamed, finally prying the door handle.

It held up.

'Spare the rod and spoil the kid, Marcella!' she wailed, nearly defeated. 'I've heard about teenagers, but I didn't think Annie'd ever turn into one!'

Then they left me alone again. D.G. My trouble was always being too good. Madness was the only thing left for me.

'Boldness! Downright boldness!' Marcella grumped, returning hours later to find the food untouched.

Sometime I fell into an exhausted dream about searching Florentine streets for a sight of Dante. But he was nowhere to be found. No one came to disturb my studies again, and I

122

finished the first canto in rough. I wasn't hungry. I had a funny floaty feeling. Night ran into day and day into night. Either was immaterial to me. Time stopped, now that I'd eschewed the path of dalliance. I was a watcher of the skies. And silent upon a peak in Darien.

I awoke to a voice speaking Italian. 'Anna, mi scusi, Anna!'

Thinking it another dream, I turned into my pillow.

But the voice persisted. 'Anna! Bella Anna! Parla mi!'

Virgil came to Dante in his dark wood, but he wouldn't know about me.

'Anna, parla, per favore!'

I still couldn't recognise the voice.

'Anna, parla mi!'

'Ombra od omo certo?' I asked haltingly, which was what Dante had asked Virgil. 'Are you a real man or a shade?'

'Ombra od omo certo?' the voice repeated, puzzled.

There was a pregnant silence, followed by frantic thumbing through a book.

'Ombra od omo certo? Hmm . . . Ah, yes, omo's man . . . and certo, I have it! Oonagh!'

It was Father Mullane's Cork accent.

'Omo certo, Anna!' he declared triumphantly. 'Omo certo!'

I didn't answer.

He thumbed his book again. 'Anna, mi mostra la stanza!'

Stanza might be something to do with poetry, but I knew no modern Italian.

'Annie, open up!' he coaxed.

Father Mullane had been with Daddy when he died. Later he'd arranged the funeral, ringing up people to come and digging the grave with Cousin William – the newspapers and grave-diggers were on strike at the time.

'Open up, Annie!'

He'd been waiting at the church when we brought the body.

'Be a good girl, Annie! Open the door!'

At the funeral Mass he'd assisted our grumpy P.P., reminding him Daddy wasn't a *her*.

'Annie,' he grumbled, rattling the door knob. 'Will you please open up!'

'Will you go out again?'

'I will.'

'Promise!'

He sighed. 'I promise.'

So I let him in.

He's middle-aged and balding and fattish with a red nose. In his voluminous and stained black habit, he had to squeeze sideways past the washbasin.

'Hmm . . . Very cosy!' He squelched his glower and smiled companionably. Sort of, then nodded at my row of books in the medicine cupboard: my Brontë and other novels; *Leaving Certificate Prose; Flowers from Many Gardens;* and *The Christian Brothers' Higher Literary Reader.*

I got back into the bath tub.

He sat on the loo, facing me. Rummaging in his pocket, he took out an Italian guide book, which he quickly stuffed back in and took out his pipe instead. 'Mind if I smoke?'

I shook my head.

He filled his pipe 'Nothing like a well stocked library!'

This annoyed me, but I just stared at my Dante.

He let out mushrooms of smoke, making me cough. It drives me crazy the way people pollute the atmosphere. Just crazy.

'Bath comfortable?' he asked, the pipe going.

I nodded. If I said anything, he might stay.

He puffed away, silently scrutinising me.

'Annie,' he sighed, at last. 'What's all this? You're usually such a sensible girl.'

That was the last thing I wanted to hear.

'Annie,' he went on. 'I know you don't have to be reminded of the respect due to a mother . . .'

I sighed, bored. My privacy was nothing to do with my mother.

124

' . . . A mother is given to us by God,' he went on preachily. 'To watch over our life . . .'

In our case it was the other way around.

'When we're infants she guides our first steps. And later – later, God speaks to us through our mother. Don't you realize that, Annie?'

If God was speaking through my mother, no wonder he didn't always sound sensible.

'To sneer at her wisdom is the path to perdition, Annie.'

I raised my left eyebrow, a feat which had once cost hours of practise.

'And the Devil leads us down it.'

I stared at my book.

'Tell me, are you saying your prayers? No!' He seemed to be about to pounce on me, but calmed down. 'William says it was an accident! Now you must accept that! Annie, have you ever noticed a tree? A tree is a very beautiful thing. It does its job perfectly. It looks at God all day, and lifts its leafy arms to pray.'

'Joyce Kilmer?' I sniffed. 'Huhh!'

His pipe had gone out, so he masticated the stem noisily, making no moves to go. 'You're upset about your father, aren't you, love?' His voice was preachy again. 'I know he died very painfully.'

I wanted to scream.

'But God gives us these crosses to show His love. Now don't block your ears!'

'You promised to go soon!'

His brow furrowed. 'But God's love is boundless, Annie!'

I grabbed my Dante. 'I'm studying!'

He glanced at the cover. 'Isn't – ah – Dante – a little advanced for you?'

I looked at him pityingly.

'Eh – of course – it takes an intellectual to understand an intellectual's poet!' He puffed his pipe. 'Tell me, have you read any philosophy?'

'N-no.'

'Well, I've just the thing for you! Kant's *Critique of Pure Reason*. Have you read it? No! Well, tell you what, I'll lend it to you. Meantime, there's the happy medium, yes, the golden mean.' He paused, then went on casually, 'Your mother – ah – says you've fallen for some fellow?'

My heart started thudding.

'Some solicitor?'

It was madness telling my mother anything.

He cleared his throat. 'You've taken it too seriously, love. Sure, you're too young to know what love means.'

'I can find out!'

He perused my face. 'Did anyone–?'

'What?' I feigned innocence.

He studied me, then shook his head. 'Sure, you're only a child, Annie.' Then he tried again. 'Did anyone –?'

'What?'

Narrowing his eyes, he blurted. 'Did anyone interfere with you?'

I went back to my book.

'You can tell me, Annie.' His voice was gentle.

Oh, he was broadminded enough. There was my mother's liking him. And their visits, etc. And once when the school sex education priest had scared us with the story about a girl getting pregnant in her brother's bathwater, he'd said it couldn't happen. 'Wash the bath though,' he added. 'You can't be too careful.'

'Annie, you can trust me.'

If I told him about Anton, there'd only be a stupid fuss. 'You said you'd go!'

He puffed irritably.

I pretended to read.

'Well, blast it!' he said angrily. 'If you won't talk to me, will you do me a favour?'

'What?'

126

'A – favour!'

'But what?'

He eyed me cautiously. 'Will you see someone?'

'Who?'

He avoided my eyes. 'Someone who'll help you.'

'But who?' I knew he was afraid to say doctor.

'Never mind *who*!' He stood up, brusquely pocketing his pipe. 'Get dressed!'

I returned to my book.

'Get dressed, Annie! I'll tell you on the way!'

I thought it might be interesting to see a doctor, but I wanted to get on with my studies. I flicked through my dictionary for the right words to explain this in Italian 'Eh . . . andare . . . all'estro . . .'

'Andiamo!' he roared, grabbing me and hauling me into the hall.

That very evening found us squeezed on the couch outside Dr Nirmal's office in a wide corridor of Saint Patrick's Hospital, Dublin.

I was in the middle. My mother flanked my right side, maintaining the tearful silence she'd observed since my exit. And Fr Mullane my left, telling me between pokes of his elbow and puffs on his pipe the hospital was a gift from Jonathan Swift to the people of Dublin.

'Ahem . . . yes.' He cleared his throat, pointing upwards with his pipe. 'This's the original building. Swift left instructions for the location in his will.'

The place looked sort of worn-in OK, but not that ancient. The long wide corridor had a waxy smell, reminding me of school. Along one side, quaint little doors opened into rooms – of which Dr Nirmal's was the first. And on the other, tall windows looked across a patch of grass to a parallel granite wing.

'That's the men's section,' Father said, seeing me stare through the window behind us.

I could see a priest pacing the opposite corridor. It connected to ours at the hall where a Cerberus-like guard sat.

'I'm glad it's co-ed,' I whispered.

'Co-ed? Ah, yes! Swift saw to that!' He lowered his voice. 'The will specified "Aged lunatics, idiots and – eh – others".'

I looked warily at the man sitting on the next couch. He was reading a magazine perfectly normally.

Then a group of women passed, joking cheerfully.

'They look OK,' I whispered.

Father frowned in puzzlement. 'What?'

'They don't look like lunatics!'

This brought a poke from my mother.

'What? . . . Ah, but they're intellectuals! It's for intellectuals now, Annie!' Father puffed his pipe. 'Have you read Swift?'

'Only *Gulliver's Travels*.'

'A good children's story. His best. His other work's ruined by coarseness. Went mad, poor –.' He stopped himself in time. 'Went to Trinity, poor fellow. Ruined a lot of people.'

I studied the man on the next couch. My trouble was not knowing what madness was like. The *impasse* in the bathroom had convinced my mother and Fr Mullane, but would it convince a doctor? Should I kick and scream? Or tear out my hair? Mrs Rochester was mad enough to be chained down. But Swift had been a great writer.

Unless he was pretending too?

The only mad person I ever met is perfectly normal. He's my mother's favourite Healy cousin, a Classical scholar *manqué* who lived in St. John of God's Hospital. Except that he called it Stillorgan Castle, he seemed OK too. Basically he was more than OK, he was very kind. He regularly took us to operas, arriving at our house in a taxi with tickets for the *Merry Widow* or *Maritana,* or *La Bohême*. Or whatever was on at the Gaiety. We always had a theatre-box and chocolates. And coffee or a mineral during the interval. The only odd thing: he'd talk at the top of his voice all through the performance. I suppose that was cracked, but at the time I had only worried that people were looking. Maybe he had terrible depths I'd not plumbed. From some shock in childhood. I've read that madness is often caused by a shock – Miss Havisham's bridegroom not turning up and that. Hmm . . .

Nothing unusual had ever happened to me. So how would I convince a doctor? Oh, an English girl in school once said our class were War babies, but I wasn't born till 1945. Maybe I could make up funny dreams. Say Emily had appeared to me. Or Dante.

Just then Dr Nirmal opened his door, showing another patient out.

I watched as they shook hands and chatted. The doctor was tallish and sort of pigeon chested, with a whitish countenance and whitish wavy hair. He wore a dapper red dotted bow-tie with matching pocket hanky, but his suit was baggy and rumpled.

The other patient moved on and he came over, his hand tremblingly out. 'F-f-father.'

As they shook hands, he glanced expectantly at my mother. 'Is th-th-this?'

'Ah, no!' Father interrupted his stammer, yanking me up. 'It's Annie, here!'

'Ah! Annie!' The doctor's smile oozed cheerfulness. 'Would you l-l-like to have a ch-chat with me?' His voice was Englishy.

Nervously I nodded.

Then, glancing knowingly from Fr Mullane to my mother, he led me into his sanctus sanctorum.

'Keep nothing back, darling!' Tearfully my mother broke her silence.

The office was tiny and reeked of stale cigarettes. A couch took up one wall and a filing-cabinet and desk the rest of the space. Dr Nirmal sat at his desk, pointing me to the couch.

'Will I lie down?'

'What is c-c-comfortable.'

129

I sat bolt upright.

Dr Nirmal lit a cigarette, puffed once and laid it tremblingly on the ashtray. He made a steeple with his nicotiney fingers, missed, but got it right the second time. 'F-f-father tells me you're h-having a disagreement with your m-m-mother.'

I weakened under his honest blue gaze. Like Dante at the gate of Hell, I was smitten with cowardice. Fooling Fr Mullane was one thing, but this man was highly nervous. I'd have to go home and be normal like everyone else.

'My mother and I get on very well,' I said at last.

'Hmm . . .' He scribbled this down. 'Then w-why d-d-did you l-l-lock yourself in?'

I said nothing.

'You're upset about your d-d-dog's accident?'

Defeatedly I shook my head. Explaining that Cousin William had turned out to be a murderer would take too long. Besides, the doctor might ask to see him instead of me. 'It's the only room in the house with a lock.'

He scribbled this down, reaching for another cigarette.

As I wondered whether to remind him about the first, he lit the second, puffed it and laid it as before on the ashtray.

'B-b-but why did you w-w-want to l-l-lock yourself in?'

'For privacy. I'm translating Dante.'

'Hm . . .' He looked up from scribbling. 'The Italian D-D-Dante?'

I nodded. There was no other as far as I knew.

'And w-w-why D-D-D- – Why him?' His eyebrows lifted curiously.

'He understood things.' I coughed from the smoke. My asthma could start any minute.

'W-w-what things?'

'Why we're living and that. He went through Hell, then Purgatory, then Paradise. He had a vision there.'

'And t-t-tell me, Annie. D-do you think you'll have a v-v-vision?' He looked alarmed.

'I hope so.' I broke into more coughing. I should've said I had visions all the time.

Waiting for me to recover, the doctor lit up again, following the usual wasteful procedure.

I couldn't stop coughing.

'Wh-wh-what is it?'

'Nothing! Just my asthma.'

He scribbled this down. 'D-d-do you get it often?'

'Now and again.' It'd be rude to tell him I was allergic to tobacco.

'Hmm . . . Psychos-s-somatic.' He chewed the end of his biro. 'F-f-father tells me your D-d-dad died.'

I shrugged. 'We are but dust.'

The room reeked of smouldering butts, but he lit up again. 'D-d-does your D-d-dad's death depress you?'

I nodded, thinking it a weird question.

'D-d-do you f-f-feel worst morning, noon or night?'

'Eh . . . When I think about it.' I hadn't felt sad at the funeral, the way Doone had. I had sort of watched myself. Silly things worried me now, like would he be cold in winter?

He looked up from his note-pad. 'T-t-tell me about your D-d-dad!'

I thought for a moment. 'Well . . . he was a gentleman farmer.'

'Y-y-yes . . .'

'He went to Clongowes.'

The doctor nodded encouragingly.

'He liked the cinema. And the races. And having lunch in town.' I racked my brains. 'He went on a ski-ing holiday once. To Bavaria. Before the war . . .'

'G-g-go on!'

'He liked to sing John McCormack's songs . . . "Love's Old Sweet Song," that sort of thing.' I sighed heavily. 'He hadn't any luck. You need luck.'

The doctor nodded sympathetically. 'D-d-do you have any

131

special memories?'

I breathed in lungfuls of smoke. 'Well . . . Once at our old house . . . we saw a fox . . . running over the fields. And we chased it for miles to the nest . . .'

'Y-y-yes?' The doctor's eyes rounded in horror.

'There were babies in it.'

'Oh!' He sighed disappointedly. 'D-d-do you have other m-m-memories?'

He was probably trying to discover some shock in childhood. I could tell him about my rabbit being eaten by our cat, but he'd only think me a coward. The rest of my life had been disgustingly normal. And I'd loved my father from the cradle's arms. The evening we found the fox's nest was the happiest moment of my life. A dusk had fallen over the fields. We walked for miles and miles. Then back to the house through the apple orchard and over the cracked tennis court . . .

'T-t-take your time.' The doctor was lighting up again.

'I can't remember anything else.' I couldn't explain how the house went. Like everything. How I saw that life through the wrong end of a telescope.

The doctor waved away some smoke. 'F-f-father Mullane thinks, and I have to agree w-w-with him, that ah, your father's d-death has d-d-depressed you.'

'Yes – well –.'

'W-w-we both think you n-n-need a rest.'

'Ah! I'm mad then?' I sat bolt upright.

'N-n-now Annie, d-d-did I say th-that?' he frowned sternly.

'No.'

'It often h-h-happens that a b-bereavment c-causes a depression. Which l-l-leads to a disturbance.'

'A disturbance?'

He nodded, accidentally snapping his biro in two. 'Oh d-dear! Yes, a psychiatric illness. Now I w-w-want you to be reasonable, Annie.'

'I will. I will.' I kept the grin from my face. Without even

132

trying I'd convinced him.

'W-w-will you stay here with us?'

I hesitated, not appearing too eager. 'Can I've a room to myself?'

'That c-c-can be arranged.' He stood up, groping again for the cigarettes but pushing them away. 'M-m-must give up smoking!'

Then Dr Nirmal took my mother into his office and I waited with Fr Mullane.

When they came out, my mother was dabbing her eyes.

She hugged me forgivingly. 'Annie, darling, Dr Nirmal wants you to stay here.'

Stiffening, I pulled away.

'Darling, please co-operate!'

I stared at the three anxious faces. My mother's eyes were redrimmed, her green silk head-scarf askew. Fr Mullane's shoulders were hunched, his coat half-mast over his soutane. And the doctor, his white hair wild, looking ready to grab me.

With him I hadn't pretended anything – ironically he thought I *was* mad. So it was sinful to continue with my mother and Fr Mullane. But I couldn't go back now. Like Macbeth I was in too far.

'I'll bring your things tonight,' my mother placated, retying her scarf.

'My books?' I whispered. 'And my blanket-bit?'

'Of course, darling.' She put her arm round me.

'I'll drive her back with them.' Fr Mullane stepped forwards, gripping my mother's arm. 'If you co-operate with the doctors!'

I had every intention of doing so, but looked bewildered.

My mother's mouth tightened as she held back tears. Oh, Angel of God, what was I doing? She'd go to bits without me. To absolute bits. And how would I manage without her? I nuzzled into her baldy fur coat. Then, just as I was about to confess, Fr Mullane nodded at the doctor and led her firmly down the corridor.

133

Feeling like a serpent, I watched the fur coat out of sight. 'My mother'll never manage without me!' I whispered to the doctor, starting after her.

'C-c-come, Annie!' He gripped my arm. 'Your m-mother's one of the m-m-most sensible women I've ever met.'

I knew otherwise, but allowed myself to be led up the endless shiny corridor. Further up we passed more couches on which people chatted happily. And through all the quaint little doors, I saw into neat bedrooms, wondering if one would be mine. I kept thinking we'd arrived, but the doctor kept walking on, his shoes squeaking oddly. At last we reached the top, turning left into another short corridor which led to a ward with beds.

'That was Ward Five, Annie,' he said. 'And th-th-this is F-f-five Solarium where you'll b-b-be c-c-comfortable.'

I panicked. 'But you said –.'

'Y-y-you'll h-h-have your room!' He nodded vigorously.

Then a nurse stepped towards us, bristling with efficiency and crackling with cheerfulness. 'Is this Anne? I'm Sister Hackett!'

As we shook hands, I examined the array of badges on her starched bosom. There was no sign of the Mater, my mother's old hospital.

The doctor whispered something to her, then took his leave of me. 'S-s-sister will show you y-y-your room.'

'I – eh –.' I watched bereft as he turned his back and squeaked back down the long corridor. I didn't know what to expect next: maybe for Sister Hackett to come at me with a straightjacket or injection, but she just opened the door behind us.

'Have you been in St Pat's before?' she asked, smiling stiffly.

'Eh – no.' It was a smallish bedroom, but mine own.

'You should be comfortable here!' Briskly she untucked the white bedspread.

As well as a bed, there was a dressing table and chair. And best of all, a view of an old walled garden with bare ruined choirs of trees. The branches were stark against the sky, making

134

a lacy pattern. Fr Mullane's right, I thought, there's something about a tree . . . As yet, no sign of Wordsworth's immortal daffodils. But if winter comes . . .

'Get undressed now!' Sister went out, coming back immediately with a nightie. 'Put that on for the moment!'

I dragged myself from the window and, with her watching me, undressed.

'Get into bed, now!' She folded my clothes neatly and carried them out, my green tweed coat over her arm. 'We'll hang your coat out here!'

As I lay down, very tired now, she came back with a handful of little yellow white and blue pills and a glass of water. 'Down the hatch, there's the good girl!'

I swallowed them. She crackled out again, saying, 'Supper will be in an hour, Anne.'

The door closed.

And I was summoned to the sessions of sweet silent thought.

A bird chirped ominously in the garden. I decided to write a poem to celebrate, but a woozy feeling knelled the death of that day's life.

My sleep was long and fretful. I seemed to fall through years of dreamless dark. I awoke sometime, wondering what kind of country I had come to. What would its inhabitants be like? Nervously I looked out to the murky passage, hoping to find a bathroom. There was a light in the room opposite which turned out to be it. Everything seemed normal. But would I discover tiny trees? Or grass of twenty feet? Would lunatic Lilliputians or diseased Brobdingnagians seize me?

Groggily I got back into bed, awaking again to cheerful humming and clinking delph.

A bird-like woman of about fifty stood over me with a tray. Her wispy hair was dyed pink. She wore pink tinted glasses and a pink diaphonous dressing-gown. 'Are you awake, pet? Sit up, that's the girl!'

I did. She laid the tray on my lap.

135

'Here, let me puff your pillows!' She perused me, tapping her jutting chin. 'No, you're too young for Rosalind!'

I blinked nervously. 'Eh – what?'

'But you'll do very nicely for Desdemona! Don't look so alarmed, pet!' She plonked on the end of my bed. 'I'm Mrs Greene, formerly an actress, presently Directress of the Dean's Dramatic Society! To keep in practise, I'm organizing a reading of scenes from Shakespeare!'

'But I've never acted.'

'Of course you have!'

She has extra-sensory perception, I thought.

'You're probably like me and have a natural talent. Your food's getting cold! Don't look so worried, it's not poisoned!'

I took a bite of the poached egg on toast. There was more buttered toast and a scoop of marmalade on a side plate.

Mrs Greene chuckled. 'You're asking yourself what kind of a raving lunatic is this? Now admit it!'

Luckily my mouth was full.

'I'm no lunatic, pet! Just an alcoholic!'

'I was President of the Pioneers in school,' I said, knowing well the curse of drink. When my father drank, my mother always moved into Buswell's Hotel. But he'd always get sorry and beg her to come home. So she would. And all would be well until the next outbreak – except Doone and I'd be dragged out of bed for early Mass when he was repenting. 'Can you not give it up?' I enquired politely.

Her eyes rounded in horror behind the pink glasses. 'I darned well have to! Do you think I could stay here, otherwise?'

Knowing the feeling, I stared at my tray.

'Pet!' She pointed upwards. 'One drink and I'd be swinging from that light! I'd swing myself out of here!' She jumped up, doing a ballet leap. 'Probably to Hong Kong!' Then she leapt across the room landing with a thump. 'I was there once!'

'Were –.'

'And in Ceylon.' She took off again, landing with another

136

thump. 'And in Jamaica!' She stopped, breathless. 'Last time I ended up in Papua New Guinea. The captain was really worried –.'

'Who's the captain?'

'My husband, pet! Next time it might be Afghanistan! Pakistan! Some other stan! I'm allergic to alcohol, pet! I have the geographic syndrome. Tea?'

'Please.'

'Milk and sugar?'

I nodded.

And she leapt balletically out, returning with a cup of tea. 'I've put in two sugars, unstirred. Now will you be Desdemona?'

I hesitated. 'Can't I be Ophelia?'

'Ophelia? Why not!' And she floated out of the room, murmuring, 'Nymph in thy orisons, be all my gins remembered.'

The idea of reading Shakespeare was exciting. Anew McMaster had read scenes from the tragedies in our school once. And our class had seen Orson Welles acting the part of Falstaff in *Henry IV*. We got piles and piles of autos afterwards, and the actors were so nice I decided to be one. It was only a matter of cultivating a nice manner. Mrs Greene certainly had one. And I finished my first breakfast, picturing her disembarking from a Hong Kong plane and leaping across the runway to the amazement of slitty-eyed officials. The geographic syndrome sounded more like a spy story than a disease. Was there a historical syndrome? And an archaeological syndrome? The possibilities were endless. Drink did funny things to people.

But who can judge another? Let me not cast the first stone.

Mrs Greene was my first friend in St. Patrick's. As Virgil was to Dante, she became to me, guiding my steps in that Nirvana of Happiness.

As I finished eating, Sister Hackett came in with more pills. 'Down the hatch! That's right! Did you sleep well, Annie?'

'I woke sometime. Then I dozed back.'

'Your mother left your things last night. You were out for the

137

count. She wouldn't wake you.'

I said nothing. The sight of my mother would only weaken my resolve.

Sister took out my tray, coming back with my mother's leather trousseau case. We had used it in our fatal flight to London and the memory made me queasy. But I was now in happier fields. My blanket was there, D.G. And a new white nightie and new blue silk dressing gown. Also a neatly packed washbag with soap, toothbrush, shampoo, etc. And my Dante.

'Have a wash now! The bathroom's across the corridor! Then I'll weigh you!' Sister Hackett bossed, crackling out of my room.

Groggily I went out, peeping into the adjoining ward. It was quite crowded. Some of the patients were in their dressing gowns and some were dressed, but all were busy. Either making beds. Or dusting. Or sweeping. Despite the Dean's specifications, everybody looked the picture of normality and nobody was particularly aged.

The next person I met was my age.

I was washing my teeth at the basins when an Englishy voice called, 'You the new inmate?'

A pale girl with lank blond shoulder length hair pouted into the mirror. She wore a grubby pink towelling dressing-gown and too much black eye make-up.

Quickly rinsing my mouth, I held out my hand. 'Eh – I'm Anne O'Brien.'

'Tina Snellgrove. Never shake hands! A bourgeois hangup! What you in for?'

'A rest.' My face twitched oddly.

'They all say that.' She sighed knowledgeably, plunging her hands into her dressing gown pockets and lounging against the basins. 'You look depressive.'

'Do I?'

'The question is . . . exogenous or endogenous?'

'What?'

138

'One's from the outside, and one's from the inside.'

'Oh! Well, the doctor –.'

'Who? Nirmal?'

I nodded.

'Daft as a coot!' Her accent was thicker now, like an English coal miner. 'What'd 'e say exactly?'

'That I'm disturbed. Eh – about my father.'

Her eyes rounded in horror. 'Your father?'

'He died.' My face twitched again.

'Oh!' She seemed relieved, but continued perusing me. 'Did you attempt anything? Wrists? Pills?'

'Eh – What?'

She held out her hands, wrists upwards. 'Wrists are messy! Slit me own three times!'

I gaped in horror at the healed pink slits. Locking yourself in the bathroom was one thing, but –.'

'With wrists there's blood everywhere!' Her eyes looked blacker. 'Last time I tried aspirin. Swallowed a whole bottle in the middle of Old English! Woke up 'ere! Never liked Old English!'

I dragged my gaze from her wrists.

'Back with Nirmal!' She grimaced into the mirror.

Just then a piece of toast fell from somewhere under her dressing gown.

'You won't tell, will you?' She stooped to pick it up.

'Tell what?'

'About this!' She blushed, shoving the toast into her pocket. 'It's me breakfast! The food's rotten 'ere!'

As I shook my head, she made for the W.C.

Maybe I'm just boring and like everything – even school porridge – but I thought the breakfast delicious. I mean, toast's my favourite food.

'You a student?' Tina shouted, flushing the chain. 'I'm reading English at Trinity.'

'I'm at Halfpenny's. Eh – Miss Halfpenny's College.'

139

She came back out. 'What do you read?'

'Nothing at the moment. I'm translating Dante.'

'Oh!' She gave me a puzzled look. 'Where is Halfpenny's, anyway?'

'Clare Street!' I went on quickly, 'A new Dante is badly needed! All the others made him sound like bad Milton!'

She took eyeshadow from her pocket, smudging it messily on. 'Me boyfriend's doin' a thesis on Milton. Thinks it's super stuff.'

I shook my head. 'Not compared to Dante! He was the greatest poet since Homer!'

She nodded placatingly into the mirror, fingering her lank locks. 'Got any shampoo? Jim's comin' tonight. Better wash me 'air.'

As I gave her some from my washbag, Sister Hackett called from the door. 'Have you made your bed, Tina? And buy your own shampoo! Hurry Anne, I want to weigh you!'

My face was twitching like mad now.

'What is it?' Sister grumped as we walked down Ward Five's long corridor.

I had my hand to my face. 'Eh – my face's twitching since breakfast.'

She pulled away my hand, perusing me. 'I don't see anything! It's your imagination, Anne!'

The scales were in a little room in a corridor connecting the men's and women's wings.

'Hop up there!' Sister ordered, balancing it.

I was seven stone four.

'You'll have to eat, if you want to get better, Anne!' Sister grumped. 'Don't let that Tina put ideas into your head!'

'What ideas?'

'Just eat what's put in front of you!'

As we made our way back, I decided not eating must be a *sine qua non* of madness and *de rigeur* for staying. As one traveller in the dark wood of deceit, I recognized others. Mrs

Greene had given up drink to stay. And Tina food. I sensed murky depths to her. Why for instance was she so gloaty about the slits? And why was she so embarassed about me seeing the toast? And why on earth, with going to Trinity College and having a boyfriend – even one who liked Milton – did she want to stay here?

I wondered if she wore a gown at Trinity. My mother had wanted me to go there, but the Hound blamed the ills of the world on the place. Any bad news, say a murder or something, and she'd mutter 'Trinity College' under her breath. Basically this was because one of our past pupils had defied the Archbishop's ban and gone there, ending up marrying a divorcé (Protestant) – according to the Hound a fate far worse than death: eternal damnation. Although I had never before met anyone from Trinity, I had often looked through the gates, not venturing further. Oh, not because of religion. It just looked so learned . . . so grand and forbidding. Except for the grass, it was completely grey inside, both the quads and the buildings. And outside grimy statues of Burke and Goldsmith stared across at Grattan, ignoring Moore with his halo of pigeons. It was silly I know, but I dreamed there might one day be a statue of me: Anne B. O'Brien, Translator of Dante.

But there wouldn't be. They were all graduates, and I as a Catholic couldn't really go there without a dispensation. Anyway, without my exams I wouldn't get in.

My mother brought us up free of religious prejudice. D.G. Ironically, she didn't mind whether we went to Mass or not. I suppose it was being an American. Just if the Pope, or the Chief Rabbi, or even the Protestant Archbishop was talking on the T.V., she'd make us listen – she says there's only one God.

'Into bed now,' Sister ordered, when we came back to my room.

I obeyed, cuddling under my blanket. It had been on my bed for years and was now almost worn out. In school they'd said I was mad not to be able to manage without it, but my mother said nonsense. That everyone needed something to comfort them. Although still tired, I couldn't sleep now. I could only think about Tina's suicide attempts and, after a while, sat up and found the bit in Dante where the suicides were condemned to be trees:

> *Ma fronda verdi, ma di color fosca*
> (Not green, but of a dusky hue).

Later that morning, Evelyn came in to sweep my room. She was a small redhaired girl with hair cut in a childishly straight fashion who wore anklesocks with a housecoat. And, although only a year younger than I, worked as a maid in St Patrick's.

'Let me do that!' I jumped out of bed, feeling a complete fraud.

But she kept on, smiling cheerfully. 'You don't do jobs till you're up!' Her accent was pure Dublin.

'How long will I be in bed?' My face still twitched.

She shrugged, 'Some stay six months. Some longer.'

'*Six* months?' I got back into bed. 'How long are you here?'

'Dunno . . . maybe six months. I've had six jobs since school.'

'Six? Do you not miss school?'

She shook her head disgustedly, then brightened. 'I'm emigratin' to America. Have ya ever been?'

'No, but I'm half American.'

She gaped in awe, her chin resting on the brush-handle. 'Half American . . . Half American . . .'

'Well, sort of. My mother's an American citizen. She was brought up there.'

Her eyes went dreamy. 'Did she ever meet Debbie Reynolds?'

I shook my head.

Then Dr Nirmal came in, his stethoscope dangling round his neck. He wore the same rumpled suit, but his bow-tie was blue-dotted with a matching pocket hanky.

Seeing Evelyn, he immediately put his hand to his eyes. 'N-n-now, Evelyn. D-d-don't nag!'

142

'How many did ya smoke today?' She thumped the floor with her brush.

'N-n-now st-st-stop!' He waved her into silence.

'Ya didn't give them up at all!'

'Oh, r-r-run along!' And he ushered her out.

I wondered if he'd give me inkblots to describe, like on T.V. But he just said, 'H-how did you s-s-sleep?'

'I woke up once, but dozed back.'

He rubbed his chin worriedly. 'D-d-do you often wake early?'

'Usually.' It was the way my kidneys worked.

'At the s-s-same t-t-time?'

'Early – I'm not sure!' My face twitched oddly again. 'Doctor, what's wrong with me?'

'Hmm . . . I'll ask Sister to give you something.'

'Doctor, my face.'

He just perused me nervously.

'Doctor! Did you see that?' I held the side of my face. 'My face!'

'V-v-very p-p-pretty! Now let's listen to the old t-t-ticker.'

As he put the icy stethoscope to my chest, I got a fit of the giggles. Not from embarassment or anything stupid, just the shock of the cold.

'Doctor!' I gasped, as soon as my fit abated. 'What's wrong with my face?'

He ignored me, moving the cold knob further up. 'T-t-take a deep breath now!' Then he pocketed the stethoscope and sat on a chair. 'I s-s-see you're reading D-D-Dante?'

'Yes! For my translation!' My face went again. 'Doctor, what's wrong with me?'

'You'll be f-fine, Annie. W-w-would you think of b-b-being a writer yourself?'

'I keep a diary.'

'D-d-did you ever think of t-t-trying a n-n-novel?'

I shook my head. My life was too dull to be written of, my circumstances too unlike anything in a book.

143

'Y-y-you have r-r-remarkable insights, Annie.'

My face was going like mad now.

'I h-h-ave five children and can't get one to open a b-b-book.' He stood up, staring sadly out the window.

I think that was the moment I began feeling fond of Dr Nirmal. I felt so sorry for him. 'Try reading to them! Eh–Doctor!'

His blue eyes were round, his white hair unruly. 'R-r-reading to them? . . . Hmm!' He dabbed his nose with his hanky.

'Doctor! My face!'

He perused me, finally noticing. 'It's twitching!'

'I know! I've been trying to tell you!'

'Hmm . . . How long h-h-has that b-b-been hap-p-pening?'

'Since breakfast!' It was the beginning of some creepy crawly disease. I'd read they started like that.

'P-p-robably a r-r-reaction to L-l-largactyl. I'll ask Sister to give you something to c-c-counteract it.'

I thought it'd be better to stop taking the first pill.

He stood up to go.

'Doctor, when can I get up? Will it be six months?' I looked at him glumly.

'Now who told you that?'

'Eh – that girl who was here!'

'Evelyn? She's a w-w-worrier!' He chuckled. 'Don't worry, Annie! I'll get you b-b-better!' He turned at the door. 'T-t-tell you what! You c-c-can get up for b-b-breakfast in your dressing-gown. How's that?'

'OK.' But I watched dismayed as he went out humming.

Getting better was the last thing I wanted. Or getting up. It had been a fatal mistake to ask when. Blister it! Next they'd be sending me home. But, as I'd no idea what the doctor was thinking, I didn't know what to do or say. The only clues on madness I'd picked up so far were not eating and not sleeping. So I left my lunch that day – even the delicious meringue and custard dessert. And that night I fought sleep, prowling the

144

narrow corridors to make sure the night nurse saw me.

The next morning's breakfast was served in the adjoining Solarium. As I walked groggily in, the other patients were already seated at a centre table. There was no sign of Tina and the only familiar person was Mrs Greene who wore slacks and sat at the top, exuberantly serving porridge.

'Annie, pet! Sit here!' she called, pointing to a chair beside her. 'Will you have porridge?'

'She will!' Sister grumped, fussing around the ward. 'And take her down to the shop after breakfast, Mrs Greene! Annie, your mother left you some money!' And she handed me an envelope with my name in my mother's slanty American handwriting. There was a fiver inside and a note. I put them in my pocket to read later.

'It's my day to help Evelyn with the dishes,' Mrs Greene was saying. 'The Volga will take her!' And she forced a smile to the end of the table. 'Won't you, dears?'

I thought I was seeing double as two identical blue-haired ladies dressed identically in baby-blue twinsets and pearl necklaces said simultaneously, 'We will!'

But one was taller than the other.

'I'm Victoria!' she said, offering me her hand.

'And Olga Sheehan,' the smaller one followed suit.

'The Volga for short!' Mrs Greene quipped, ladling out a spoonful. 'Like Mary and her lamb! Everywhere that Olga goes, Victoria's sure to follow!'

The sisters glared huffily as Mrs Greene introduced me to the others. I don't remember everyone, but I know Madeline was sitting opposite me. She was a beautifully dressed woman of about forty. Her fine drawn features and wispy pinned up hair and long swannish neck reminded me of a ballet dancer. The only thing: she had the saddest green eyes.

'Madeline's reading Desdemona!' Mrs Greene had finished serving. 'Annie's agreed to do Ophelia! So you two'll get to know each other!'

145

I thought her too old for that part, but just smiled. I felt an instant rapport with those eyes. They were very green, but red-rimmed as if she'd just stopped crying. And behind them, saucers of more tears seemed ready to brim out if someone so much as nudged her.

'Isn't Annie pure Botticelli?' she said, acknowledging my stare with a smile.

Mrs Greene peered at me pinkly. 'She is!'

Before I could ask what that meant, Olga passed a snap from the end of the table. 'Our grandnephews, dear.'

'Not here!' Victoria muttered, reaching for the photos.

'Café au lait! Café au lait!' Olga wrenched it free, passing it along.

They were two little Indian boys. 'They're lovely!' I passed it back.

'Our niece married an Indian.' Olga smiled rapturously.

'A half-naked fakir!' Victoria snapped. 'Now eat your break-fast.'

'Humbug Victoria!' Mrs Greene shouted. 'Flatulent humbug!'

'Café au lait!' Olga muttered, peering lovingly at the snap and putting it away.

Victoria stabbed her bread vindictively. 'A half-naked fakir! The young generation!'

'The age of chivalry's gone,' I said, to say something.

'Café au lait!' Mrs Greene called out, echoing Olga.

I thought there was going to be a row and poked nervously at my porridge. But the rest of the breakfast passed without incident. Mrs Greene and Madeline talked volubly and the only interruptions were sporadic shouts from Olga of, *'Café au lait!'*

'We'll wait for you in Ward Five, dear,' Victoria said, finally rising.

'On the first couch,' Olga added.

I nodded, saying I'd have to wash my teeth. Then in the privacy of my room, read my mother's note:

146

Darling Annie,

The doctor thinks you need a bit of a breather, so I won't visit for a while. They have a shop if you need anything. So buy yourself some *Lucozade* darling. I know you like that.

Doone is well, but misses you. The trip to the Kibbutz is postponed for a few weeks more. Poor Mr Freeman has legal problems.

Get well, darling. Please understand about my not visiting.

Love, Mummy.

The Volga were sitting primly on the first couch in Ward Five, a suitcase parked on the floor between them.

'We'll have to hurry!' Victoria creakingly arose, taking my elbow.

'But we haven't checked the list!' Fussily Olga laid the case on the couch, clicking it open. 'Something might be missing!'

'Oh, all right!' Victoria groped in her handbag for a list. 'Tin whistle,' she shouted, turning to me. 'In case of fog, dear!'

'Present!' Olga touched a whistle sellotaped neatly to the cardboard case lid.

'Blankets?' Victoria read, and to me. 'For frost, dear. And East wind! Most treacherous elements! Woollen underwear?'

Coincidentally a doctor once told me those very elements had caused my asthma.

'Dinghy?' Victoria went on. 'For flood, dear. Those foolish people on the Titanic!'

'Present!'

'Emergency rations?'

'Present!'

'Salt tablets?'

'Present!'

'Chocolates?'

147

'Present!'

'Gas stove?'

'Gas stove? Wait a minute, I –.' Olga groped deeply in the case. 'I'm sure it's here. Ah! Yes, everything present and correct!' She clicked the case shut. And the three of us made a slow and stately progress down the long wide polished corridor.

Halfway, I stopped dead.

Tina was walking groggily towards us, supported between two nurses. She looked like death, hardly recognizable from yesterday.

'What's wrong?' I asked, stopping beside her.

'She's all right! She's just had treatment.' One of the nurses said calmly.

Tina stared vacantly, eerily through me.

'Treatment?' I wondered how it could help.

'You won't know her in an hour, dear,' Victoria consoled, pulling me on.

'She'll be a new girl,' Olga added knowledgeably.

Then I looked into a ward full of unconscious people, lying clothed on beds. 'Who are they?'

'Outpatients, dear.' Victoria hurried me on. 'They come in for treatment.'

Olga shook her head sympathetically. 'They're not lucky enough to live here.'

As we walked through the connecting corridor, the strange smells made me nauseous. The conked-out figures in the ward reminded me of a dream about Nazis injecting people for experiments. Oh, Angel of God, would such treatment ever be given me? There was nothing wrong with me, nothing. I just wanted to stay here, somehow to find myself. And carry out my my life's purpose of translating Dante. That's why I went into the bathroom. But my mother and Fr Mullane and Dr Nirmal thought I was cracked. Well, I wasn't. I just couldn't live at home.

148

The hospital shop was on the men's side near the hall and had all sorts of sweets and things. I bought a bottle of *Lucozade*. In our country house, I had a long bus journey home from day school. So my mother would always revive me with it. The familiar bottle comforted me now and banished thoughts of Tina and the other stricken patients.

The next week passed happily. The only disturbances were visits from Dr Nirmal, during which I grew fonder and fonder of him. And from Evelyn who gave me chewing gum and talked non-stop about America. At meals in the Solarium, Sister Hackett watched every bite I took, insisting on my drinking a glass of *Complan* with every meal – it's white gooey stuff, something like liquid glue. Ugh. So I started putting on weight. And with all the pills, I was too groggy to do any Dante. So I made up stories about myself as an heiress in decline and Chris as a sardonic and smitten suitor. Our vast estates bordered so, when I was out driving in the governess trap, we'd meet accidentally. I loved Chris, Dear Reader, and could not cast him out or measure deed for deed. Maybe he was an alcoholic like Mrs Greene and in need of pity, woman's true domain. So I wrote him a letter and gave it to her to post.

Dearest Christopher,

Thank you so much for accompanying me to Nicola's *début*. I enjoyed myself so much.

What could not be said that evening, can be expressed in the intimacy of a letter. I will not profane a 'word' too often profaned. I will just say I feel a deep *tendresse pour toi*. I realize my feeling may never be reciprocated. So from now on, it will burn like a silent flame in my heart. A flame which no storm will ever extinguish. It and the memory of our evening together will warm me in the lonely years ahead.

By the way: sorry for dashing off! I had to see about

149

our dog. I am now here, recovering from his sad demise. If you have a minute, do write. It's a bit boring here.

Your friend,
Anne O'Brien.

The new pill didn't cure my twitch. So one evening after supper I asked Mrs Greene if it was normal for Largactyl to have that effect.

She perused me. 'I don't see anything. Largactyl, you say? Hmm!'

'Dr Nirmal gave me another pill to counteract it. And now the other side feels funny too!'

She slapped the bed quilt. 'He's trying to make an Irish dancer out of you!'

'Wh-what?'

She straightened her back, doing a mock jig around the room. 'They give Irish dancers one pill to make the top stiff and another to make the legs jerk! Except in vaster quantities!'

'Oh!'

'Ha!' She shrieked with laughter, clapping her hands. 'You believed me! Down to serious business now! We've got to practise our reading!' And she went out to get Madeline.

Madeline smiled hello in her usual gentle way and, while Mrs Greene thumbed through a vast tome, stared sadly from the end of my bed.

'Madeline's nervous about her first A.A. meeting tomorrow!' Mrs Greene said. 'Wait till she's an old hand like me!' She handed her the tome. 'There's Desdemona's speech! Begin there!'

Nervously Madeline cleared her throat. 'I've never acted.'

'You might be like Annie and me with a natural talent!'

'I forgot, I was a shepherd boy once.' I sat up on my pillow. 'Maybe she could be Titania – "these are the forgeries of jealousy." Or Cleopatra, whom age cannot wither or custom

150

stale.'

'You certainly know your Shakespeare,' Madeline said, studying me.

'Annie's an intellectual,' Mrs Greene sighed. 'She's translating Dante.'

'Shakespeare's OK,' I said begrudgingly. 'We read a lot of him in school.'

'The Captain's very fond of Shakespeare!' Mrs Greene adjusted her glasses.

'Stick to your Shakespeare and your Dante, Annie,' Madeline said slowly. 'Never get married!' And then she burst out crying.

'Now! Now! Stop this!' Mrs Greene rushed to comfort her.

'Annie reminds me so much of Caroline!' Madeline said between sobs. 'My children –.'

'But, you'll be back with them soon!' Mrs Greene's arm was around her.

'But I can't live there. I can't live there ever again!' And she burst into worse crying.

'You won't have to,' Mrs Greene consoled. 'Something will turn up. We're one happy family here, aren't we, Annie?'

I nodded, wanting to put my arms round Madeline too. But I just watched, frozen. She cried inconsolably, in a way I'd never seen an adult do. Even Mrs Greene could not prevail against her tears, so we abandoned our reading for that evening.

In the bathroom that night I asked Mrs Greene if Madeline was OK.

She nodded, flicking her wispy pink hair in the mirror. 'It's a very sad case, pet.'

'Why can't she live with her children?'

'Oh . . . Annie, you're too young to know how . . . marriage doesn't always work out.'

'I'm not! My mother tells me everything!'

Mrs Greene sighed, and went on, carefully choosing her words. 'Oh, it's no secret here. Madeline married a brute. Oh! a respectable brute! A Fitzwilliam Square doctor. Who wore her out!'

'How?'

'Having nine children! Just look at her! The youngest is three months!' She shook her head grimly. 'I don't know what the end of it will be. The husband committed her here, and won't let the children visit.'

'But they're her children too!'

'The father's the guardian in Irish law! He's got big guns behind him, pet! The Catholic Church! The medical profession! As an inmate here, Madeline has no rights to anything! I can tell you, the Captain'd have a bone to pick with that man!' She shook her head.

'Could they not get separated?'

'In Ireland?' Mrs Greene sighed heavily. 'You're young, pet!'

'But you can get separated! A Mensa et a thoro! My mother was going to.'

'And her children?' Mrs Greene stared at me over her glasses. 'But run along, time you were in bed. And it's not your worry!'

But Mrs Greene was wrong about that. In my new family of friends at St. Patrick's, each member was concerned about the other. The Volga fussed over me and Tina, worrying about my thinness and her boyfriend not visiting. And every evening Mrs Greene brought Madeline into my room for our readings. We made good progress. Madeline read the speech where Desdemona begs Othello to kill her tomorrow. And I read Ophelia's ramblings about rue and rosemary. Although I was getting fed up with her. Richard III was more my bag, but Mrs Greene said a priest was doing him.

In the middle of one rehearsal my mother burst in, carrying parcels. 'Oh! I've interrupted something!'

'Not at all!' Mrs Greene hopped up. 'We were going!'

Madeline looked hesitantly from my mother to me. 'Ah – we'll see you later, Annie.'

152

I should've introduced them, but just lay there till they'd gone.

My mother leant to kiss me. 'Darling, I've brought you a radio!' She opened one of the parcels, placing a shiny new radio on my bedside table. 'And your favourite black grapes . . . Some scones from Marcella . . . And a letter from Doone!'

I looked from the radio to my mother. It was a week since I'd seen her, but I felt none of my old joy, just a terrible tiredness.

'You're looking better, darling!'

'Am I?'

There was an awkward silence.

'I'll get a plate for the grapes!' As she went out, I read Doone's letter.

Dear Sis,

I miss you. Do not be sad abowt Pete. Pleese! He's in Heevan now. Mummy's quiet tired. Marcella and me is making her go to bed. (fairly often!!!) I miss you so very much even if I do not write much. I just freeze with pen in hand . . .

'What happened about Killiney convent?' I asked as my mother came back with a plate.

'The nuns wouldn't take her! I'm trying the Protestant schools!'

'What happened about the Kibbutz?'

'They've postponed it! Mr Freeman's in Mountjoy! After all the employment he gave!' She snatched at a grape.

'Oh, dear! But what –.'

'Stop worrying, darling! That's why you're here!' She wriggled out of her leopard skin coat. 'How do you like the radio?' She flicked it on and music blared.

'Well . . .' It was probably purchased on H.P. so I had visions of men taking it back.

'It'll be great company!'

'But I don't want company!'

153

My mother snatched at more grapes. 'Well! Sharper than a serpent's tooth!'

I put my fingers in my ears. 'Please turn it off!'

My mother flicked it off. 'Annie! Dr Nirmal tells me you're disturbed. But I know you! I know something happened at Nicola's ball to make you ashamed of me!'

'Oh, don't be silly.'

'Then why didn't you introduce me to your new friends?'

'We were just practising Shakespeare!'

My mother sighed. 'Annie, you can't blame me for Cousin William!'

'I don't.' I picked up a book.

'Annie,' she pleaded. 'If you'll come home, you'll have your own room!'

'I can't.'

'You'd prefer a dump like this?' Her voice broke. 'But you're my clever girl! You can't stay here! Darling, if you come home, I'll pay for a grind. You'll fly through the Trinity Matric! I'll find the money somewhere!'

I put my fingers in my ears again. 'Mummy, please!'

'It's all Aunt Allie's fault! Forcing you to type!'

'It isn't! You always blame her!'

'Tell me what happened at Nicola's ball.'

I went back to my book. She didn't own me, any more than Cousin William had owned Pete.

'Annie, darling, remember when you were little? You'd always come home with a handful of buttercups for me?'

I couldn't look up.

'For me, Annie. For me.'

She was crying, but I still couldn't look up.

After a moment, she grabbed her coat and bag and left.

I lay back, crying too. I didn't know why I behaved like that. Maybe Mrs Greene was right about me being young, too young to understand anything. But I felt so old. I had always loved my mother more than anyone in the world. But love, the poets say,

154

is but the opposite side of the coin to hate. Now I felt only a vast indifference. I was on a lonely and distant mountain and couldn't find my way back down. There were too many vapours surrounding me. It's true I blamed my mother for everything: Cousin William, Pete, Chris's cheque, the *début*. I even blamed her for me taking her side against my father. One incident in particular haunted me. I had heard my parents quarrelling about something, I forget what. My father said that we were all against him, then, seeing me, 'Except you, Annie.' 'I couldn't love a drunkard,' I snapped back. 'And I'll certainly never marry one!' Oh, God! How could I have said that? When he'd sung so often to me:

> *And for bonnie Annie Laurie*
> *I'd lay me doun and dee.*

He was dead six months later. Of a brain tumour. Which was why he couldn't think straight. It wasn't drink at all. Why hadn't my mother known and told me he was sick? To prevent myself thinking, I read Doone's note again. She missed my father more than I did. And now, how was she managing without me? Was she getting her comics? Come Thursday and no money for her weekly ration of 'The Silent Three' or 'The Chalet School' etc. and she'd be miserable. Ironic, considering she didn't like school. But I banished such thoughts.

My mother rang me from work that night, accepting the *status quo*. She didn't visit me again, but established a *détente* by posting me money. Sister would wave the weekly letter, which I'd always hope was from Chris. But it was always from my mother.

To pass the time, I imagined Chris answered me, and I actually wrote out a draft of what he might say.

Mon Coeur,
I looked for you everywhere. I had planned to take you for a midnight spin to see the lights of the city and plight

155

our troth. *Un autre temps, n'est-ce-pas?*

How, *ma chère fille,* could I disdain your feeling? *Au contraire,* I *aussi* have been smitten since our fateful meeting in the Shelbourne. For this reason I hope you will one day do me the honour of becoming *engagé.*

Your loving,

Christophe.

Then I addressed an envelope to myself, stuck on an old stamp, wrinkled it up, and propped it on my dressing table for Mrs Greene or Madeline to see.

And Mrs Greene did, the very next evening. She had come to my room for our reading, rather late and without Madeline.

'I'm afraid we'll have to cancel tonight, Annie.' She plonked on the end of my bed.

'What is it?' I sat up.

'Madeline's had a relapse. And I haven't the heart.'

'Is she back in bed?'

'Yes. Upstairs in Ward 6,' Mrs Greene frowned, changing the subject. 'I see you've had a letter!'

I sighed, feigning boredom, stretching for it. 'Yes. From my boyfriend. He might be visiting me. Read it, if you like!'

She hesitated, then scanned it quickly. 'Goodness, he does seem keen, pet.'

'He is. We're getting engaged.'

'What does Mama say?'

I lay back despairingly. 'She's dead against it. Everyone is!'

'Well, you're young. How old is the young man?'

'Thirty-fiveish.'

'A little old for you, pet.'

I felt stabbed by her words.

'Of course, an age difference sometimes works very well. It's just that – well – you're too young to settle down. Mama's right.' She looked sharply at the letter again, then sharply at me.

I grabbed it back. 'Can I visit Madeline, sometime?'

Mrs Greene just peered at me through her pink glasses, perusing my very soul. 'There's only one thing wrong with imagining things, Annie,' she said at last. 'They're just not real.'

I nearly died of mortification. Did she really suspect that I had written the letter. And if so, how?

'I'll ask if you can visit Madeline, pet!' She broke the silence and went out.

Mrs Greene obtained permission for me to visit Madeline with her the next afternoon. Ward 6 was on the women's side, directly above Ward 5. We went through a locked doorway and up a flight of narrow stairs, opening onto a similar wide corridor with the same little doors opening off one side. But where Ward 5 had couches along the window side, this was crammed with beds. Some were occupied and some were made, with dressing-gowned women sitting on chairs beside them. The patients were of all ages, but, unlike those downstairs, they were listless, and one old woman had no teeth.

'This is a chronic ward, Annie.' Mrs Greene noticed my dismay.

Just then a fattish dressing-gowned girl asked me if I had a cigarette.

I said I'd get her some but Mrs Greene pulled me on, saying sharply, 'She doesn't smoke, Judith!'

I watched her slink away, thinking that like in Dante, St. Patrick's had different circles of despair. The souls here were more lost than those downstairs. And the hospital wasn't quite the Nirvana I had thought. But I didn't want to dwell on such things.

Madeline lay in bed in a bleak little room. Her hair was loose and dishevelled, her face white, her sad eyes circled and drugged.

'Provisions! Provisions!' Mrs Greene put a bottle of shampoo and a 7UP on her bedside table. 'And I've brought Annie to cheer you up!'

'Hello, Annie.' Madeline smiled wanly, pulling herself up in bed.

I couldn't get over the deterioration in her.

'Did you ring Caroline?' She gripped Mrs Greene's wrist, anxiously searching her face.

'Yes! The Reverend Mother let me speak to her. I told her you're much better.'

Madeline flopped back on her pillows. 'I'm not allowed to visit my own daughter, Annie!'

'Now, now . . .' Mrs Greene busied herself with opening the 7UP and pouring it. 'This too will pass.'

Madeline laughed hysterically. 'I'm dragged back here like a convict for trying.'

'Hush, now! Drink this!' Mrs Greene soothed.

'Why can't she visit you?' I asked awkwardly. It seemed a simple enough request for Madeline to want to see her child.

'My husband doesn't want her corrupted.'

I just stood there, feeling a spasm of guilt about my own mother. Mrs Greene fussed around the room, straightening the quilt and tidying the bedside table. 'We promised not to stay long, pet! I'll come back tomorrow and see if you need anything.'

And so we left her.

'It seems very unfair,' I said, going back down the stairs.

'I don't know where it'll all end,' Mrs Greene muttered. 'She's had a break . . . and tried to leave. She was picked up in Wicklow near her daughter's school. The husband's inhuman, inhuman . . .'

I didn't see Madeline again for some time. As she was laid up, our readings were cancelled. So to pass the time, I often stood on my bed, reciting poetry to myself. Because of the Brontës, I loved anything about moors. In school, when unable to sleep, I'd be hauntingly sad Lucy Gray, singing and wandering over them. Or else I'd be the only daughter of proud Lord Ullin – it was silly but I wanted a title. One day a highland chief would tramp across the heather and fall instantly in love with me. He used to look like Alan Breck, but now he was Chris. Of course my father, Lord

158

Ullin, forbade our union. So we eloped, meeting our damp fate . . . to my father's woe.

> *'Come back, come back!' he cried in grief.*
> *Across this stormy water.*
> *'And I'll forgive your highland chief*
> *My daughter! Oh, my daughter!'*

Reading that line always made me cry for my father. Unluckily, Tina burst into my room and saw me.

'What's wrong?' she quizzed, staring up at me. 'Nirmal's not bullying you too?'

Hastily I jumped down, wiping my eyes. 'No! It's just this poem . . . "Lord Ullin's Daughter".'

She grabbed my book, giggling. 'Christ! That's not poetry!'

'What is it then?'

'Only an old ballad!'

'A ballad is poetry!'

She snapped the book shut. 'Not in the modernist sense.'

'I've read modern – eh – modernist poetry. I've read . . . "The Scholar Gypsy".'

She grimaced. 'Matthew Arnold's a bore! No one ever reads him now! Except for "Dover Beach". Do you know that?'

I shook my head, wanting to murder my mother for thinking me clever and the Hound for always reading out my essays.

'Ah, love,' Tina began to recite in her rich Northern English accent,

> *Let us be true*
> *To one another. For the world which seems*
> *To lie before us like a land of dreams*
> *So various, so beautiful, so new*
> *Hath really neither joy, nor love, nor light*
> *Nor certitude, nor peace, nor help for pain . . .*

She paused, catching her breath. *'And we are here as on a darkling plain . . . Swept with confused alarms of struggle and flight . . .'*

159

'Go on! Please go on!' I said, not noticing that Tina was crying. 'But, what is it?'

Messily she wiped her eyes. 'Jim's a swine, a Trotskyite swine! They're all the same!'

'Trotskyites?'

'Swine! He drives me to slit me wrists, and then goes off with another bird!'

'Are you engaged?'

She shrugged. 'I suppose. We were livin' together.'

'In the same house?'

'The same bed! Except he wanted it all the time!'

'The bed?'

'No, sex!'

'Oh . . .' I felt myself redden at the thought of anything like that with Chris.

''e wanted to get married, but I couldn't decide.'

'Well, maybe you don't like him.'

Tina blew furiously into a hanky. 'I do! I luv 'im! Dr Nirmal says it's just depression. He's givin' me me last shock treatment tomorrow.' She put on a shocking pink lipstick at my mirror.

I quaked inwardly at the memory of seeing her unconscious. She sighed. 'Then I'll be goin' home. Christ! To recuperate! Trinity won't pay for me anymore!'

'Don't you get on with your parents?'

'Haven't lived there since school. Nirmal doesn't want me to go back. But there's nowhere else. Oh, me mum's OK. It's me dad. He's a vicar and pissy-mean. Never lets us have heat in winter, and there's never enough for the kids to eat.'

'We're often short too,' I admitted.

'Oh, he's got the money! He's just a maniac. A piss artist. He nearly died when I got me grant to Trinity.'

I always imagined vicars to be kind befuddled people who took tea at four, before the war. But he sounded even worse than Cousin William. Although he had often no money, my father never complained about our house being a blaze of light in

160

summer, or a furnace in winter. And when his ship came in, he was sending me to a Swiss Finishing School and buying Doone a pony. His only fault, in my book, was being too religious and dragging us to novenas, etc.

I was just going to tell Tina about my father when Mrs Greene burst in, looking very agitated. 'We'll have to do something! Evelyn's got herself arrested!'

I was dumbfounded.

'What? Where is she?' Tina snapped.

'In Donnybrook Garda Station! The American Embassy have charged her with assault!'

'But why?' I sat weakly on my bed. 'She told me she was emigrating to America.'

'It's a wonder she didn't tell you she was emigrating to the moon! She has this obsession with America . . .' Mrs Greene sighed. 'Well, yesterday she was meant to visit her married sister. But instead she stood outside the American Embassy, looking in. She wanted a visa or something. So they sent out a Marine to tell her to move on, and she hit him!'

'Capitalist Fascist swine!'

'She couldn't have hurt him,' I suggested. 'She's so tiny.'

Mrs Greene made for the door. 'I know, but she's appearing in court tomorrow. I'll have to be there.'

Dr Nirmal appeared in the doorway, putting Evelyn's troubles out of my head. 'L-ladies, I n-need a little word with Annie.'

As Mrs Greene and Tina went out, I sat up in bed, smiling. On Dr Nirmal's night on duty, he was wont to come in for a chat.

'I've good news, Annie. You c-can g-get up tomorrow.'

'But . . . Do I *have* to?'

He sat down, crossing his legs. 'Y-you're much better.'

'Better?' I stared at him in disbelief. 'I . . . didn't tell you I wake up bumping my head against the wall. Is that better? And . . . And those trees in the garden . . . sometimes I see them getting bigger and bigger!'

'Hmm! . . .' He stood up, looking out the window. Then the

puzzled look in his blue eyes changed to one of amusement.

'I never told you I was a war baby!'

He started chuckling. 'N-now stop this nonsense. If y-you b-b-become a complete r-recluse, you'll never be able for the stresses and s-s-st – troubles of daily life.'

They were harpies waiting for me at the hospital gates. 'Please don't make me get up!'

'B-but there are all s-sorts of things to d-do. Oc-c-cupational therapy. Or art-t-t therapy!'

'But I have my therapy here!' I held up my book.

'You can r-r-read in the evenings. C-come n-now! . . . Cheer up!'

I was crying.

He sighed heavily. For awhile he just sat there, then said gently, 'You know, Annie, I t-t-tried your suggestion. I r-read R-Robinson Crusoe to my t-twin sons. But after a chapter I l-l-looked up, and they were gone.'

I blew my nose. 'What age are they?'

'Three!' He stood up, looking dolefully out the window. 'And g-g-gone!'

'Try something easier! . . . My mother started us on Fairy Tales!'

'And your m-mother's done a w-wonderful job on you!' He looked down at me kindly. 'But y-you k-know, Annie, p-parents are for little children . . . Oh, in comparison, I'm quite a f-failure as a f-father! My older ch-children read c-comics!'

'You aren't a failure. My little sister reads School Friend.'

'Hmm . . . Does she?' He brightened. 'She's living at home?'

'The wind bloweth where it listeth,' I said, not wanting to talk about home.

'The wind b-b-bloweth where it listeth? Hmm! You're so wise, Annie. Why d-d-didn't I think of that m-myself?' And he went out smiling.

I stared glumly at the ceiling. Unless I thought of something *aussitôt que possible*, home was next.

The next morning I was given my clothes. And after breakfast, I tidied my little room where joy forever dwelt and went down to the art room with the Volga. It was in the garden in a sort of glass extension. Tables and chairs and easels were arranged in a circle like school.

As the Volga sat fussily down, the Art therapist, a small blond tweedy woman bustled up. 'You must be Annie. Dr Nirmal told me you might be down.' Her accent was like the Queen of England.

Then she showed me to a place beside the only other patient in the room. He was a beaky old man in a wheel chair, wearing a raincoat and a Churchillian straw hat.

'What'll I do?' I asked, as the therapist gave me paper and a pencil.

'Try Mr de Burgh Whyte's geranium!'

The old man painted delicately, beautifully, in complete silence. But I shook my head, thinking it too normal for me. 'Could I do something abstract?'

'What a good idea!' The therapist pointed to the cupboard. 'You'll find poster colours and brushes there.'

I got paints and water, deciding to do a face. Firstly I blobbed on white paint for the face. Then reds and blues in insane wavy lines like Munch for the hair. Then I did the mouth as a frantic red slit, and the eyes as lit coals. The effect was spooky.

'What do you think?' I turned it towards the old man.

He looked glassily through me.

Thinking he must be deaf, I shouted, 'I'm Anne O'Brien. Originally from the North side of Dublin. We had a farm . . .'

He returned to his painting.

I attacked my painting again, and after a few minutes tried to talk to him again. 'Je suis Anne O'Brien, de Dublin. Aimez-vous ça?' He looked a bit foreign.

This made him look tiredly up. But he still didn't say anything, just tore a page from his notebook and scribbled out a message which he passed to me: 'I'm neither deaf nor French. My name is

163

Grundig Radio. I do not speak any human language.'

Radio sounded Italian, if said in a certain way, Ra-*di*-o, But Grundig?

I wrote a reply on the other side: 'I'm very glad to meet you. I won't disturb you again. But *why*?'

He read it, glared at me and wrote: 'I cannot but conclude the bulk of your natives to be the most pernicious race of little odious vermin.'

He looked so grumpy, I wrote nothing more. Anyway, the therapist appeared behind me saying, 'That's very – interesting. Hmm . . . I should think Dr Nirmal will be interested in seeing that.'

'It's my inner state!' I said. 'A self portrait.'

Then the Volga gathered round.

'Umm, it shows sensitivity, dear,' Victoria said.

'And promise, don't you think, Victoria dear?' Olga added.

At elevenses the three of us went over to the hospital café, where they insisted on paying for my coffee.

'Isn't Grundig a queer name?' I asked when we were cosily seated at a table.

'His real name's Gearoid de Burgh Whyte,' Victoria explained.

'But he changed it by deed poll to that of a machine,' Olga continued.

'He has eschewed humanity, dear.'

Olga shook her head sadly. 'Tut, tut.'

'And such a good family too,' Victoria went on. 'He's the Earl of Mayo's cousin. And in Debrett's.'

'Is that anything like Stubb's,' I asked. 'We're in that. For debt!'

The two of them paled, saying, 'Hush, dear!'

'Only the best people are in Debretts,' Victoria explained.

Olga squeezed my arm. 'Some of the best people are in Stubb's too!'

'Oh, hush!' Victoria said irately. 'The de Burghs came from France originally. And changed to the Protestant Faith in the

Eighteenth Century.'

'Late,' Olga sighed. 'Very late.'

'What were they before?' I asked.

'Papists!' they both snapped.

I gulped my coffee.

'Poor Grundig won't have anything to do with the family,' Victoria whispered. 'He had a breakdown as a student and was sent here.'

'He was a student of Mahaffy's.'

'After he was discharged originally,' Victoria went on slowly, 'he wanted to come back. But the family wouldn't agree, so he jumped out the castle window.'

'And broke his spine,' Olga said. 'In two places. One! Two!'

Victoria sighed. 'He's partially paralyzed now.'

'He'll never be able to walk again.' Olga stared sadly into space.

I quaked inwardly. Slitting your wrist was one thing, but throwing yourself out a castle window?

'Victoria dear, do you think Annie looks cold?'

Then Olga rooted in her case, while Victoria felt my hands. 'You are cold, dear!'

'Go and put that on!' Olga whispered, taking a woollen vest from the suit case.

So I did.

That evening I was helping Mrs Greene with the dishes when she told me Evelyn was in Mountjoy in solitary confinement. 'The poor child badly needs a radio. I'm collecting among the patients.'

'She can have mine!' I said.

Mrs Greene was hesitant. 'But what would Mama say?'

'She won't mind! If she knew, she'd buy her one!'

'Well . . . the child needs one badly.' She wiped her hands. 'She's a schizophrenic . . . and should be in hospital, not prison!'

'A schizophrenic?'

'She lives in a fantasy world. For instance, she thinks she can go to America! Oh! I'm amazed they didn't notice it here! The Americans charged her with soliciting!'

'What's that?'

'You've heard of prostitution? And disturbing the peace! And assault! She got six months!' She hesitated, looking past me to the corridor. 'Is this a visitor for you, Annie?'

'I don't –.' But I turned to see Doone in the scullery doorway. 'Yes! It's my sister!'

She seemed to come from another life. She was leggier than ever, her navy school coat was above her knees and too short in the sleeves. 'Mummy said I could come!'

'Of course!' I led her into my room. 'Is everything OK?'

She looked at me through hay-like hair. 'Are you OK? Mummy says I can't worry you.'

'Tell me if anything's wrong!'

She thrust a crumpled newspaper cutting at me. 'The police were all over the house.'

'The police? When?' I scanned the cutting: ANTIQUE DEALER CHARGED WITH FRAUD. 'Mr Gerald Freeman, 30 Westminster Road, Foxrock, today appeared before Justice Barry on charges of fraud. Detective Murphy of the fraud squad testified that for the last five years Mr Freeman has passed off imitation brass beds as antiques. He also sold imitation corner cabinets as antiques. Detective Murphy claimed the Irish public have been defrauded of thousands of pounds. The case was adjourned and bail was set at £1,000.'

'God,' I whispered. 'Poor Mr Freeman!'

Doone's lip was quivering.

I put my arm round her shoulders. 'Now listen, Mr Freeman's a genius! He'll get out of it!'

Grimily she wiped her eyes. 'The police searched the house . . . Susie was crying –.' This made her start.

'Listen . . . maybe they *are* antiques!'

'You think so?'

'They looked it!'

'But Susie's school friends will jeer.'

'She has you! And remember, "Sticks and stones . . ."'

She was momentarily soothed by my mother's motto, then burst into more crying. 'Come home, Sis!'

'Oh God! I can't! I – eh – I'm disturbed. Please don't cry!'

She wiped her eyes. 'I – I got that horrible thing!'

'What horrible thing?'

'That . . . p-p-period thing!' She could hardly say the word.

'But that's nothing. It means you're a woman.'

Her thin shoulders began to shake again.

I poured her a glass of Lucozade. 'Listen, nothing will change! In three days you'll be exactly the same as before.'

'You're sure?'

'Yes!' I didn't realize then nothing can ever be the same, once the moving finger writes. 'You're wearing a pad?'

Grimly she shook her head.

'But you must! For a few days.'

'I won't!'

'Not even for me?'

'Well . . .' She looked at me suspiciously.

I got her a pad and belt from my drawer. 'You've told Mummy?'

She shook her head. 'She was asleep. When're you coming home?'

I changed the subject, telling her all about my new life. Funnily we didn't speak of Pete or Cousin William. I told her to tell my mother about her period and she promised to. It brought home their lack of rapport. Even though my mother had prepared me, I had got a shock with mine. But my mother had been at my side. Oh, I was the favourite one, like the Prodigal Son in the Gospel. Doone got on better with my father, but he was gone. And once she'd told me she could hardly remember our fat years, living in the country. Only our lean years of vagrancy from flat to flat. And now she'd never even get a pony. Oh, my father had bought her a donkey once, but we'd nowhere to keep it. And now she had

167

lost Pete. And the Kibbutz would probably fall through. I knew all that. I knew she was lonely, and about my duties as an elder sister. I knew it all, but I still couldn't go home.

Being up wasn't bad. The hospital was a haven of learning. A Utopia of artisticness. As well as art therapy and the café, there was occupational therapy where you could make baskets. Gym therapy where you did exercises. And even industrial therapy where you could earn money by making plugs or something. On most mornings there was a lecture on different stimulating topics: alcoholism caused by depression, depression caused by alcoholism, elation, drug addiction, cross addiction, suicide, attempted suicide, etc., etc. All the doctors took turns. And sometimes the Hospital Secretary. And sometimes Matron.

My tenth day up was Dr Nirmal's turn.

As usual I sat between the Volga in the front row of the lecture hall, sharing their knee rug. The other patients were scattered on the tiered rows behind us. Fragments of their conversation floated down, hushing as Dr Nirmal squeaked across the wax floor to the podium.

'G-g-good morning!' He smiled nervously, tremblingly lighting a cigarette which he puffed and put out. 'T-t-today we'll continue our discussion of what is n-n-n-n-n--.'

'Normal!' a man's voice shouted from the back.

I breathed a sigh of relief.

'Thank y-you!' He lit another cigarette, puffing and putting it out.' L-last time we d-discovered that f-f-fantasy is a n-n-n - ordinary trick of the mind. The d-d-dictionary definitions of f-f-fantasy were a t-t-train of thought indulged in to g-gratify one's d-desires, whim, an illusion, a h-h-h-h-h -.'

'Hallucination!' the man shouted again.

'Thank y-you!' Dr Nirmal took a deep breath. 'We discussed fantasy as a l-l-literary f-f-form too. And we s-saw that it r-ranged from the f-f-fantasy stories of G-Grimm, to L-Lewis C-Carroll, to the s-s-s-s-science fiction of J-Jules Verne and H.G. W-W-W-W -'

168

'Wells!'

'Exactly!'

As Dr Nirmal lit another cigarette, I noticed Victoria and Olga had fallen asleep, each with a head on my shoulders.

'We looked at the Secret L-L-Life of W-Walter M-M-M-M –'

'Maugham!'

'Mitty! But thanks! We s-s-saw a hero inventing interior worlds to c-compensate for the drabness of life. But another w-w-way of l-l-living in f-f-fantasy is evasion . . .'

Olga and Victoria were snoring loudly in harmony.

' . . . In his famous t-t-tragic-comedy, *The Cherry Orchard*, Ch-Ch-Chekov shows a whole family refusing to f-f-face up to bankruptcy. A n-n-newly rich business m-man s-suggests a w-way of s-saving them by s-selling their b-b-beautiful orchard for b-b-building land –.'

'Café au lait!' Olga shouted, violently awakening.

'A half-naked fakir!' Victoria jerked awake too, then seeing where she was: 'Shh!'

Dr Nirmal coughed and went on. 'B-but the family refuse to l-l-listen.' He read from the play, 'If there is one thing interesting, one thing outstanding in the whole country, it's our cherry orchard.'

As Dr Nirmal walked to the end of the podium, I thought of our apple orchard in the country.

'The only outstanding thing about this orchard is that it's very large. It only provides a crop every other year, and there's nobody to buy it!'

'Café au lait!' Olga jerked awake again.

'Shh!' Victoria nudged her.

Dr Nirmal continued walking up and down the podium reading lines from the play. But I was lost in my own thoughts of the past. Of selling our farm. And the animals Doone and I had as pets. It was just the same with us. We had refused to face up to bankruptcy. Our whole family was depressingly normal.

'The p-p-play closes to the sound of an axe. Old R-Russia dies. The Cherry Orchard is a s-s-symbol of the p-p-past . . .'

169

When I explained to Doone that our cherry-tree Aunt Allie was minding was a symbol of our past, she just said it wasn't because you couldn't play it.

'Each of us h-h-has a Ch-Cherry Orchard. S-s-someplace in the p-p-past where happiness has b-b-been.'

Mine was dancing with Chris.

' . . . Ch-Chekov laments the p-p-passage of time. B-but shows us w-w-we must all axe our orchards . . .'

As he stammered on, I sat entranced. It didn't matter about the university any more. Here in the broader school of life, I could continue my education. I'd heard of the Russian writer Tolstoy OK, but never of Chekov.

There was so much I didn't know.

I have read that the uneducated view of life is entirely personal and unaware of the intangible. And that great minds discuss ideas, average minds discuss events, and small minds discuss people. The types of minds that discuss dogs, I suppose, come lower on the scale . . . I must read Chekov, I thought. I must. Dr Nirmal would surely lend me the play.

After the lecture the Volga gathered their things, and we moved out of the hall towards art therapy. As we passed through the garden, a nun paced up and down, praying. I thought she must be a visitor. But the habit was Sacred Heart, and there was something familiar about the petite erect figure.

It couldn't be the Hound? Although Dante had met his teacher in Hell.

Then the figure spun round, pacing towards us. 'Anne!'

'Mother!' I ran up to her, amazed.

'What are you doing here?'

'I'm committed! For being disturbed!'

'Nonsense, child!' She snapped her prayerbook shut and, nodding warily at the Volga, pulled me aside.

They went on to art therapy.

As we went up to Ward Five to find a couch, I pondered on the coincidence. When Dante met his teacher Brunetto Latini in the

170

Inferno, they couldn't stop or they'd be stuck in the same place for a hundred years. 'Why are you here?' Dante asked him. 'When in the world you taught me what makes man eternal?'

When we sat down, the Hound's brown eyes bored into me, just like of old. 'Now tell me what happened, Anne!'

'Daddy died in the summer. And – I was doing typing. I – got fed up.'

She squeezed my hand. 'Death is God's will, Anne. How's your mother?'

'OK,' I shrugged guiltily. They had never clicked, but the Hound showed no animosity now.

'I didn't think you'd like commercial college! I begged Mrs Grubb-Healy to leave you in school for another year.' She sighed. 'You were my best pupil, Anne. The only one who wasn't a Machievellian.'

'You taught me what makes man – you taught me everything.'

She took my hand. 'Thank you, dear. Don't tell anyone, but I'm leaving the order. I'm giving up teaching and joining the Poor Clares.'

'But you won't see anyone!'

'I don't want to. I'll have God.' She stared dreamily ahead. 'The world is too much with us, Anne.'

I shivered. God's so cold and eerie. I mean, I had begged Him to make Daddy better.

'You're still a dreamer, Anne.' She squeezed my hand. 'Don't look so sad, dear! How long have you been here?'

'Since the beginning of November.' I'd lost all track of time.

'Hmm. It's probably a spot of depression. I'm just here to see Dr Moore. I'm out in St. Edmundsbury's convalescing. You must come out and visit. Now tell me about Doone!'

'She's going to a Kibbutz!'

The Hound stared in silent horror. 'With whom is she going?'

'Eh – our neighbours, the Freemans.'

'Not those – those –.'

'Jews?' I knew she was afraid to say the word.

171

She stared, as if she'd just caught me talking in study. 'I remember them visiting Doone. But to allow a child of Doone's age to go on holidays with pagans!'

'They're not pagans!'

'And not Christians either. I begged Reverend Mother to keep her in school!'

I felt myself redden at the mention of money. 'They'll be visiting Jerusalem.'

'But in what company! Take care whom you associate with here, Anne! Those women are Protestants!' She took out her watch. 'Now should you be someplace?'

'Art therapy.'

'I'll walk down with you.'

It was weird. The Hound hated Protestants and believed everyone from Cork an imperialist. And the British were a red rag to her, because of Cromwell and the Lane Collection of paintings. I had asked her, wasn't it sorted out now that they hung in our gallery half the time? But she said centuries of wrong could never be righted. Of course, she was a Gaelgóir like Aunt Allie and spoke Irish fluently. In that I had disappointed her too. When I got my exam results, she had written saying, she'd hoped for more spectacular marks. And that it was a sad chapter in the history of my life. I suppose it was. But Irish had never clicked in my mind. Probably because of my mother always saying, 'No child of an American citizen is learning that gibberish!' Also Parnell didn't know it. Still I liked Irish History, even though it was sad, and worked into every essay:

> *Unequal they came to the battle*
> *Fine linen shirts on the race of Con*
> *The foreigners one mass of iron.*

At the artroom the Hound gave me a medal. 'I want you to wear this, Anne. Our Lady will look after you.'

'Eh – thanks!' I put it round my neck.

Then she came in to see what I was doing, kissing me goodbye.

172

That kiss proved she loved me as I loved her. And by meeting here we were now equals. I had never even thought how tiring teaching must be. And all morning pondered on the pity of her decision to quit. Her mind was an absolute beacon in darkness. Nothing was ever too much trouble for her to explain. Except when I asked why Brunetto Latini was in Hell for sodomy, she'd snapped, 'Remember your body's a Temple of the Holy Ghost!'

And now she was quitting this world for the next. They say Heaven's like eating strawberries and cream forever. But I couldn't imagine that. At my father's funeral, Fr Mullane had said the angels were leading him to Abraham's side. But what would they say to each other? And how would I ever find him again among so many millions? Although my heart had grown cold towards God, an idea took root: if I was sent home, I'd join the Poor Clares.

The days passed, melting into each other as they tilted into winter. Christmas loomed in the distance. Most of the patients were going home, either for the week or the day. In my weekly chats with Dr Nirmal there was no discussion about me going home. And I avoided it, knowing if I left my Eden I'd never get back. I still didn't sleep, which I thought was perfectly normal, but which worried Dr Nirmal. The result was a stronger sleeping potion. Once a Trinity Psychologist tested my I.Q., giving me all sorts of inkblots to describe and a word association test. I acted as crazy as possible, saying, 'Bread pudding' for 'Depression' and 'Murder' for 'Brother'. Although the tester looked at me oddly, I felt sure he'd end up finding me normal.

So I avoided Dr Nirmal, hiding in the loo on his night.

But he sent a nurse to find me.

'You d-d-did well in y-y-your test, Annie.' He studied my chart. I waited for the blow.

'Especially v-v-verbally. You h-haven't started w-w-writing your s-s-story yet?'

I shook my head. The Hound said a novel needs a beginning, middle and end, but I wouldn't know where to start. Also your style had to be like clear water and convey meaning exactly. But I preferred Goldsmith who touched nothing he did not adorn.

'H-h-have you thought about Christmas?' Dr Nirmal looked right at me.

'Can I go home?' I thought that was better strategy.

'W-well, y-y-you are much better.' He sighed. 'L-let me think about it!'

I had to do something *très vite*.

The next day an RTE TV crew were making a documentary on the hospital. They came into art therapy, one wielding a mike, the other lugging a camera and lights, etc. When they'd set everything up, the man with the mike made for Grundig, 'Excuse me, Sir!'

As usual, Grundig didn't even look up.

'Eh – excuse me, Sir!'

The Volga stirred nervously beside me. Victoria embroidered while Olga painted.

'Sir! Could I have a few words!'

'He doesn't like to be disturbed!' Victoria snapped.

Olga nodded. 'He has eschewed humanity.'

'Would you like to chat with us?' The man made for her.

Olga looked frantically to her sister.

'My sister cannot be troubled!' Victoria blurted. 'Can I help you?'

The TV man beamed. 'Indeed yes! You can tell us how you came to be here!'

Victoria folded her hands on the desk. 'Papa thought it best for Olga. And I came to accompany her.'

'Oh! And when was that?' the TV man said into the mike.

Victoria lapsed into thought. 'It must be thirty years.'

'Thirty-one in May, dear,' Olga corrected.

'Oh! Ah! You must've seen some changes in your time!'

'Changes, yes. 'Victoria picked up her embroidery. 'Mostly for the worse!'

'Mostly! But not all!' Olga added.

'Ah! Hmm! Yes!' The TV man then spotted me. 'I see a young

174

lady here who has something to say.' He held the mike to me.
'Would you tell us how old you are?'

'A hundred and fifty,' I said innocently.

He blinked, swallowing nervously. 'Well . . . Ha! Ha! You've
lived to a great age!'

I shook my head. 'Not really. Trees live to be old. I'm a
Mimosa.'

If Grundig could be a machine, I could be a tree.

'A Mim – Yes, well . . . And would you like to tell us what
you're painting here?'

I was copying a Turner landscape. 'Well . . . this is water and
this is a bridge, and that's a wood . . . I'm sailing down the river to
that wood.'

'Ah! I see. How interesting. What made you choose a wood?'

'Trees live in woods!'

'Ha! Ha! So they do! So they do!' He backed nervously off and
the other man filmed me painting.

The film was on TV the next week, making me a celebrity
overnight. Everyone, just everyone congratulated me. No one
seemed to think it funny that I'd become a tree. I suppose they
thought I was just being imaginative.

Every morning I looked for a letter from Chris, but none came.
One day, though, I got a letter from Evelyn:

> Form P.12
> Number: 37   Name: Evelyn Allen
> Mountjoy Female Prison
> N.C. Road,
> Dublin.

> Date: December 14th 1962

Dear Annie,

Just a few lines to let you know i was very glad to get your
radio what you sent me, as i was needing it very badly, and i
can get Luxemburg on it. i'm glad you still like St. Pat's so

much. That makes tow of us, this place is a real dump, and I mean it. Tell everyone I was asking for them, and think of the old gang often. I have a little niece, she is ten days old, I'm hoping to get out for the christing. i hear the marine i hit had to go to hosbital with a bad green injury. He was a big black man and quite nice. i hope this will not keep me out of America. maybe i will write him a nice letter. they are giving me shock treatments here, i don't mind too much but would rather be listening to your lovely radio.

well, that's all i can think of. Tell Mrs Greene and Madeleen and Tina and the rest i am sorry for the trouble i cause. Love,

Evelyn.

My mother sometimes came in for a flying visit on her way to work, but mostly she rang me.

'Listen,' she said one evening. 'Doone's off at last! The Freemans are emigrating to Israel and taking her for a while. I don't even have to buy clothes! Apparently Susie has oodles.'

'What about Mr Freeman?' I shivered at the word emigration.

'He's following as soon as he gets out of Mountjoy.'

'C-can I see them off?'

'You're not well enough, darling!'

I said nothing. If Doone stayed forever, it'd be dreadful.

'Darling, are you still there?'

'Yes! . . . She'll be coming back?'

'Of course! After Christmas. And listen! Cousin William's emigrating to Australia. He got all sorts of brochures from the embassy! Won't it be lovely to be rid of him?'

I pictured vast and sandy deserts. Cousin William might die there like a soldier of the Legion with 'lack of woman's nursing' and 'dearth of woman's tears . . .'

'Darling, you're not upset?'

'Eh – no!'

'What other news have I? Oh, Brown Thomas are trying to get

176

money out of me! Remember the day we tricked them?'

'You mean my bra?' I could never forget the day I met Chris.

My mother was chuckling. 'Idiots! They won't get a penny out of me!'

'Mummy –.'

'Yes, darling?'

'What did the letter *say*, exactly?'

'Can't remember! Tore it up! Now stop worrying! That's why you're there!'

So I put the letter out of my head. I didn't think of Cousin William either. I just imagined us meeting again in old age and me forgiving him. By now I had decided he'd murdered Pete out of spite. He was angry about the land being sold. And I had once said he was getting like Heathcliff. So he must've read the book and discovered Heathcliff had hung Isabella's dog. The coincidence was ironic. And the cruelty. My father always said the just man showed mercy to man and beast alike.

About a week later Madeline was up and in the cafe with a girl in a school uniform. Although youngish for fifteen, I guessed her to be Madeline's daughter and that the father had relented and allowed a visit. The sight of them reminded me of outings with my mother in school. Mount Prospect was so strict we were never allowed out. Not even to sit in the car during parlour. Except on Saturdays for games – if you were on a team. Because of my asthma, I wasn't. But my mother could wangle anything. She told the Hound I had a rare dental disease and had to see a dentist weekly. Of course, the Hound was suspicious but had to agree to this. And, of course, we never went near a dentist. My teeth would've been drilled to nothing from going that often. My mother and I spent the morning in the Metropole Café, having tea and club sandwiches. Talking, talking, talking. And then we went downstairs to the matinée. Once we saw Dirk Bogarde and Capucine in *Song Without End*. He was the temperamental musician with the Divine Gift and she the woman he loved. I cried all through it because I wasn't beautiful or divinely gifted. And all

177

the way home in the bus, because I wouldn't see my mother for a whole week. It's funny how things reverse. Like, then I thought the temperamental part of me consisted in being 10% mental and 90% temper over maths. And now I suppose it's 90% mental and 10% temper. Funny . . . Oh, the happy autumn fields.

Just then Mrs Greene carried a cup of coffee to my table. 'You're looking very miserable. What is it, pet?'

'I was-was thinking of my mother.'

She sat down. 'I haven't seen her for ages.'

There was an awkward silence.

'It's hard on mothers, Annie.' She sipped her coffee. 'One day your swallows fly – and that's hard. Look at poor Madeline!'

'What about our Shakespearian readings?' I blurted, frantically changing the subject. 'We haven't been practising.'

'Oh! There was no support!'

'But what about your career? Keeping in practise?'

'The theatre's dead, pet! Besides, who'd give an old hag like me a part? I'm trying my hand at fiction.' She dug into her handbag, pulling out some tattered papers. 'Here's the first chapter of a novel!'

Silently I read the grubby manuscript. 'It was the temptation, the final creeping temptation which made it difficult. If there had been somewhere to put the temptation, some handy box, she could have withstood the suffering caused by her own transgressions. Alas, she had transgressed so often!'

'What do you think, pet?'

'Well, ah . . . well, ah . . .' I didn't know what to say.

'It's my own true story! With all the names changed, of course, to protect the guilty.' She adjusted her pink glasses. 'The *Irish Times* may be interested in serial rights. Just think of all that lovely money. I could go to Istanbul. Or pay for staying on here.'

'Is it dear here?' I had just assumed my mother would pay for everything with a cheque, like in hotels.

'Dear?' Mrs Greene's eyes widened behind her glasses. 'What do you think Evelyn's doing in Mountjoy! Her sister wouldn't pay for her anywhere. Oh, I can manage a few months at a time. I have a small allowance from the Captain.'

'An allowance? He's not dead or anything?'

Mrs Greene stared sadly into her coffee. 'He left me, pet. No one wants to live with a drunk. I have a bedsit.' She sighed. 'I'll soon have to go back there.'

Panic brushed aside my surprise about the Captain. 'You're not leaving?'

She winked at me. 'Oh, I'll be back, pet. Be lonely out there! You're too young to understand loneliness, pet!'

'I'm nearly eighteen.'

'To be nearly eighteen and have everything in the future!' Mrs Greene stared dreamily into space.

I was going to say it wasn't that great, and to admit everything to Mrs Greene about wanting to stay, when an apparition appeared in the café doorway.

Aunt Allie!

I thought my heart was going to stop.

She just stood there, staring. As usual, she was dressed in the black trappings of woe from her feet to her black cloche hat which pulled her eyes into frightening Chinese-like slits. 'Your mother said I'd find you here! Hmph! Consorting with lunatics!' she shouted at last.

Everyone gaped, just gaped as she charged over to our table. 'Explain yourself, Miss!'

'Eh – I'm disturbed, Aunt Allie!'

As she sat down, Mrs Greene blinked unbelievingly.

Aunt Allie pealed off her black leather gloves. 'Your mother has certainly seen to that! She's turned you into a double crosser!'

I began crying.

'Just a minute!' Mrs Greene butted in.

'Stop that and explain yourself!' Aunt Allie fumed.

'Just a minute!' Mrs Greene tried again. 'I won't allow this!'

'Who is this woman, Anne?' Aunt Allie snapped, not even looking at Mrs Greene.

'A friend, Aunt Allie.'

'Kindly ask her to leave us!' Aunt Allie shouted.

I looked in desperation from Aunt Allie to Mrs Greene.

'I refuse!' Mrs Greene sat bolt upright. 'Absolutely refuse to leave her alone with you!'

'Ask your friend to go, Anne!' Aunt Allie's face was coming out in red blotches of irritation.

'Mrs Greene – I – eh –.'

'I've no intention of leaving, Annie!' Mrs Greene snapped, turning on Aunt Allie. 'I shall have Sister eject you! You – you bully!'

Oh God! I thought, Oh God!

Aunt Allie rose to her feet. 'That will be quite unnecessary! I'm leaving!'

'Good riddance! To bully a sick child!'

I put my head in my hands.

'Lunacy runs in the family all right!' Aunt Allie snapped. 'But I can tell you one thing! There's nothing wrong with her!'

'Qualified people think otherwise!' Mrs Greene quipped.

Aunt Allie pulled on her gloves, saying, 'I only came to say Anne, I'm washing my hands of you! I'm folding my tent and disappearing!'

Oh God, I thought, lifting up my head.

'Don't let us detain you!' Mrs Greene waved theatrically. 'Stand not upon the order of your going! But go at once!'

I should've said wait. Or told Mrs Greene to go. But I just sat there.

'Just one thing, Anne!' Aunt Allie went on. 'People end up here because they can't accept life! They're have-nots who envy the haves!'

As Aunt Allie stormed out of the café, I stayed glued to my chair. I should've run after her, said I was sorry for always letting her down. After all, I understood her in a way Mrs Greene could not. All she ever wanted was for me to be able to earn my living. To have a sense of responsibility for my life. Not to turn out 'soft' like the Healys. She had failed badly with my mother – she thought. And now she had failed with me.

The row upset me dreadfully, but it was nothing to the blow which followed.

I was in bed that night when Mrs Greene burst into my room, her eyes red from crying.

'Wh-what is it?' I thought my mother was dead.

'Madeline's attempted suicide. She's –.'

'But I saw her today in the café!'

Mrs Greene was shaking her head. 'She drank a bottle of Jeyes Fluid. They've brought her to hospital. But –.'

'But I saw her in the café! With a girl!'

'Her daughter.' Mrs Greene spoke in a low urgent voice. 'The father's sending the children to English boarding schools, so Madeline would never see them.'

'But why?'

Mrs Greene shrugged. 'Why? Who knows why?' And she went out, still shaking her head.

I was back in my dark and savage wood. I lay awake all night, praying for Madeline to live. If she died what would her children do? And what would I do without my mother? The idea was too dreadful to even imagine. And yet my mother had suffered that loss at three months old. And only remembered her father as an old man. She hadn't even aunts or uncles, because after his wife's death, her father had taken his three remaining children back to America. The Healy aunts had sacked Marcella and on the ship a mad maid had tried to throw my mother overboard, believing a motherless child was better off drowned. For a while they lived in New York, where my grandfather practised law. Another mad maid had tried to get him to marry her and had given my mother a dress for the wedding. But when he refused, she'd taken the dress back, breaking my mother's heart. After that, they lived without help. Then one Tuesday in October 1929 the Stock Exchange fell. My mother says everyone else fell too, off skyscrapers, but her father just bundled them into a car and drove to Florida. My mother didn't even bring her coat, thinking it'd be too hot. Oh, it sounded so glamourous, going to the beach instead of school. The land of Swanee and honeysuckle grass. But it must've been lonely. My mother told me people would say she was lucky not to have known her mother. Then she couldn't miss her. But all those hot Florida nights, she'd imagined her mother as a star and talked to her nightly at the window. All through her childhood, the Healys came on visits, taking them out to sumptuous dinners and inviting my mother for a visit to Ireland. Her father said that it was a blighted country and the Irish always destroyed their great – Parnell and Collins. But my mother was determined to go when she was eighteen. As soon as she was, her father died, so she did. But except for Aunt Allie, the Healys didn't want her. She was a stranger in a foreign country and was shuttled from rich house to rich house and ended up doing nursing. She loved that, and, when the war finally came, deliberately missed the last ship back. And then she met my father in a railway station. It was her fate . . . except it didn't work out always. Then, lying in the dark, I realized the truth: I was the only person my mother had. In a way I was her mother.

Finally I got up, looking out my window for a star. But they were cloaked by December fog. And could my grandmother hear me from death's dateless night? In the darkness, I wept for her. For Madeline. And for my father. Towards morning the nightnurse came in and saw me, giving me a sleeping draught. I fell asleep, but even in my dreams I wept. For there is no medicine to

> *Pluck out a rooted sorrow*
> *Raze out the written troubles of the brain.*

The next morning I slept it out. So, as the head doctor was doing rounds, Mrs Greene shook me awake. The others had finished breakfast and were tidying the ward, while I gobbled mine.

By half-nine everything was spic and span, and we had lined the corridor to be inspected in army fashion by the cohort of doctors and Matron.

I was next to Mrs Greene.

The head doctor moved along the row, stopping at her. 'I'm afraid she's gone . . . tragic . . .'

I tried not to listen.

'A very sick woman . . . Now Mrs Greene, you can't take this so badly . . .'

As Mrs Greene rushed away, the doctor came to me. 'How are you, Anne?'

My mouth went completely dry.

'Dear me.' He took my hand, rubbing it. 'You're cold. Aren't you feeling well?'

'I'm g-grand.' But tears came to me at the thought of Madeline. One minute you're alive, but before you can say Jack Robinson you're dead. And she'd never even said goodbye.

'Now, now,' the head doctor comforted, whispering something to Dr Nirmal and Matron.

At therapy that morning, I couldn't do anything. Not even write a note to Grundig. I could only sit thinking what a dreadful person I was. In a way Nicola's ball was my apex. But in a different way than I had thought. Before it, I feared childish things. Like the dark. And strange dogs and trees. And what people thought. But the worst things in the world were invisible and inside people. I complained about other people being sophisters and calculators, but I was no exception. By leaving Pete with Cousin William, I had betrayed him. And by loving a Man of the World and trying to gain the world, I had betrayed myself. The soil of my soul had gone dry. Saprophytes and weeds grew there. I had turned my back on my sister and mother. I had run from them, as I had run from Pete and my rabbit long ago. I was Judas.

After lunch I was summoned to Dr Nirmal's office.

'We've d-decided to g-give you a course of shock t-treatment, Annie. You s-s-seem very depressed.'

Remembering Tina, I felt queasy. 'But it makes you look awful. As if you're dying.'

183

He lit a cigarette. 'You l-look awful after any ordeal – a t-t-tooth extraction. Oh, you'll g-g-get a headache. B-but we'll give you something f-f-for that. You won't feel anything.'

Before I would've been delighted to be in need of shocks, but now I was in a slough of doubt.

He stubbed out his cigarette, lighting another. 'A l-l-little current of electricity will pass through your b-brain. And it'll cheer you up!'

'But *how*?' I knew nothing ever would.

'They d-don't know. It was discovered by accident.'

I made a face.

'All g-great discoveries were. Penicillin. Smallpox serum. The important thing is it w-w-works, Annie! There'll be no ill effects. There's just a t-temporary m-m-memory loss.'

'I'll lose my memory?'

He nodded. 'P-perhaps t-temporarily.'

'OK. I'll have it immediately.'

But I had to wait till the next morning to forget.

'Sorrow is rust on the soul,' Doctor Johnson has written, and for the rest of that day it ate into mine. Madeline's sad fountains of eyes were constantly before me, reminding me somehow of my mother. I couldn't stop thinking of her fudge. And French toast. And iced tea. And her tipping. And our shopping. And Parnell's statue. Oh, my mother admired him, but it was the fallen hero that inspired her imagination. One of her famous anti-Healy stories has to do with Parnell. He had called on them for a change of linen when down on his luck, which they gave OK – they didn't turn against him. But my mother always lambasted them for not giving more. I mean she was the type who'd give her coat to a beggar. Once on O'Connell Bridge a tinker child had asked her for money, but she had only a half-a-crown and a penny. Instead of walking on like everyone else, my mother decided to give the child whatever she took out. Of course it was the half-a-crown, but she gave it. She did. But I wanted to forget all that. I wanted to stay in my cocoon. Which was impossible so long as I remembered things. Like the first time Aunt Allie brought me shopping for school clothes. We got the pyjamas in Newell's. The uniform in Switzer's. And the shoes in Bradley's – where, although I was fifteen, they tried to give me a balloon. But instead of being happy, I cried. I was young then, and didn't know a school term is but a shadow of a final parting. I didn't understand that love is but grief. But my mother understood. She understood.

It was darkly Lenten when nightnurse called me the next morning. In my dressing-gown, I followed her down the long dim corridor to a little waiting-room in the connecting corridor.

Olga was there, studying a book about the Queen's coronation. 'Isn't she lovely?'

Groggily I nodded. The Queen's OK, but the first Elizabeth is more my type.

'My granddaughter,' Olga sighed. 'I'm a widow of the late king.'

I looked at her suspiciously. She had told me her grand-nephews were Indian. And how could she be a widow of the late king? 'Eh – I thought you came from Cork?'

'Ssh!' Olga's eyes widened madly, as she put a finger to her lips. 'That's Victoria's story. She likes to be incognito.'

Then a nurse took Olga away.

As I waited, sorrow rusted into me. My only hope was to forget.

'Anne!' The nurse popped her head cheerfully round the door. 'Doctor's waiting!'

I followed, my heart thumping in terror. In the dreary adjacent room, a blond lady doctor stood beside a sort of trolley stretcher.

'Hop up!' She patted it, giving me a lipsticked smile.

I hesitated, fear freezing me. On a side table I saw a set of earphones which must be to electrocute your brain. It looked like an instrument of torture. Did I really want to forget everything? And how many other memories had been blitzed in this bleak little room?

'Come on, Annie' The nurse said, nudging me.

'Hop up! There's the good girl!' The doctor patted the trolley again, holding an injection needle behind her back.

I ran, Dear Reader, at the sight of it.

The nurse tackled me, but somehow I got past her and the doctor into the corridor. With them chasing me, I made for the hall door. Although I was in my dressing-gown, I'd go home. But the door was locked, so I made for the café, shouting at my pursuers, 'Leave me alone! Leave me alone!'

But it was no use.

The café was locked too and other nurses bore down on me.

'It's all right, Anne' they reassured me.

'I want Dr Nirmal,' I shouted, struggling. 'My mother!'

But I was dragged back like a slave in chains to the place of execution.

The blond lady doctor was waiting there, her face red with irritation.

'You're a very silly girl! Get on that trolley at once!'

Numbly I did.

Two nurses held me down, while the doctor covered me with a tartan rug and tied my arm tightly with a rubber tube. She flicked my vein with a hard red nail, saying gloatingly, 'What lovely veins you have, dear.'

I saw the needle again and struggled.

But she bore down on me too, smelling of perfume. 'It's all right, Anne!'

I felt a jab.

Fluid surged into my ears. I was drowning in a sea of misery.

Then I fell like Alice, opening my eyes back in my own bed.

Victoria stood over me with a cup of tea. 'Are you awake, Annie dear?'

I stared groggily around my room. How had I got there?

'I've brought you a cup of tea, dear,' Victoria said gently. 'Are you awake yet?'

'I – I think so!' I sat up. 'Ouch! My head!'

'Sister will give you something for that! Drink this! It'll make you feel better!' And she puffed my pillows, sitting comfortably on my bed.

Rattlingly I sipped my tea. 'Funny, I dreamt Olga told me she was the Queen's grandmother!'

'You didn't dream it, dear.'

Then I remembered. Olga reading the book on Royalty. My escape attempt. The treatment hadn't worked after all.

'Olga was always the pretty one,' Victoria went on. 'A honeypot. Papa thought her young man unsuitable though, and broke the engagement. The next morning Olga came downstairs, saying she was Queen Mary of Teck.'

'But didn't Queen Mary die ages ago?'

'Not according to Olga,' Victoria paused. 'I sometimes think Papa was wrong. There might be happiness in marriage . . . We were his pearls, all he had. Mama died, you see . . . and we were all he had.'

I didn't know what to say.

Victoria got up, looking sadly at me. 'I'll see how the poor dear is.'

The treatment hadn't made me lose my memory. Only given me an awful headache. I remembered everything about my mother. Her childhood. Parnell, the lot. How I'd left her to cope with Cousin William and find a school for Doone. How my sojourn in the bathroom must've seemed such a rejection of her. How I didn't want her to visit me, and how when she did I'd barely speak to her. Then and there, I decided to go home. To find my mother and somehow cope. It was awful leaving my friends. I'd miss everyone so much: Mrs Greene and the Volga and even Dr Nirmal. Oh, probably him more than all. For at that moment, I realized I'd come to love him. It was weird, I was meant to love Chris.

After lunch I asked Sister Hackett for permission to go home for a visit. But she waved me crossly away, saying not without Dr Nirmal's permission. And I'd behaved badly enough for one day.

So I went down to Art therapy, crossing the hall to see if Cerberus was there. He looked up grumpily. I'd never get past him. They'd never believe my confession, and running for it again would only end up in my capture. I was labelled, and all the perfumes of Arabia wouldn't sweeten my little hand.

In the art room Grundig was painting silently.

I decided to do another abstract, getting out paints. But it was no use. I just sat there, my mind elsewhere.

After awhile I felt nudging, as Grundig passed a note, saying, 'You're very pale. What's up?'

'I've a headache from shock treatment,' I scribbled back.

He read it, tossing it angrily into the wastebasket. He looked so cross, I thought I'd done something.

So I scribbled another note. 'Is anything wrong?'

After a few minutes he wrote back. 'Can you translate this? Iti sapis spotand abigone.'

It looked like Latin OK, but the words didn't mean anything. Maybe my mind was affected. Maybe I'd eventually forget everything. Although I'd wanted this yesterday, I now panicked. What if I forgot my mother? Doone? Our childhood? All my knowledge?

I passed it back, shaking my head.

He drew a few swift strokes on it, passing it back. 'It/i s/a/piss /pot and a/big/one.'

'Oh! I get it! It is a piss pot and a big one!' I laughed, then began crying.

He stared angrily at me.

'Stop that!' he suddenly blurted in a hoarse voice. 'I hate crying!'

I stopped, amazed to hear him speak. 'Eh, sorry!'

He wheeled over. 'They're out of their minds doing that to a kid like you!'

'But I wanted to forget. I'm a t-t-terrible person.'

'We're all terrible people, Annie.'

His words were like balm. And his blue wrinkled eyes were so kind.

'Have you ever seen Swift's tomb?'

I shook my head.

'Well, go and get your coat! Meet me in the front hall in five minutes. I'll show you something to translate.'

'But how'll we get past Cerberus?'

'Who? Oh, Andy! Leave him to me!'

So I pushed him through the garden, up the ramp into the café, through the corridors to the men's section. Then I got my coat and met him back in the hall.

'We're going out for a breath of air, Andy!'

'Right! Mr de Burgh Whyte!' was all Cerberus said.

We went up the steep tree-lined avenue to the street. Everything seemed weirdly new and strange outside. I felt a sense of elation, like getting out of boarding school. The James's Street traffic was noisier than I remembered, and the sour smell of brewing Guinness stronger. As we passed their sombre Georgian offices, I thought of Frog. With people like her and Mrs Greene, it was no wonder the Guinness's were millionaire's. And it was to have been my destiny to work there. Maybe it wouldn't have been so bad. Maybe it wasn't too late? But would Aunt Allie ever forgive me now? And would I ever see Frog again? By Thomas Street the sour smell mingled with the Liffey stink and the hawkers' rotting fruit.

We passed John's Lane Augustinian Church. Then High Street where we went to last Mass with my father. Dublin's a city of churches, and I remembered them all: Mount Argus, Aungier Street, Clarendon Street, Westland Row, Adam and Eve's, Gardiner Street. I remembered their funny smell of wet clothes, incense and candles.

I even remembered the Protestant Churches – although only from the outside: St. Michan's where you could see dead bodies and touch the hand of the Crusader, Findlater's, the Black Church, and Christ Church looming greyly ahead of us.

Its bells pealed over the city as we turned down to Swift's Cathedral. Like all the New Year Eves of my childhood when we

189

stayed up to toast the midnight hour with Club Orange. I could even see my father, like Banquo's ghost, holding up his glass. And for the first time his memory didn't make me unhappy. Now I understood him. After all, I'd failed too. And the Cathedral came into sight and the knacker's smell became stronger. I felt a sense of belonging. The Vikings had come to Dublin. The French. The English. Handel had first played the Messiah here. And the O'Briens had lived here for eight generations. The city was in my blood. It was silly to mourn for the country. We had never really belonged there. My father wasn't the rural type. And neither was I.

'The entrance is round the corner,' Grundig said at the main door.

'We're excommunicated for setting foot in a Protestant Church.'

'Did the Nutty Nun tell you that? Where'd she disappear to?'

'She went out to St. Edmundsbury's. Then she's changing orders. She's joining the Poor Clares.'

'Surely one's as bad as the next. Communities of religious and communities of the insane don't differ much. They're all for the inadequate.'

'She says the world's too Machiavellian.'

'Damn right it is! That fellow was vastly misunderstood.'

'Was he anything like Dante?' We were at the door.

'Well, both believed man to be a citizen. The verger will help me down these steps. Just run in and tell them I'm here.'

Two youngish blackfrocked men helped Grundig down the steps into the vast and eerie cathedral. I stared up the centre aisle to the high altar where choirboys practised 'Silent Night.' There was a smell of must and the walls were covered with plaques.

'Come over here!' Grundig called, staring up at a black plaque on the wall. 'I want to see if you can translate this. It's Swift's epitaph – in the language of your church.'

I studied the gold letters:

190

Hic Depositum Est Corpus
JONATHAN SWIFT S.T.D.
Hujus Ecclesiae Cathedralis
Decani
Ubi saeva Indignatio
Ulterius
Cor Lacerare nequit.
Abi Viator
Et imitare, si poteris,
Strenuum pro virili
Libertatis Vindicatorem.
Obiit 19 Die Mensis Octobris
A.D. 1745 Anno Aetatis 78.

I didn't say so, but I'd vaguely heard of this. 'Here is deposited . . . the body of Jonathan Swift S.T.D. . . . What's that?'

'A degree! Go on!'

'Decani . . . Dean of this Cathedral . . . Ubi . . . Where . . . Saeva Indignatio . . . indignation. Nequit . . . is no longer able . . . to lacerate, cor . . . lacerate his heart. Abi Viator. . . . go journeyer –

'Go traveller!'

'Go traveller . . . and imitate, si poteris . . . if you are able . . . Strenuum Vindicatorem . . . Strenuous Vindicator?'

'Strenuous defender!'

'Strenuous defender of manly liberty?'

'Well!' Grundig smiled admiringly. 'They haven't blitzed you completely. But don't let them do that again! And get out of the place! It's only for cripples like me!' He swung away from me, muttering, 'Imitare si poteris!'

I walked around, stopping at a white marble monument inscribed with the name of John Philpot Curran. 'He was terrible to Emmet.'

191

Grundig wheeled up to me. 'If not wanting that drip for a son-in-law is terrible, then I'm all for being terrible.'

'But Emmet was a hero!'

'I'm not sure I'd like to live under your heroes, Annie.' He made for the door. 'Come on! We'd better be getting back!'

I lingered at the monument, pondering on the irony of his daughter, Sarah Curran, Emmet's true love, marrying a British officer. After Emmet had died for Ireland, desiring not even an epitaph until his country took its place among the nations of the world. But such is life's bitter irony. On the way out, I studied the inscription under a sleeping knight: 'The issue of the Right Honourable Richard Boyle Earle of Corke and the Ladie Katheryne his wyfe and such of their daughters husbands as are married.'

'Come, Annie!' The vergers were already helping Grundig out.

'I saw a grammatical error on a tomb!' I said when we were in the street.

'Well, you can write to the Dean!'

'It said 'such of their daughters husbands as are married.' There was no comma on daughters and a husband has to be married!' I pushed his chair round the corner and past the main door.

'You're an awful show-off, Annie!' He chuckled to himself.

'But it's tautology – statement of the obvious fact.'

'Is that right?' There was a note of sarcasm in his voice.

'Well – Oh!' I was glad he couldn't see me redden. 'I'm sorry.'

'You need more than good grammar to get through life, Annie!'

All the way back through the crammed and raucous streets, I pondered on this. I was a snob about my knowledge. But Aunt Allie was right. I didn't know anything. I only pretended to know things. Tina was only a year and a half older than I and knew far more. And I had failed my matric through my own fault. Aunt Allie might've given me another chance at it, if I'd worked at boring things like Irish. Funnily, I could see now that my hatred of Irish had been a rebellion against her. And I'd behaved the same way about Miss Halfpenny's. I'd wanted to annoy Aunt Allie, to rebel against her because of always having to be so 'good' with my mother. And that was why I wanted to stay in St. Patrick's: to rebel against my mother. But now I was a woman and must think as a woman. And being a woman meant having regrets. As soon as she got to work, I'd ring my mother and say I was coming home.

No one seemed to have missed us. I left Grundig at his room, and went to mine to hang up my coat.

There was a note on my pillow.

From my mother.

Darling Annie,
All is up. I'm taking the mailboat tonight. Brown Thomas's at the instigation of Aunt Allie, cannot be dissuaded from bringing ruin on me and my children. I'm sorry, darling. I'll send for you as soon as I'm settled. I'm writing to Mrs Freeman about Doone.
Love, Mummy.

I ran out to the corridor, shouting at Sister. 'How long ago was my mother here?'

She didn't look up from her chart. 'About an hour ago. We couldn't find you.'

'I must go home immediately!'

She looked up briefly. 'You'll go nowhere without Dr Nirmal's permission. Into supper like a good girl!'

'But you can't keep me here!' I was suddenly enraged.

'Your mother has signed you in! Now go into your supper!'

I began crying. Mrs Greene heard, and came out of the Solarium. 'What's all this?'

'She says I'm signed in! She won't let me home!'

Mrs Greene nodded at Sister and, leading me in to supper, sat me down beside her. 'Now what's all this? You're annoyed with Mama for signing you in?'

193

'No! It's the opposite! I wanted to come! There's nothing wrong with me! But now they won't let me go!' I didn't care who heard.

'Wanting to come is a symptom, pet.'

'Is it?' I felt utter confusion.

'I expect most people do at first.' She squeezed my arm. 'You've had a nervous breakdown, pet. But you'll be stronger for it.' She spooned out some baked beans. 'Now eat something!'

'I can't. My mother's going to England. And I can't even say goodbye!'

'Of course you can!'

'But I've no busfare or anything! And Cerberus!'

She dug into her handbag, taking out a pound. 'Take this, and leave Cerberus to me. I'll go down to the hall after supper. You follow me in a few minutes! One thing –.'

'What?'

'You must tell me how you are.'

'Can I ring you?'

She agreed to that. I sat nervously through the rest of supper, feeling like a prisoner escaping from a P.O.W. camp. Then, as Sister gave out the pills, Mrs Greene glided out, humming cheerfully.

'Pills, Annie!' Sister smiled brightly, holding mine out on a spoon.

I took them, avoiding her eyes. Then spat them out in the bathroom. From now on I'd need all my wits. Then I got my coat, sauntering down the long corridor to the front hall.

'You're a cutie, Andy!' Mrs Greene drawled drunkenly as I rounded the corner. Cerberus was trying violently to detach from her embrace.

'I'd like to gobble you up!'

'Now, Mrs Greene –.'

'Let me out of here!' she shouted, suddenly angry.

He picked up the phone, speaking into it.

She ruffled his hair placatingly. 'Cutesie is cross! Shh!' She put a finger to her lips. 'I'll go quietly. Hiccup! 'Scuse me!' Then he caught her as she lurched frighteningly, shouting, *'Café au lait!'*

'What are you doing?' Cerberus snapped, seeing me.

'She's going to blazes! To blazes!' Mrs Greene raised a clenched fist. *'Café au lait! Café au lait!'* She said it like *Vive la France!* Or some ancient call to arms.

'I left my book in the cafe,' I blurted.

He nodded crossly, frog-marching Mrs Greene back to the ward. And I slipped into the cold air of freedom.

9

Our house was a deserted village. All the windows were bolted, the hall door weirdly padlocked.

I tried the back door.

The garage door.

Then, in desperation, broke in through the kitchen window. 'Mama!' I ran through the empty house. 'Mama!'

But there was only a mocking silence.

Rooms once filled with laughter and cheerful barking were now cluttered with half-packed boxes.

She was gone.

I was too late.

> *. . . all germens spill at once*
> *That make ingrateful man.*

In despair I wandered from room to room, remembering the day we moved in. The boxy little house was our first real home after years of vagrancy. We'd had our own furniture in storage for years. And at last could get it out. But as the men carried it piece by piece into the house, my mother had almost wept. She'd forgotten most of her good stuff was sold. What remained was damaged or lost. We only had half a dining room table. And all the chairs dribbled stuffing. But she soon cheered up, saying things didn't matter. And she made a home for us. Patients contributed some ornaments, old pots and pans, etc. And she picked up a couch on the instalment plan. It was now missing from the drawing room. Also my Combridge's print of Gains- borough's *Blue Boy*. My grandmother's photo was still on the mantelpiece though, and Doone's three white china ducks flew frozenly on the wall overhead.

I sat on the floor tormented by memories. The day we moved in, the previous tenant was in the middle of fleeing Ireland. She was a Hungarian refugee with wild greying hair and mad violety eyes who ranted nonstop about the Irish being worse than the communists and the whole country being a damp bog-hole where nothing worked. Then she had the gall, the absolute gall, to demand £5 for her odds and ends – orange boxes basically. Now my mother only had £10 for our electricity deposit but, to my horror, she fished into her bag and, ignoring my coughs, gave the refugee a fiver.

Afterwards I'd grumbled why did she do it?

'For luck, darling,' she replied. 'For luck.'

Everyone needed luck, and my mother was no exception. Throw your bread upon the waters was her philosophy. So she bled her breast for her young and gave her last crust to a hungry beggar. And now what was her return? Only the bitter bread of exile and a life of wandering.

I have read that at the moment of death your life flashes before you, and it was like that for me now, I was paralyzed by memories of my mother. Of her *joie de vivre,* bringing Doone and me to tea and cream cakes in Fullers' or the Monument Café one at a time to spare expense. Of her giving the tinkers baths, and a party for their children in this very room. Of the time I'd almost set the house on fire making a hot whiskey for her flu. You were meant to pour in boiling water, but I boiled the whiskey. And it went on fire. I had been scared, then miserable because it was wasted and she was so sick. Who would mind her now?

If only I could push back the clock.

My grandmother stared quizzically from the mantelpiece. Her *pince-nez*, tasselly Victorian dress and swept-up hair had all the romance of a character in a book. Although from a family of hoarders, she'd been a scatterer too, throwing an opal ring into the Liffey to ward off bad luck. But she couldn't help me now.

197

Although my mother would surely be back for the photo? And to finish packing?

I ran up the stairs, frantically searching her wardrobe. But no. Her clothes were gone. And my father's white leather honeymoon suitcase. I was too late.

Unless I caught her at the boat?

It sailed around nineish and it was now after eight.

I ran back to the bus stop, catching a 46A to Dun Laoghaire. As we jolted by the usual circuitous route, I wandered back through the labyrinthine ways of my mind to the time we went to London. My mother wanted to make a new start, but it was miserable. I couldn't discover how to cross the road. All the pedestrian crossings were tunnels. And they wouldn't have us in the Grosvenor House Hotel where she'd been on holiday with Daddy – even though I spent our last 15/- on afternoon tea. So we ended up in the Mount Royal where they brought us breakfast in bed. Then she couldn't find a job, and I missed Doone and Daddy so much, we decided to come home. Except then we had no fare. And one relation wouldn't lend it. But my father's wild colonial brother did, giving me a £1 which I immediately lost, and a novel by Zola which I still haven't read. Dear God, I prayed, don't let us go there again. Not to that city where everyone had a home but us. Things had turned out like this because of pretending: me about Chris, my mother that we weren't poor. Oh God, give me another chance. I'd been to a far country, but there was only this place of tears. I knew that now. I'd take my bill and instead of a hundred write fifty from now on. I wouldn't even boast about Dante, if I had another chance. But my prayers seemed to scatter before the wind outside. As the rain pattered against the bus window, I heard my mother crying. And in the chug of the bus's engine, her voice said, 'All things betray thee, who betrayest me.'

Our first flat had been in Dun Laoghaire, so I knew where the mailboat left from. Its funnel still peeped from behind the huge pier. And a queue of people still lugged suitcases through the barricades.

I ran to the top.

'Ticket please!' A guard roughly barred my way.

'I'm saying goodbye to someone!'

'Only passengers beyond this point!'

'But I'll get off again!'

He reached past me, punching another ticket. 'Not running away from home?'

'No! It's my mother. Did you happen to see a woman in a leopard skin coat?'

Grimly he shook his head.

'She may be on the boat. *Please,* can I see?'

'Only passengers beyond this point!' Doggedly he punched another ticket.

'Well, what's the fare to England?' I had the change of a pound. Somewhere I'd get the rest.

'What part? Next please!'

'Eh – London?' There're piles of cities in England, I know. But London always equals England to me.

'Seven pounds ten shillings to Euston! The man snapped. 'Next please! Move along now!'

I hated him. If he wasn't there, I'd stow away.

Just then a country woman stepped forward. 'Are you in trouble, pet?'

I nodded, walking off.

She ran after me waving something. 'Here, take this!'

It was a holy picture of Our Lady. On the back was an ejaculation to the Tower of Ivory. Nicola and I had written millions of holy pictures to each other in school. 'Dear Nicola, In mem. of sitting beside each other in study . . . Dear Anne, In mem. of the Hound's lecture today, and our last term in fifth year . . .'

Our class would be home for Christmas by now. But school was a lost world. And so was Nicola.

'Does the father know?' The woman breathed in my face.

'What father?' I thought she meant some priest.

The woman grabbed my arm. 'The Legion of Mary have a hostel for girls in trouble! There's no need to run away!'

If all came to all, I could bring my mother there. 'Where's the Hostel?'

'I'll get you a bed for the night!'

'No! No thanks!'

I ran back up the steps to the Victorian Obelisk at the bottom of the Marine Road. It was a sort of Thermopylae. Like the Persians my mother had to pass this way. On summer evenings long ago I had lingered with my father on this very spot, listening to our landlord preach brotherly love. It was non-Catholic, so my father always hurried me on. Then we'd walk the pier, out on the top wall, back on the lower. There was a summer breeze . . . And boats bobbed on the water . . . And sometimes a band played. But all I could think of was getting back to my book. Ironic, that only in the winter of discontent could I appreciate the summer of content.

'Joy to the world! The Lord is come!' a group carolled in the distance.

I ran back to the boat. Without my mother Christmas meant nothing to me. She had always made it, conspiring by hook or by crook to get everyone a present. But, Oh God, where was she now? The passengers were all aboard. And still no sign of her. If she was gone, I'd follow her, that's all. Mrs Greene would lend me the money. Then I'd just walk around London till we met. That's what Great-grandfather Healy did when his son (Aunt Allie's husband) disappeared with a man and twenty thousand pounds – which according to my mother should've come to us. 'Come home to your wife,' he had said to the prodigal, when they met in a Chelsea Street. So he did. But with tears running down his face.

It was so sad. For Aunt Allie too. Oh, I'd beg her, absolutely beg her to forgive me. I could see now what a fatal mistake giving up Miss Halfpenny's was.

Then horses galloped in my head.

A woman in an old tweed coat and flat shoes carried a white case to the barricade. As she furtively turned her head, my horses lurched to a stop.

It was my mother.

No one else would wear sun glasses on a December night.

'Mummy!' I ran down the steps. 'Mummy!'

But, seeing me, she rushed on.

'Wait! Please wait!'

'Annie!' she hissed, as I caught up. 'Don't you realize you're giving me away? I'm in disguise.'

'Where's your leopard skin coat?'

'Ocelot! How many times must I tell you that? It's in the suitcase. I might be recognized.'

'Please don't go!'

'Darling, do you think I want to? There's no choice. Aunt Allie's set the bloodhounds on me.'

'But I've spoken to Aunt Allie! Eh – She's going to settle everything. She says it's all a ghastly mistake.'

My mother looked at me suspiciously. 'When did you speak to her?'

'Just now! I phoned her. She's sorry.'

'Hmph! She should be! But it may be too late. Besides, we've nowhere to live! We've been evicted!' She made for the boat again.

I pulled her back. 'We'll find a flat!'

'But if it got into the papers! You and Doone would be ruined!'

'I promise it'll be all right!'

'But I've already put too much on you, darling.'

'You haven't –.'

'Now stop that crying! I have. I should've thrown William out! Such mad, monstrous behaviour! He's gone now! Good riddance! Forgive me, Annie!'

It was typical of my mother to mix everything up.

'But it's *me* who –.'

'Oh, stop that!' She took off her sunglasses, folding me in her arms. 'It's not what children owe their parents! You've given me so much joy. Always remember that. Now stop – I'll send for you! And I've written to Mrs Freeman about Doone. We'll all be together again.' She held me at arm's length, her blue eyes perusing me. 'As soon as you're well.'

'But I am well! Please don't go!' Hastily I wiped my eyes. 'Let's go up to the Royal Marine for a cup of tea. I've enough for a tip too.'

Dismally she looked towards the boat. 'But where'll we live?'

'We'll find a flat. Like old times!'

'You can't cross the Liffey, darling.'

'Please!'

There were alarms and excursions coming from the boat.

'Oh, Annie!'

I had won.

I linked her arm, steering her up the steps, across the road through the Royal Marine gardens to the hotel. As it was late and we couldn't go home, we checked in and were given a palatial room with a bath and seaview. While my mother bathed, I watched the mailboat go out with its nightly cargo of exiles. For the moment we weren't with them. For tonight at least we had shelter. Although I'd detained my mother by false pretences, I felt sure Aunt Allie would help. She always had before. She'd once lent my father five thousand pounds. And the last time we were being evicted, she'd organized a round robin among the Healys for the rent.

We were the only guests in the hotel dining room. A waiter with an air of *hauteur* took our order.

My mother glanced knowledgeably at the menu. 'I'll have the lobster. And how are the oysters?'

He coughed politely. 'They're the very best, Madam. Galway Bay.'

'Give me six on the half-shell to start.'

He scribbled this down, turning expectantly to me.

Frantically I scanned my menu. 'Eh – do you have any chips?'

'Have something more nourishing, Annie!'

The waiter cleared his throat. 'French fried potatoes?'

I nodded. 'I'll have those.'

He pointed to the bottom of my menu. 'They – ah – come with a mixed grill.'

'OK!' Nervously I snapped my menu shut and gave it to him.

'And bring us a wine list!' my mother ordered.

He produced one from behind his back. And while my mother scanned it, I coughed meaningfully and tried to catch her eye. I mean, how were we going to pay?

But my hints fell on barren ground.

'Give us half a bottle of Muscadet!' she said blithely. Then, as he glided away, she turned to me. 'You're not exactly an alcoholic because you like a glass of wine, darling.'

'I know.' In that regard, I had been too judgemental in the past.

'And you'll have to learn to like things besides chips!'

'But I like chips!' I argued, quaking inwardly at the thought of the bill. I mean, blister it! How were we going to pay? I sat there, contemplating Mr Micawber's words of wisdom, 'Annual income twenty pounds, annual expenditure nineteen nineteen and six, result happiness. Annual income twenty pounds, annual expenditure twenty pounds nought and six, result misery.' I could see my mother was removed from reality. From now on I'd render to Caesar the things that were Caesar's. Somehow I'd get us out of the hotel. But first I'd ring Aunt Allie. Oh, I'm not the stuff of heroes like my mother. In High School, she'd once painted a seam up her legs when ordered to wear stockings. And in training hospital she threw a bedpan at a bullying ward sister and when asked if she were sorry, replied, 'Yes, that it was empty!' Being the daughter of an ambassador gives her the courage. 'Remember who you are!' was always her advice to Doone and me when snubbed by a friend. Being a granddaughter must be too far removed, because I'm a coward. In school the Hound thought I was good, but it was cowardice. I mean, compared to Caius at Messina, or Horatius saving the bridge, or Joan of Arc, or anyone, I'm nothing. And if I were ever captured by the communists, I'd instantly deny my faith – worse than St Peter. Oh, people in books stood up to grumpy relatives, Jane Eyre and that. But books are different, I knew that now.

The waiter brought my mother's oysters. They were strange, slithery ploppy things in grey barky shells. I watched in fascination as my mother squeezed lemon and tomato ketchup on them. 'Are they dead?'

'Of course! Here, try one!'

I grimaced. 'Ugh! No thanks!'

'They're a treat, Annie!' My mother laughed. 'People pay a lot for them.' And she sucked one off the shell.

'I'm going to the loo,' I said, getting up. The phone boxes were near the Ladies in a long corridor at the back of the lobby. I'd ring Aunt Allie without another thought. Just do it, that's all. Plunge in. The only thing you have to fear is fear itself, my mother always said.

I slid the door firmly shut and dialled the number, picturing as it rang that dark religiously polished house. Aunt Allie and Frog would have finished dinner by now. And in the drawing room. One knitting. The other sipping Guinness. And Brigid Birch would be thudding grumpily up the stairs from the kitchen.

Suddenly the receiver was picked up and her thick orphan's voice said, '778023.'

I lost my voice.

'778023.'

'Eh – could I speak to Mrs Grubb-Healy, please!'

'Who's tha'?'

'Eh – her niece.'

'Her niece?'

'Yes. Anne! Anne O'Brien.'

'Oh, You? Hmph! I'll see!'

After a second there was fierce whispering in the background.

I thought my heart would stop, but then Aunt Allie said icily, 'Hello, Anne.'

'Hello, Aunt Allie.'

'How many times must I tell you I'm not your Aunt!'

'Eh – sorry Aunt –.'

'You have your insane friends eject me! And then dare to ring this house! Such bad manners!'

'I'm sorry about Miss Halfpenny's, Aunt Allie!' I blurted.

'I'm not your Aunt!'

'No.'

'And I've no obligation towards you!'

'I know – but I need money badly!'

'Ha! So you've turned into a begging O'Brien!'

'It's –.'

'I knew it! I knew it!'

'It's for my mother,' I said levelly. 'She's being brought to court by Brown Thomas's. For charging stuff to your account!'

'Stuff indeed! Fifteen pounds worth of underwear! But they're sueing her, are they?' Her tone changed to one of curiosity. 'They tried to stick me. But I washed my hands.'

'But Aunt –.'

'It'll teach her a lesson, Anne!'

Then I played my last card. 'But if you don't help, she might go to jail!'

'Oh, she'll definitely go!' she retorted coolly. 'For fraud, Anne! Fraud!'

'Oh!' Tears came to my eyes and panic choked me.

'I've washed my hands! And as for Miss Halfpenny's I've folded my tent!'

Click went the phone.

I hung up too, staying in the box to recover my breath. Damn Aunt Allie, I sobbed. Damn her. She always treated us like scum. Even when she wasn't on the outs with my mother, she'd never visit. The memory of her parked outside, and holding court in the car with Tommy listening to every word would always sting me.

Always. Damn her. She could keep her filthy lucre. What did she expect me to call her? She was married to my mother's uncle, wasn't she? Didn't that make her some sort of Aunt? And look at how she treated Frog! I'd never speak to her again. I'd get fifteen pounds somewhere. I'd get a job, then ask for an advance on wages. The important thing was to keep my mother from suspecting. The court wasn't till Friday morning. I had two whole days to find the money and give it to Brown Thomas's.

On the way back to the dining room, I heard the receptionist shout at a manager. 'Did anyone come from the agency?'

He shook his head. 'I'll have to do the bedrooms myself! Chamber maids are impossible to keep!'

It was fate, that I'd heard.

My mother had begun her lobster. 'Are you all right, darling?'

I stared at the red monster on her plate. 'Ugh.'

'Would you like a bite?'

'It looks vicious!'

'Oh, don't be so childish. Your father always ordered lobster and he was a gourmet. You pick out the meat. And dip it in butter. Here try a bite.'

I wouldn't.

'Well, have a glass of wine.'

So I did.

'Annie,' my mother went on gently. 'I've run your father down to you. But don't think we didn't love each other.'

'I know you did!' I stared at my grill, damming back tears.

'And I've never been unfaithful to him, darling.'

'But –'

'Not even since his death. When you're older you'll understand how people –.'

'Mummy, I am grown up! And I do understand!' I attacked my chips. If only my father were here now. Even Aunt Allie was charmed by him. He would just phone her and tell her not to be a nervous girl. He called all women girls, no matter what age. But I was on my own now. I'd have to cope somehow. My mother had always supported me. From now on I'd support her. It had been an omen, hearing the manager complain about needing a chambermaid. In the morning I'd apply for a job in the hotel. I'd disguise myself like my mother had done. Except I wouldn't tell her. Although I'd vowed to walk in the grey of reality, I'd have to pretend for just a little longer. Otherwise she'd run away again.

After dinner we had coffee in the T.V. lounge, and then went upstairs to our room. As we lay in our half-acre of bed, I sang her to sleep as Daddy often had. 'Just a song at twilight . . . when the lights are low . . .' and 'The sea, oh, the sea! Long may it roll between England and me!'

Finally she dozed off and I lay awake. To have her back was. . . . oh, love's old sweet song. Like her kissing me when I was little. Or when we lay awake wondering where Daddy was drinking. Or the time she told me about Father Mullane. Or our dentist visits to the Metropole Café. The Hound says you can't be too happy in this life, that perfection lies in the next. Maybe that's true. But my mother – I'm not saying to anyone *else* – but to me she's the Queen of France. Maybe that's just a child's vision. When they become sixteen, children are meant to judge their parents. Maybe that's it. Except I'm backward. Like waiting till seventeen for my first bra, I waited till then to judge my mother.

The next morning I ordered breakfast in bed, hiding under the sheets as the maid carried it in. Then, telling my mother to rest for the day, I put on her sunglasses with my green tweed coat and went downstairs to the hotel lobby.

'I'm from the agency,' I said to the receptionist.

She gave me a disdainful look. 'We were expecting you yesterday.'

I said nothing.

'Take a seat! I'll ring for the housekeeper.'

After ages a big fat redhaired woman in black appeared, beckoning to me. I followed her up to a small office on the first floor.

'You've brought your cards?' she asked in a wheezy mannish voice.

'Cards? . . . I've just left school!'

'Hmm. So you've no experience? Have you a school reference?'

'I can get one. I went to Mount Prospect.'

She fiddled with some hairs on her chin. 'We don't get many Mount Prospect girls here.'

'Oh! But my father died! I'm working to help my mother.'

A look of sympathy softened her hard face. 'Can I ask why you're wearing sunglasses?'

'Doctor's orders! My eyes are sensitive to light.'

'Hmm . . . I suppose if the agency have sent you . . . We can give you a trial. Can you start right away?'

I nodded. 'What's the salary?'

'The wages are £5.9.11 a week. You work a long day and a short. Today's a short day. We'll give you tomorrow off to get your cards. She reached for a chart behind. 'You work every second Sunday. Any questions?'

I shook my head, deciding to ask about the advance later. She gave me a maid's uniform and showed me to a cupboard full of dusters and brushes and cleaning stuff. Then she allocated my rooms to me, about ten at the top of the hotel. It was tiring but fairly straightforward: I had to change the sheets, wash the bath and toilet, and hoover the floor. The only thing: I was very slow. I was meant to be finished by one o'clock, but I had three more rooms to do at three. But I finished, and when my rooms were being inspected broached the subject of an advance.

'I'm afraid that's impossible!' The Housekeeper leant wheezily over my clean bath, turning off a tap. 'Be careful about the taps. If the plug was in, it could flood!'

'But when'll I get paid?'

'Not for two weeks! It's hotel policy!' And she waddled off calling. 'Check the taps in your rooms!'

There was no use in crying. I'd just have to plan another strategy. I changed into my clothes, sneaking back to our room.

My mother believed I'd been with Aunt Allie all day, paying Brown Thomas's and arranging with our landlord.

'Was she sorry?' she asked me in tones of injured innocence.

I nodded, saying we'd have to rest up to have energy for a move as the landlord still might insist on it. She agreed to order dinner in our room – I was afraid to be seen in the dining room. Immediately after eating, I fell into an exhausted sleep, dreaming all night about my father. It was a weird dream. I was on a beach, watching swimmers. Suddenly I saw my father among them, and ran into the water. He waved me back, shouting furiously, 'Go, back! Go back, Annie!' And instead of coming ashore, he swam further out to sea. Just as he reached the horizon, he turned, saying, 'I'm going now. I won't come again. The water's too dangerous.' And I turned sadly away, bumping head-on into Mr Jennings.

It was an omen.

I awoke with my strategy planned: to see Mr Jennings first thing. So, after breakfast in bed, I bussed into town.

The Jennings Group Head office was in a big concrete building in Nassau Street, near Miss Halfpenny's, my old haunt. I pushed open the heavy glass door, crossing the plant-filled and carpeted foyer to the receptionist.

'Can I help you?' she asked.

'Could I see Mr Jennings, please?'

She arched a pencilled eyebrow. 'Have you an appointment?'

'An appointment? . . . Yes!'

Frostily she dialled the phone. 'Who shall I say?'

'Miss Anne O'Brien.'

She examined her long red fingernails, snapping into the receiver. 'A Miss O'Brien for Mr Jennings . . . What? Hmm . . .' Then turning to me, bored. 'There's nothing in the book! When did you make your appointment?'

'Nicola Jennings made it for me!'

She cleared her throat. 'She says Miss Jennings made it!'

'I'm a family friend.'

'What? Send her up? All right!' Then smiling brightly at me. 'Take the lift to the third floor!'

I did, pressing the three button to be shot queasily upwards. I stepped out onto more soft carpets and crossed a sort of corridor to another wax-like secretary.

'Mr Jennings is engaged at the moment. Take a seat!' She pointed to a big leather couch.

I sank down. There were magazines on the low table in front of me, but I couldn't read. I just sat, breathing deeply to stop the horses going mad in my head and rehearsing my speech to Mr Jennings. 'Daddy had back luck . . . And Mummy had to work . . . But she couldn't get used to being poor . . . She wasn't meant for it . . . She wanted us to have things –.'

'He won't be long now,' the secretary was saying.

'Eh – what?'

'I said, Mr Jennings won't be long.'

I swallowed nervously. 'I'm in no hurry.'

Inserting a page in her typewriter, she asked curiously, 'Were you in school with Nicola?'

I nodded, hiding behind a magazine. My mouth was completely dry. Maybe I should run for it. Maybe it was crazy expecting Mr Jennings to help. But my father and he had served Mass for the Jesuit Saint, Fr John Sullivan. And when the school bully had spattered my father's best suit with mud, Mr Jennings had stuck –.

The phone was buzzing.

'Mr Jennings will see you now,' said the secretary's manicured voice.

I followed her to Mr Jennings' door, the horses going mad in my head and dots dancing before my eyes.

She opened the door. 'Miss Anne O'Brien.'

Mr Jennings sat redfaced behind a huge desk, bumping his tummy as he stood up. 'Ha! It's Anne-Marie! The cigarette girl!'

I just stood there, remembering the burnt table.

'What can I do for you?' He brushed his few strands of

hair. 'Sit down!'

I did.

He did too.

'Good!' He hooked both thumbs into his waistcoat pockets. 'Good! Given up smoking, have you? Good! Good! Nasty habit. Nicola quit. Off in Switzerland now! Ever been in Switzerland?'

'No.' Maybe he didn't see me with the butt.

'Lovely country! Great air! Good for you!' He flicked through a desk diary, shaking his jowly face. 'Let's see . . . my secretary says Nicola made an appointment. Can't recall it . . . the memory . . .'

'She didn't, Mr Jennings.'

His face purpled. 'Wh--What?'

'I just came.'

He gaped unbelievingly. 'You told a lie?'

'Only a white lie.'

He broke into explosive coughing, snatching a breath. 'I don't care what colour it is!' He snatched another breath, shaking his head. 'Ah, no! A lie is a lie! I can't waste my time with liars! I remember now! You're the little girl who was born in the West Indies. Bill O'Brien's daughter. Your poor mother has her hands full!'

'It's my mother I came about.'

'What's wrong with her?'

'A shop is sueing her. She bought me . . . clothes. And couldn't pay.'

He sighed knowledgeably. 'I suppose you pestered her?'

I nodded. It was like making up sins for Confession. 'She may go to jail. If – if you'll lend me £15, I'll –.'

'What? What?' He shook his jowls. 'Lend you money? I can't believe my ears!'

'I'd pay you back, if you possibly could.'

He leant over the desk. 'How?'

'I have a job in the Royal Marine Hotel.'

'Hmm! Have you?' He paused, going on angrily. 'But I can't stand the improvidence of today's youth! Living beyond their means!'

'I don't!'

He wagged a finger. 'You pestered your mother!'

'I'd pay you back,' I pleaded, controlling tears.

He looked hard at me. 'How do I know you're telling the truth?'

Weirdly I went beetroot, as if I was lying.

He went purple again, snapping, 'Why didn't your mother come herself?'

'Eh – she wouldn't.' The galloping started in my head.

He began coughing again. 'Your mother's a respectable lady. If she wanted help, she'd come herself!'

I knew she'd rather drown herself.

'Ah, yes! I'm on to you! Yes indeed.' He picked up the phone. 'Miss Coffey show this girl out!' He stood up, shaking his head. 'It's tragic when children turn out like you! Tragic! My God, if Nicola got up to a game like this! Have you stopped going to Mass?'

Everything blurred as the secretary showed me out. As if in a cloud, I went down in the lift, past the first secretary, and out into Nassau Street where faceless crowds jostled me all the way to Bewley's of Grafton Street. Now we'd have to go to England. And be bra refugees. We were ruined.

There's comfort in the smell of coffee.

But the chatter and clattery-clink of cups seemed to stop as I went into the ground floor café. Then everyone looked up. They could all see I was a liar with no money. Without money, you're eyeless in Gaza. You're David without his sling. So I dashed out, hiding behind the shop window and looking over plates of sweets to the street.

There was a familiar face in the crowd.

Father Mullane.

Like an Angel of God, he came into the café.

'Father!' I whispered from my corner. 'Father!'

'Annie!' he hailed, coming over and heartily shaking my hand. 'Better, are you? Good! Come and have a coffee!'

I tried to dam tears, but it was no use.

Nervously he looked round. 'Now what's wrong? Aren't you better?' He edged me into the corner. 'Stop that! That's the good girl! Haven't they helped you in that hospital?'

I succumbed to more tears.

'You need a doctor, love.'

'I – I –.'

'Come on and have a coffee!' And he led me into the noisy café.

The cups and cutlery clinked obliviously now, and no one looked up. He found a table with two free seats – a man and a woman occupied the other two. As we sat down the man folded his paper and left.

'I'm disappointed you're not better, Annie.' Father sighed heavily. 'How long have you been in St Pat's?'

'Since the beginning of November.'

'And what's this, the twentieth of December? Hmm . . . Ah, God is good. You'll soon be out.'

'I am out.'

'What? . . . We'll have two coffees and buns, please!' He hailed a flitting waitress, and as she cleared our table went on, 'How's Dr Nirmal?'

'He's having problems with his children.'

Fr Mullane nodded sympathetically. 'He thinks you're well enough to be out?'

'He doesn't know.'

'Don't tell me you're out without permission!' He shook his head.

'I've left! I'm working!'

'Left? Working? Where?'

The waitress clattered down our coffee and buns.

He attacked a bun. 'Ah, Annie, why couldn't you wait?

213

What's going to become of you?'

'My mother has a very worrying bill,' I whispered across the table.

'Sure, we all have worrying bills! Eat up! God is good!' He pushed the bun plate to me.

'Brown Thomas's are sueing her for £15 worth of underwear.'

'What?' His mouth was full of bun.

'Of brassieres. She bought them for me.'

He glanced at my chest. 'Hmm . . .Sueing her? Ah, God is good. Eat up!'

Ignoring the curious stare of the woman beside me, I whispered, 'Can you help? Otherwise she might go to jail.'

He frowned. 'Annie, do you honestly think God will allow your mother to go to jail? Have you prayed about it? No, I can see you haven't!' He attacked another bun. 'Faith can move mountains, Annie. And have you done what I asked you? Looked at the trees? No! Taken a lesson in simple faith? No! Trees carry out their task, Annie. Lift their leafy arms in love –.'

'But we're not *trees!*'

There was a pregnant silence, as he munched irritably.

'Would you lend me £15?' I blurted.

'Annie, you know I've taken a vow of poverty!'

I nodded miserably.

He suddenly dived into his pocket. 'Tell you what, though! I'll lend you ten bob. No, I'll lend you a pound.' And he pressed a wrinkled note into my hand.

'I can't –.' My mother was paying for her fidelity.

'Take it! I insist! Although, if it's in the hands of the law, she'll need a solicitor. Has she got one? No. What about your young man? Eh, waitress!' He waved for the bill. 'The children of this world are wiser in their generation than the children of light, Annie.' He stood up. 'Get her a solicitor, love. And do one thing for me?'

'What?'

'Smile! God loves you!' He smiled himself and got up.

I watched his large black figure cross the café to the waitress who scribbled out a bill. Then he went to the cash desk and out of sight. Faith probably moved mountains, but I was the only person who could help my mother. Except I was failing miserably. But I did know a solicitor. Maybe Chris was wise in his generation. Maybe if he helped, we could die with harness on our back. Instead of wandering homeless in England.

I hurried out of the café, crossed Grafton Street to Anne Street and then Dawson Street. Fossil Forsyth was at the top, directly opposite the Marie Jean flower shop. For a while, I studied the brass plaque outside. Ironic, although I loved Chris, I dreaded meeting him. Just dreaded it. I was afraid of him. At last I got the courage to push open the door and go up the stairs.

But halfway I stopped dead, remembering Nicola's ball and that long walk home in the dark. I had fled that banquet of life.

Then I heard footsteps at the top and fled again.

'Hello,' someone called behind me. 'Hello, there!'

I turned at the door.

It was Chris.

In panic, I closed my eyes.

'What the hell are you doing here?' Laughing, he stuffed a bundle of letters into his grubby raincoat pocket.

I was still taller. His eyes were still the grey-blue of Peter Finch. His pock-marked skin the hue of Dirk Bogarde's. And he smiled the same crooked smile, cutting the same notch in my heart.

'Did you get home all right? Christ, I was pissed that night! Everyone was!' He looked irritably down at my high heels.

My mouth was completely dry.

'That Nicola's a boring bitch when she's drunk! Great spread, though! Old man Jennings just clinched another land deal!' He shook his head appreciatively. 'Eh – What do you want?'

'I'm employing a solicitor.'

'You need a solicitor?' He glanced at his watch. 'Well, come upstairs! I'll see what I can do.'

He ran ahead of me up the stairs, pushing open the door at the top and ushering me through a hall where a secretary typed behind a counter.

'I'm using the conference room, Angela!' And he led me into a large room, furnished with bookcases and a big mahogany table.

'Take a pew!' He pulled out a chair, took off his raincoat and sat down. 'Now, why do you want a solicitor?'

'My mother's being sued.' I gripped the edge of my seat. 'By Brown Thomas's for £15.'

He drew a sharp breath. 'Shoplifting?'

I shook my head. 'No. Fraud.'

He scratched his bald patch. 'Can she pay for a solicitor?'

I put all my money on the table. 'I have nearly thirty shillings.'

He put his hands to his face, laughing. 'My God! . . . You don't come to a solicitor with thirty shillings! Frankly, it wouldn't pay for the stamps!'

'I can get more,' I heard myself say.

He tilted his chair forwards. 'Frankly, your mother owes me fifty quid already! Did you know that? She consulted me about your brother's inheritance –.'

'I have rich relations,' I pleaded. 'The court's tomorrow morning.'

'Phew! That's tricky!' He sat bolt upright. 'Can you get a hundred pounds?'

I nodded, thinking I could owe it to him.

He took out a notebook. 'In that case, tell me everything. And no fabrications!'

So I told him everything from the beginning.

'Brown Thomas's should've checked the account!' He perused my countenance. 'Were you charged?'

'I don't know.'

'You'll know it if you're in Mountjoy! How did you get so wild?'

I just looked at him.

'Well, I have Mrs Grubb-Healy's number! Are you on the phone?'

216

'We're staying at the Royal Marine for a few nights. 'I was in St. Patrick's –'

'St. Patrick's hospital?' He banged his forehead with the heel of his hand. 'That's right! You wrote to me. I thought it was the name of your house! Still, it might be useful.' And he jotted it down. 'What doctor are you under?'

Then he jotted down Dr Nirmal's name, showing me out. 'Get on to your relatives for a hundred quid! And be back here at nine in the morning with your mother!'

'Can I owe you the money?' I blurted in the outer office.

'No chance! I must have payment in advance! I'll have to pay a barrister!' And he closed the door in my face.

In a slough of despondence, I walked back down Dawson Street. The field was lost and all was lost. There was no hope of getting a hundred pounds before the morning. We'd have to take the mailboat tonight. Suddenly I was filled with a nameless loneliness for Doone. Where would she live when she came back? Would she ever again make scones in the kitchen with Marcella? That was her favourite thing in the world. Unlike me, she's a good cook. My mother always said the one good thing about having so many troubles was that we wouldn't marry young. I never would now, but it'd be a pity if Doone didn't. She'd make such a good wife. What if I never saw her again for years? Or Mrs Greene and my other friends? I decided to go up to St. Patrick's to say goodbye and get Mrs Greene's address. Then we could write to each other at least.

I rang my mother from the Hibernian.

'Anne' she said before I could explain anything. 'You'll never believe it! Some stupid new chambermaid left a tap running upstairs! And our bathroom's flooded!'

Oh, blister it! I thought.

'She was wearing sunglasses! They can't find her anywhere! . . . Annie . . .'

'Mummy! Listen carefully. You'll have to leave the hotel at once! Wear all the clothes you can. Remember, like London?'

217

'I understand, darling!'

'Meet me outside the Hibernian in an hour!'

'I'll be there, darling.' And she hung up the phone.

I took the bus to St. Patrick's.

Dr Nirmal was talking to Cerberus in the hall, as I went in.

'S-S-So there you are!' He grabbed my arm.

'I have to leave! I only came back to say goodbye!' I wrenched free.

Cerberus made a dive for me.

'It's all r-right, Andy.' Dr Nirmal led me up the corridor towards his office, groping for a cigarette. 'S-s-see you're making me s-s-smoke! P-p-people have been w-w-worried about you, Annie!'

'Doctor, I can't stay. There's nothing wrong with me. There never was! I didn't want to live at home –' I broke off, embarrassed.

'Wh-when did I ever s-say you'd l-live at home?' He tremblingly lit a cigarette.

I gaped at him.

'D-didn't I s-s-say parents are for little children?'

'Well, yes – but –.'

'I w-would never h-have sent you home, Annie.'

'But I can't stay. We can't afford it!'

He looked aggrieved. 'N-Now h-has anyone ever mentioned m-money to you, Annie?'

'Frequently!'

'Not here! The s-s-secretary has agreed to w-wait for p-payment.'

'But we're paupers! We'll never, never, never be able to pay!'

'B-blast it!' He stubbed out his butt on a matchbox and pocketed both. 'Good afternoon, Mrs Greene, Mr de Burgh Whyte!' He smiled as they passed. 'Annie, a M-M-Mr. M-Murphy, a solicitor, has r-rung me. He t-told me your m-mother's in difficulties, and I've agreed to appear in court for her.

W-where is she now?'

'She's meeting me in an hour! Will you say she's mad?'

He looked apoplectic. 'We don't use that t-t-t-phrase! I've told you that b-before!' Then he lowered his voice. 'I'll say your mother's s-s-uffered a g-great deal of s-stress. F-first, your father's death and then your illness.'

'My illness?' If life's an illness, I supposed I'd got it OK. But I'd never be able to persuade the doctor.

'B-back to the ward now!'

'Can I go back tomorrow? I'm meeting Mummy in town!'

He groped agitatedly for a cigarette. 'B-bring her back here t-tonight. She can stay the n-night. Yes! . . . Now p-promise me!'

I nodded miserably. We'd be on the high seas tonight, so I couldn't honour my word. Oh, blister it! I hated deceiving Dr Nirmal.

As I made for the hall door, Grundig wheeled after me.

'Annie! I heard all that. Do you need money?'

'I need a hundred pounds,' I said numbly. 'And there's no hope of getting it!' Stupidly I began crying.

'Oh, stop it!' He took the minature from round his neck. I had often seen him wearing it, but never had the courage to ask about it. 'Here, take this down to the Dawson Gallery. It's my great-grandmother. Painted by Reynolds! She might as well finally serve a useful function. I'll give you a note for Leo Smith.' And he wheeled towards his room.

'I-I'll pay you back. But –.' Relief came in the form of more tears.

'Now, for God's sake, stop!'

'You're very good!'

'I'm just a fool among knaves, Annie.'

Then and there he wrote a note to Mr. Leo Smith of the Dawson Gallery, at 4, Dawson Street, Dublin. He told me to bring it right down there. So I did, catching a bus to town.

Mr. Smith looked at me grumpily over his half-moon glasses.

'Are you a friend of Mr de Burgh Whyte's?'

'Yes, Anne O'Brien.'

'Hmm . . . A dullish name,' he mused, beckoning a boy from the corner. 'I'll have to send round the corner to the bank.'

I thought he had extra-sensory perception, saying that about my name. But it was mine after all and lately I had grown to like it. But I didn't argue with the man, just wandered around the gallery looking at the pictures. I didn't even know such a gallery had existed.

After fifteen minutes the boy came back.

'Take care you don't lose it!' He handed me a thick envelope. 'And give my regards to Mr de Burgh Whyte!'

I ran jubilantly down the stairs to the street and across the road to the Hibernian. My mother was sitting in the foyer. I made a V sign like Churchill and waved the envelope. There were twenty new tenners inside. More than enough for our needs. More than enough for tea and cakes and a decent tip. In the cosy warmth of the lounge, I told her Chris would go with her to court in the morning. And Dr Nirmal would say she was stressed. And for tonight, we'd have to sleep in St Patrick's. She was agreeable to everything. My one worry was the Royal Marine. 'Never mind, darling!' my mother said. 'I gave them a false name!' So I didn't tell her about my adventures as a chambermaid, or that it was I who had caused the havoc.

As I'm nearing the end of my story, there's no need for every detail. Enough to say we went up to St Patrick's that night, where my mother was given a royal welcome by the Volga and Mrs Greene. Later on, she had a long chat with Dr Nirmal who gave her some tablets for sleeping and a bed in the Solarium.

I had difficulty in waking her the next morning, but we were at the bus stop at eight-thirty. Then, blister it, there was no sign of a bus!

None.

'It must be another strike, Annie!' My mother suggested.

So I ran back to the hospital and Cerberus called a taxi.

It came quickly, tearing all the way in. As we screeched to a

220

halt half-an-hour late at Chris' office, he was standing outside, pacing the pavement with an older man.

I looked frantically at my mother.

'Say we got a flat tyre!' She passed ten shillings to the driver. She had not lost her touch.

'We've got to be in court by ten!' Chris stormed over.

I handed him the envelope of money – £100. 'We got a flat tyre.'

'Did you?' He turned furiously to the driver.

'Ah, yes, sir! Had to change a wheel.'

As Chris yanked open the front taxi door, my mother smiled at me.

'Take us to the Four Courts!' he shouted. 'Not you, Anne. You wait in St. Patrick's. Go on! Out!'

So they both bundled in, and tore off leaving me on the pavement.

I went back to the hospital, and waited nervously on one of the couches. I felt that Chris would somehow make things turn out all right. Maybe he couldn't love me, but it was a far, far better thing to help my mother. Our adventures were the stuff of fiction, but I didn't like the idea of telling the whole world. Dr Nirmal said later to imagine telling one person. Dear Reader, you've become that person. I have told you everything. Having read so far, do you understand or condemn us? He said there's no such thing as a normal person. And that without knowing it, I'd had a nervous breakdown. I was like a cracked piece of china, which would be stronger for being repaired. That my mother would be too. He said not to blame myself. But I still do. Although not as much as that day on the couch. I am a sinner. But even saints were sinners and wrote their confessions: St Patrick and St Augustine.

Just before lunch my mother and Aunt Allie walked up the ward.

Both chatting normally.

Lay on, Macduff! I thought, going to meet them. But like old warriors, they'd laid aside their weapons. My mother was wearing her leopard skin and Aunt Allie her black Persian lamb. Their coats, lion and lamb, were the opposite of their characters. And I couldn't help thinking that only in a story would the two lie down together. But life is often stranger and has as many surprises. Art, I have read, is only a lie which makes us realize the truth.

'Oh, Annie! I wish you'd been there!' My mother kissed me. 'It was my finest hour! Mr Murphy was so nice. And there was a barrister in a wig. And Aunt Allie turned up at the last moment and said it was a mistake. A terrible mistake!'

'Hmmph!' Aunt Allie grumped. 'That young man made a liar out of me!'

I wouldn't look her in the eye.

'And the judge said I'd have to stay here for awhile. And Aunt Allie agreed to pay.'

'A pleasure!' Aunt Allie tried to catch my eye. 'You can live with me, Anne!'

At least my mother would be safe with Mrs Greene and Grundig and the Volga.

'Isn't it funny how things happen?' She went on. 'Is it all fate, darling?'

'Man is a torch, blown in the wind,' I said, not caring if Aunt Allie heard. It was the sort of unanswerable question that irritated her. Not that I know the answer either. I suppose it was fate about my grandmother wandering the nurseries of Heaven, I don't know.

'You can live with me, Annie!' Aunt Allie repeated. 'Frog has pleaded!'

I still wouldn't look at her.

'One condition though! You go to Miss Halfpenny's!'

I nodded, thinking at least Birdie would be there. Then Doctor Johnson's famous words brought tears to my eyes. 'Is not a patron, my Lord, one who looks with unconcern on a man struggling for life in the water, and when he has reached the ground, encumbers him with help?'

Maybe I'd teach Birdie that.

'You can go to night classes, Anne,' Aunt Allie went on gruffly. 'Try your Matric again. And then, who knows?'

'C-can I?' I looked up.

Man is a torch OK, blown in the wind. But, for the future, I had a task: to be my mother's mother and like Horatio to live to tell her story. For the moment, we had found honour in a losing day and ended our adventures tired but happy.